THE SUMMER OF HIM

STACY TRAVIS

FAST TURTLE PRESS

THE SUMMER OF HIM

STACY TRAVIS

Cover Design: Alyssa Garcia, Uplifting Author Services

Editing: Red Adept Editing

Publicity: Social Butterfly PR

THE SUMMER OF HIM

Summer is hotter with the perfect guy

CHAPTER ONE

Los Angeles International Airport
July

THERE WAS STILL TIME. The plane hadn't taken off yet. And that made me nervous.

He could still show up. Maybe he would.

I looked at my phone again. I'd already checked it too many times to remember, sneaking a look while dodging questions from my Lyft driver, going through security, and boarding the plane. Not to mention glancing behind me constantly like a fugitive who was being tailed.

I wasn't ready to give up on him yet. He could still get his act together. He could decide to apologize and admit that all the things he'd done and said were a blip in the larger, more important constellation of our love.

I hoped to God he wouldn't do that.

That's right. I hoped against hope that Johnny Royce, my now-ex-boyfriend, wouldn't call me or come to the airport or try to get on the plane. Yes, it was supposed to be our vacation together. And no, there wasn't a law against him traveling.

Except there was. It was the universal law of bad breakups: don't try to follow your ex-girlfriend to France, especially when the relationship ended badly. Especially when it was all your fault.

I'd been clear on that point, but logic didn't always mean anything to Johnny Royce. He was guided by different laws and principles than most people. He liked to do anything that seemed dangerous and fun. And while coming anywhere near me would definitely accomplish the dangerous part, I hoped— for once—that logic would pay him a visit and he'd see there was no fun to be had.

But I knew him.

He would think it was fine to travel together even after what had happened between us, which was a total shit show that I'd tried my best to block from memory.

Tried and failed.

So I didn't want him calling the airline and trying to reinstate the ticket I'd bought for him and later canceled. I didn't want to fight with Johnny in Paris or try to force the romance of an incredible city on the sad remains of what had sort of passed for barely-friends with mediocre benefits.

I looked down the aisle of the plane once more and exhaled an audible sigh of relief. He wasn't coming. Thinking about our yearlong relationship, I felt a mixture of 'we had our sweet moments' and 'wow, I should have seen that train wreck coming.'

If our breakup was as inevitable, so was our initial hookup. I'd walked into the bar where he worked and flirted with him. I'd planned it because I was a planner, and Johnny went along with it because, well... fun and sex. He wanted one thing from life—a party. He made a pretty decent effort to find a party on a daily basis, looking for a cliff to dive from or a door to sneak through if it seemed like something interesting lay on the other side. Johnny made everyone around him have a better time, no matter where he went.

What he didn't want was commitment. Or rules. Or sobriety, apparently. I told myself I was fine with that.

I was lying.

Johnny Royce worked as a bartender at Moby's, a tiny craft-beer and fancy burger place a dozen blocks from my apartment. He always looked like he'd just come in from playing beach volleyball—suntanned with streaks of blond in his sandy-brown hair and sunglasses on top of his head, even at night. He was always in motion, swinging out from behind the bar to wipe down three tables, scooping up empty pint glasses and dumping them in a grey kitchen bin, and wiping his hands on a long white apron without letting a single customer wait more than a couple of minutes at the bar.

He'd fill a glass, holding the tap open with the same hand so he could use the other to wipe off the bar or pop a napkin down for a newly arrived customer. Moby's had a steady flow of people, and Johnny kept up. It made me think he had to be smart if he was able to stay on top of everything without letting a task go unfulfilled.

The reality was he just didn't like people do go too long without a fresh beer.

His friends were bartenders or surfers or bartenders who surfed. After a few months of persuading, he even managed to get me on a surfboard. He guided me patiently and held onto the board until the waves came up and under me. "Okay, stand up now. Just hop into a squat, and when you're balanced, rise up and ride the wave." It took a half dozen attempts and more than a little water up my nose each time I fell, but I did get up on that board. I was having more fun than I'd had in ages, and it felt like the wave would keep on building.

That just showed how little I understood about relationships. Or surfing.

So I sat in my aisle seat on the plane—so far with no fellow travelers in my row—and thought back on the year that had led me to this moment: promising start, moments of irresponsible fun, differing life goals, and a crash and burn ending so bad it made me question my judgment for hooking up with him in the first place.

Final score: Judgment 0, Inevitable Realities of the Universe 1.

THE PLANE WAS STARTING to fill up. Flight attendants were closing some of the overhead bins and I was telling my irrational self not to worry. He wasn't coming.

But I feared the grand gesture.

It was just the kind of thing that would appeal to Johnny's adventuring spirit, trying to ignite a dashed relationship— forever, this time—at the airport in the moments before the plane was due to take off. He'd buy a ticket he couldn't afford just so he could get past the gate. He'd push his way through the line of passengers, who would all turn to see his grand romantic gesture.

"Hold on. Don't close the door. I have to get on and tell this woman I love her... that I was meant to be with her... that I was wrong... that I was an idiot... that I want to spend the rest of my life with her... Nikki, it's you. It's always been you."

He'd bend his forehead to touch mine and look into my eyes,

searching to make sure I felt the same way. I'd nod and he'd give me the best kiss of my life. People on the plane would applaud.

Then I'd have to deal with him again and look like the jerk who was turning away a guy with a cute smile making a grand gesture.

"Excuse me," said a voice to my left. My heart dropped to my feet because the voice was deep and sounded like Johnny trying to do a comedy bit: "Excuse me, Miss. Is this seat taken?"

I looked up at the tired, balding man staring at me and almost hugged him. His laptop case dangled awkwardly from his wrist while he waited for me to get up and let him into the window seat. He had a hipster beard and serious eyes, the kind that were focused on getting settled in and buckling his seatbelt.

"Sorry," I said, quickly unbuckling, standing, and moving into the aisle to let him get to his seat.

Then, because I was newly single, I checked him out. Above the beard, he wore nerdy glasses, maybe just for effect or maybe for reading, since he was leafing through a copy of *Sports Illustrated*. He'd already put his eye mask on his forehead in preparation for sleep. He'd already stuffed earbuds into his ears to block me—and anyone else—out of his life for the duration of the flight.

I turned back to the seat pocket in front of me and tucked in my iPad and the bottle of water I'd bought at the airport.

My thoughts drifted back to Johnny. Ten hours on a plane begs for topics to think about. I intentionally only remembered the best times—the sun-kissed afternoons sitting on the roof of his 1930s apartment building, where we'd have to climb out a window and hoist ourselves over a railing to crawl onto a flat patch that was perfect for watching the last half circle of sun slip into the Pacific Ocean.

At about six foot one with an athletic body he was lucky

enough to have been born with, Johnny was good at pretty much any sport he tried without a lesson. I'd trained for months to get through a century bike ride, and Johnny hopped on a borrowed bike and joined me at the last minute without suffering a sore muscle. He could sink three-pointers easily and surf waves that would frighten most people.

But it was his smile that I found the most appealing. He had a blond-streaked shock of hair that fell over his green eyes and a guilty-looking teenage-boy ear-to-ear grin. His happiness felt contagious, and I was a born rule follower who was used to having things work out if I dug in and gave it my full effort. Maybe that was why it took me a year to figure out that Johnny and I should've only lasted a couple of dates or a couple of months at best. Instead, I convinced myself that if I tried, I could make a relationship work with a fun guy who brought out a playful side of me.

The rooftop always beckoned with another sunset. He'd stuff a couple of beers in his pockets and swing a leg deftly over the rail before helping me over. My legs were shorter, so I needed the boost. There was a perfectly placed half wall where he could rest while I leaned on him. Johnny would wrap his arms around me, and we'd sip our beers, silently watching the sky change colors, never disturbed by another soul venturing up there.

"It feels like we should be drinking rosé from tall wineglasses," I'd said more than once, thinking the chilled pink drink would look pretty set against the setting sun. And I liked the way it tasted.

He'd tip his pinky finger out like he was holding a teacup, mocking me. "Oh, *oui, oui*," he'd say, laughing at himself. "People who drink wine are kinda pretentious, don't you think?"

Like a million other things, I let the semi-insult go. Up on the roof, with the warm breeze wafting across my face and Johnny nuzzling my neck, I didn't think he meant to mock me or my interest in beverages made from grapes.

I didn't think he had a mean streak. I didn't think he'd ever cheat on me.

Until he did.

CHAPTER TWO

Santa Monica, California
One Month Earlier

A LITTLE OVER a month before the trip, Johnny had convinced me to go to a high school reunion with him. I tried to convince him to go without me.

"Trust me, I went to my ten-year reunion a couple years ago, and my friends who brought boyfriends or husbands ended up regretting it. The poor guys ended up huddled together because all the high school friends wanted to hang with each other. There was guilt. There were fights. I'm saving you from that."

My offer wasn't all for him. I honestly didn't think it would be that fun for either of us.

"It won't be that way. I don't even remember the people I went to high school with. I probably won't want to stay more than an hour, but I feel like I should make an appearance."

"Great. Do that, and we can do something later. Just call me."

"No, I want you there. Please? If I do run into someone I know, I'll want to impress people with you. It'll be awesome.

Someone'll say, 'Who's that pretty brunette?' and I'll be able to say, 'She's with me.'"

He gave me the look that always charmed me—the bashful grin of a teenager who wanted to convince his parents he was a perfect angel who wouldn't think of sneaking beer from their bar fridge. It bugged me, though. After a year of dating, he still planned to refer to me as "with" him.

I was never his girlfriend. Never would be.

Against my better judgment, I agreed to go. In my jeans, high-heeled wedge sandals, and an off-the-shoulder top, I tried to look semi-fashionable without trying too hard. I put on mascara—which I hated because I often ended up stabbing myself in the eye—and lip gloss. I left my wavy brown hair down so it looked beachy and casual and tried to look extra put together just in case Johnny did run into someone he wanted to impress because that's the kind of thing a person did for the guy she was 'with.'

When we got there, Johnny fished a can of beer out of a metal tub and put it on the cushion of a lawn chair for me like he was occupying a small child with an iPad. "I'll be back in a sec," he said.

He immediately ran into an old friend named Zeke, clapping him on the back and following him to a corner of the yard where he started hugging other people and whooping it up. He never came back. I didn't need a babysitter, but I didn't know anyone at that party, so I sipped my beer and made small talk with strangers for an hour.

Eventually, I went over to where Johnny was laughing with the friends he hadn't remembered an hour earlier, and he nodded at me as if I was someone he barely knew. "'Sup?" He immediately turned away from me to talk to a tall, pretty brunette who hand her hand on his arm.

Wasn't I was supposed to be the pretty brunette in his scenario?

So I didn't walk away. I told myself to cut him some slack because he was excited about seeing old friends. He just wasn't handling it very well with respect to me. "How's it going?" I asked, noticing the empty beer cans piled up on the table in front of Johnny.

"Good. I've got a lot of catching up to do," he said, turning his back on me again and not even trying to hide the fact that he now had an arm around the brunette, whose name I might have learned if he'd acknowledged that I was 'with' him.

Hadn't I warned him about exactly that type of thing when I'd suggested he go without me?

Reunions were never fun for the dates or spouses of the people who were reminiscing about a time before we existed in their lives. He seemed too caught up to have a wandering thought about how boring it had to be for me, but since we'd already had the conversation, I figured he'd understand if I didn't want to stay. Things had gone a different way from how he'd expected. He was having fun. It was fine.

Fine, I tell you! Give me a night on the couch any day.

"It's been three hours. I kind of want to go," I told him later, feeling tired and not even caring that he was ignoring me. I knew I'd have a better time watching old arthouse movies at home. But Johnny couldn't tear himself away from his new old friends long enough to talk to me about it. He was drunk and people were laughing and crowding around him. He was right in his sweet spot.

It wouldn't have been the worst thing for him to call time of death on his party before someone had to half carry his slumped-over, staggering ass out of the place. Given how much taller he was than me, it was never easy for me to guide him to my car or get him up the stairs to his apartment when he got that wasted, but I'd persevered because sometimes we did that for people we sort of loved.

Back when we'd first started dating, it was kind of silly and fun. He was the life of every party, spreading his joy far and wide. Johnny would grow more amorous the more he drank. "You're adorable. Did I tell you how much I love your sweet rack?" he'd ask in the middle of a crowd of friends. I'd roll my eyes. He was a goof, but he was *my* goof.

Then he'd put his arms around me and rock side to side, nuzzling my neck. That would lead to him turning me toward him and dancing in the middle of a crowd, oblivious to whether there was even any music. Or a game of beer pong taking place right next to his slow waltz. He'd lean down to kiss me, channeling all his feelings into a small gesture, like a brush of his hand against my cheek. In those moments, I couldn't get enough of him.

Then abruptly, he'd pull away and spin me off to the side like he was completing the final move in his dance. He'd move off in another direction to wherever the supply of beer happened to be. Eventually, he'd return to say something charming like, "From across the room, you're stunning."

It was cute for a while. But the night of the reunion was the polar opposite. When I told him I was leaving, he eyed me like an annoying mosquito and told me how much fun he was having with his friends. "We have a lot of catching up to do," he said again.

"Okay, well, I'm still gonna go."

Instead of remarking that I was stunning and adorable—his two favorite words for me—he said something different in a tone I'd never heard before. "Why are you being such a bitch?"

"Excuse me?" I was in the middle of convincing myself I hadn't heard him correctly when he continued.

"You're always trying to do this to me. It's not cool." He popped the cap on another beer. He missed his mouth when he tried to take a drink, and it dripped down his chin. He wiped the suds off with the back of his hand, blinking heavily at me.

"Doing what?"

"Trying to crush my buzz," he said, a little belligerent. The brunette was still hanging all over him, and she looked at me like I was an intruder she wanted to assassinate with her pointy fingernails.

"Oh my God. I'm not trying to do that. You should stay and have fun. I'm just ready to go," I said.

"So go. What do I care?" It was the first time he'd ever talked to me like that. I couldn't tell whether it was brinkmanship or the alcohol, but I didn't want to be there. Not at this party, not with him.

I walked toward the house, fully intending to leave.

Then I felt a pang of guilt. He just wanted to have fun and maybe I was a buzzkill. I decided to find a quiet spot in the house and wait a little longer to see if he'd leave with me.

It's what a person in a relationship did. Unfortunately, I'm pretty sure I was the only one who believed it was a relationship.

AN HOUR LATER, I looked around the yard and didn't see him in the spot where he'd been hanging out for most of the night. The only way out of the party was through the house, and I'd have seen him if he'd passed by me there.

Then I noticed a pool house in the corner of the yard—bright lights streamed through a window—and figured people must be hanging out in there. But when I walked through the door, I didn't see people. I saw Johnny. Getting a blowjob from the brunette he'd been with earlier. Her tank top and bra were on the floor.

I stood, frozen, first wanting to un-see what I couldn't get my brain to process. It had to be an easily explained misunderstanding.

How, exactly?

I was having trouble forming words.

As if he felt my eyes on him, Johnny turned and blinked a couple times at me like he too was confused by what was happening. The now-topless woman had extracted his dick from her mouth but she did her best to look away from me. "I thought you left," was all he said.

Because *that* would have made it cool.

I didn't cry over him, and I didn't wonder if I should forgive him and try to salvage some part of our pointless non-relationship.

At thirty, I knew I wanted more. So I did what any self-respecting woman would do—I packed for my trip to France.

After shredding his nonrefundable ticket and telling him never to call me again.

CHAPTER THREE

A Plane on the Tarmac

THE FLIGHT ATTENDANTS, who each wore their hair wound up in a bun under a navy blue cap, walked down the aisles, handing tiny headphones in plastic wrap to anyone who needed them. The ones I'd brought didn't fit in the two holes in the armrest, so I took the small bundle and unwrapped the earbuds.

"Excuse me," a female voice said.

I looked up and saw a petite brown-haired woman with E-cup breasts that formed a shelf above her midsection. I don't normally size up other women's breasts but they were eye-level. I coveted her dark velour sweatsuit and realized she'd perfected the comfortable travel outfit. In my jeans, I was in for a long night of wedgies.

She was looking at her boarding pass and eyeing the row number over my head. Hers was the middle seat, so I moved so she could stow her purse and buckle in.

"Debra," she said, extending a hand. She held a stack of magazines with the other hand, *People* sitting on top.

"Hi. I'm Nikki," I said, wondering whether she'd be chatty or if she just figured anyone about to share a four-by-six-foot space for ten hours ought to get acquainted. She looked over at the bearded guy on her other side—he now had the eyemask over half his face—and turned back to me with a shrug. Now that we'd met, I just might ask to borrow her *People* magazine when she was done. Since I worked at a public relations firm, I heard —and generally ignored—celebrity gossip and it couldn't have interested me less. But on vacay, bring it on.

It turned out Debra was the last to board. The flight attendants closed the plane doors and began their safety demonstration. Debra rolled her eyes at me when they asked us to give them our undivided attention. I smiled like we were on the same team of scofflaws, but I watched the demonstration because... rule follower.

The man by the window had already fallen asleep with his mouth open. I'd seen him shake a tiny pill from a bottle and down it with some water. I'd never flown for ten hours before, so it hadn't occurred to me that medically-induced sleeping might be a good idea.

I'd only left the country a couple of times—once in college, when I crossed the border south of San Diego and spent a night in Tijuana, and a second time when I spent a semester learning Spanish in a small town near Quito, Ecuador. I realized that my high school Spanish would be of no use in France, so I'd been using a language app on my headphones while jogging.

"*Le train est grand,*" the language program would prompt me to repeat. It was great vocabulary to have in case someone asked me about the size of a train. I wouldn't know how to get to the train, but that was beside the point.

I was happy to be taking this trip. I didn't need a boyfriend or a travel companion to have a great time and I was looking forward to waking up each morning and coming up with my own plan for the day. I was independent. I could do this. Traveling alone would be good for me and it would push my boundaries. It would force me to be light and spontaneous on my own. In a foreign language. With jet lag. On unfamiliar territory. In a country where I knew no one.

No, I'm not at all freaked out.

And because I was completely freaked out, my thoughts drifted again to Johnny, as if my brain was caught in a loop, rehashing our relationship and wondering if it made me a weak feminist to think that the wrong guy was better than no guy.

Don't answer that. I know, it's no guy. No guy!

My friend Annie had known the answer to that question long before Johnny and I ever had a fight. We always fought about the same thing; how I wasn't spontaneous enough and how he wouldn't take anything seriously. And even though Annie was my closest friend and I trusted that she always had my back, I chose to ignore her concerns. At least initially.

"I get that he's fun. But is that all there is?" Annie said, after meeting Johnny for the first time at a wedding last year. She lived in San Francisco, so we didn't see each other much anymore, but we'd been roommates for all four years of college and I loved her like a sister. She was my polar opposite—impulsive and insistent with her opinions where I tended to think and consider. She had a sleeve of flower tattoos and the wiry, lean body of a triathlete, where the thought of doing three different sports in a week exhausted me, let alone in a single race. But our hearts understood each other and she was my go-to for everything.

Thus, I put stock in her unvarnished view of him. She'd seen me at all hours of the day and night in various stages of relationships, excited about a new guy or depressed about a shiny new fraternity pledge who wouldn't give me the time of day. "You're an ambitious early riser, and he brags about drinking late and sleeping late. You plan for every eventuality, and he was just talking about skydiving later today just, you know, because."

"Don't you think it's good for me to get out of my comfort zone?" I said, still trying to hang on to the idea that he made me better. "Wait, he said he's going skydiving?"

"You're going too. Apparently, it will be 'off the chain,'" Annie said. I could hear Johnny saying exactly that. "He's also planning to have you pay for it. Listen, I just want you to be happy. I don't think you have to prove you're adventurous. I love your neurotic need to plan, and I still find you fun without the skydiving."

"That's because you're like that too," I said.

"True, and I want you to be the person you are. Not the one who proves she's fun by jumping to her death from a plane. I don't like that he makes you doubt yourself and your instincts just because he doesn't think about tomorrow."

The idea of jumping from a plane invoked abject panic in me, but I continued to cling to the benighted conviction that two people with different outlooks could complement each other. "I'm serious enough for the two of us," I said. "Don't you think he brings out something better in me? A lighter, spontaneous side?" Annie would never lie to me. She was the smartest woman I knew and the youngest person to make partner at her lawfirm, while fostering six rescue dogs on the side.

"If anything, he brings out your more anal, responsible side because you always have to clean up after him," Annie said.

Whelp... there you have it. Truer words were never spoken.

IT TURNED out Debra liked to chat. That was okay with me since I knew there was very little chance of me sleeping on the plane. I could really only sleep fully-reclined, which meant that unless I wanted to lie on the floor at Debra's feet, I'd be awake.

"You traveling to see family?" she asked.

"No, just doing my own thing."

"Ah, sounds like heaven. I'm in a wedding, and my entire time in France is planned, right down to the ride from the airport. Though I guess I can't complain about the ride."

"Who's getting married? Friend?"

"My sister. She lives in Provence. Ever since she spent her junior year abroad, she's been dying to marry a French guy, and wouldn't you know, she met Allain in New York. He swore he would never go back to France, not after he'd just finished getting his green card to stay in the US. But he was no match for my sister. When she gets her heart set on something, watch out." Debra laughed.

"Have you been before? To France?" I asked.

"Nope, never. You?"

I shook my head. "First time."

She looked awed and impressed. "First time and you're off on your own. You're so brave."

I didn't feel brave. I felt like I was putting on an empowered facade when inside, I was clinging to my mom's pantleg and begging her not to leave me at preschool. I wanted to be brave. But I just felt tired.

"I'm not sure it's bravery. But I'm going, regardless."

"That *is* bravery. You just *defined* bravery." I liked Debra. I considered asking if I could tag along with her to the wedding. I'd make myself unobtrusive and I wouldn't eat. But at least I'd have a plan.

Debra kept going on about my bravery, however, so I chickened out.

"It's gonna be amazing. You're gonna find yourself. Maybe you'll have some kind of *Eat, Pray, Love* adventure and not come back for two years," she said.

The thought evoked abject panic and I assured her there

would be no two-year adventure. "I have a return ticket, and I intend to use it."

"I'm just sayin'."

"I guess. I don't feel especially brave. I just feel nervous."

"Of course you do. You're going alone. You'll be eating dinner alone. I've never done that," she said.

Nor had I. As if I needed reminding.

I would be eating dinner alone. Every night.

Debra must've seen something in my face, possibly the sudden pallor of a dead woman, because she started stammering. "I mean... it's gonna be great. You'll figure it out as you go. That's what people do in Europe. They backpack around and figure it out."

Despite myself—and the lack of a backpack or a parachute—I felt her enthusiasm start to embolden me. "You're right. I'll figure it out," I said.

"We each have to follow the path in front of us," she said,

And she was right. This was mine.

When the captain asked the flight attendants to secure the doors, something shifted in me. I felt suddenly at peace. My momentary panic was supplanted by excitement because the only direction was forward. I also felt freed, finally, from blaming myself for not making an adult relationship work with a guy who didn't want one. I needed to get back to being myself. I didn't need a relationship. I needed to remember who I was before Johnny. Independent and self-sufficient—that was how I would be for the next two weeks and for all the weeks to come.

As Los Angeles faded into the distance beneath the plane, so did any lingering doubt that I would be fine. I already felt better. *Onward.*

I was going on my own, and whatever lay in front of me would be mine to choose and determine. I needed to get away—maybe ten thousand miles away—in order to put my relationship behind me and get into the right frame of mind for what-ever came next.

I could tell the flight attendants wanted us to be sleeping because they turned up the heat, turned down the lights, and asked us to draw the window shades. Debra had to reach over and do that because the man in our row still hadn't surfaced from his Ambien haze. The fact that the rest of the passengers managed to fall asleep didn't stop my active brain from churning through topics like it was on steroids.

Debra put her eye mask on and took off her shoes to settle in for a nap. I felt self-conscious about turning on my reading lamp in the dark plane, but with most of the people around me blocking the light with eye masks, I decided no one would mind if I burned a little midnight oil.

My eyes felt bleary, but I tried to read one of my books, a mystery that should have hooked me by the end of the first twenty pages, but I lost interest. I leafed through the airline magazine and saw that someone had completed the crossword puzzle and ripped out one of the articles. I read Debra's *People* cover to cover. I played solitaire on my phone, which bored me so much I decided staring at the headrest in front of me was more fun. Boredom and staring, however, did not translate into sleep.

I shifted positions, closed my eyes, tried again to read, and then gave up. I repeated that sequence innumerable times, stuck in my own personal wakeful hell.

But ten hours later, we were landing.

CHAPTER FOUR

Paris, France

I WALKED like a zombie through customs and picked up my luggage, then I followed the masses to a bus stop where something called the Roissybus would arrive and take me somewhere near the center of Paris. It was relatively cheap and easy to find at the airport terminal. No cabs on my meager vacay budget.

A throaty female voice came over a loudspeaker and thanked us for riding the "Wassy Bus." That was how she pronounced it. Even with my limited French-language skills, I knew enough to recognize a clunky Americanized pronunciation. But it was oddly comforting to hear someone butchering the language as badly as I was sure to do. I'd heard rumors of French people having little tolerance for American tourists, but the recorded voice on the bus made me feel like I was in good company.

Before I knew it, we'd passed along the outer highways and crossed into the eighteenth arrondissement, down a busy avenue, and into the center of Paris. *Paris!* I had to take a moment and pinch myself to believe I'd actually made it there. As the bus drove, I looked out the window and saw the majestic Arc de Triomphe in the distance then the Eiffel Tower soaring above the rooftops of the city.

When the bus pulled over in front of the Opéra Garnier, I hopped off, grabbed my overstuffed blue duffel bag and a roller suitcase I'd borrowed from my parents. As the bus pulled away, I surveyed my surroundings. The streets teamed with tiny cars and mopeds. Well-dressed people hustled past on the sidewalks. I was thrilled to be in a foreign city and also scared shitless because I had no idea where to go.

Channeling Hemmingway and Georgia O'Keefe, I Googled left-bank hotels, picturing myself drinking absinthe with a present day Ernest. There were a few I could afford in the four-teenth arrondissement, near the one skyscraper in central Paris —the Montparnasse Tower—but I couldn't see a skyscraper from where I stood and had no idea where that was in relation to where the bus had stopped.

So I did the only logical thing.

No, I didn't cry.

The next logical thing.

No, I didn't get drunk.

I quickly retreated to the closest cafe I could find and plopped myself down at an outside table to order a cup of coffee. Coffee could fix anything.

It wasn't busy. About half the tables were filled, and I noticed other people sitting alone, which made me feel a little bit better. At a table in front of mine, two women who looked my age sat with bottles of Perrier and tall glasses in front of them. One of them held the leash of a small white dog, who licked water from a saucer under the table. The other had a motorcycle helmet on the seat next to her.

Johnny rode motorcycles... *Stop it, stop it, stop it.*

Two men to my right seemed like they were talking business, based on the yellow legal pad between them, the drawings they couldn't seem to agree on, and their continued head shaking and discussing. Everyone had a purpose, even the man who sat alone, writing in a small blue notebook, and the older woman eating a plate of smoked salmon and drinking wine with the dignity that a formal lunch warranted. I remembered the term *café society*, and for the first time, I understood what it meant. There was something magical about people sitting in conversation with each other. Almost no one was snapping selfies of their food or texting while sitting in front of a perfectly good person to talk to. They were doing what humans were meant to be doing—talking, connecting, and interacting. I felt myself longing to participate somehow, someway, and speak in some combination of English and Duolingo French with someone I'd yet to meet. I couldn't see my way clear to how that would happen, but I committed to staying optimistic.

I could already see that being in Paris would be good for me. I badly I needed to get away. I needed to reboot my life in the next two weeks, and even if I spent most of my time sitting in cafés like this one, I'd come away better for having been here.

I didn't need a travel companion, and I definitely didn't need a bad boyfriend. I did feel, however, that I might enjoy myself more if I had an activity other than people watching. I didn't want to feel like a lurker. Maybe if kept a journal in my bag I'd have something to do in café society.

There wasn't a lot of personal space at French cafés. The tables were tiny metal circles, and woven bistro chairs faced the street. That was perfect for having a conversation with the person the next chair over but less great if someone sat down at a nearby table and started smoking, which had just happened. Three guys in white T-shirts and jeans had just taken a table behind me, and the wind had shifted to send the smoke right into my face. I blinked it away and tried to tell myself that breathing smoke was a hallmark of Parisian life. I tried to see it as exotic and cultured even though I felt like I was eating an ashtray.

I looked around for another table, but a moment later, the wind shifted again, and I could breathe. I was trying in vain to shove my luggage inconspicuously under the table when a waiter in black pants and shirt with a white apron appeared in front of me. He put a clean ashtray on the table along with a paper coaster and a tiny bowl of peanuts.

"Bonjour," he said matter-of-factly. It was more like a statement than a greeting. I braced myself for rudeness, expecting exasperation because I didn't speak perfect French. Or he might just ignore me once he figured out I was a tourist. He had salt-and-pepper hair, which I figured put him in his forties at least.

He didn't wait for me to open my mouth. Apparently, I had "tourist" written all over me, because he grabbed a menu off a table behind him and handed it to me. It was all translated into English.

"Um, bonjour..." I went blank. The stupid lessons from Duolingo were useless, and my jet-lagged brain wasn't helping.

"You would like...?" he said, saving me from the Google search I was about to do on my phone for the French word for coffee.

"Um, coffee. Please. *S'il vous plaît.*" Maybe he'd give me credit for trying or at least wouldn't spit in my coffee.

"*Un café.*" He turned to go.

Right. "Cafe" meant coffee. I'd heard that on the plane, and I couldn't even keep that in my brain. It was quickly dawning on me that I was in over my head to come here on barely any sleep without even knowing what I planned to do for two weeks. What if all the restaurants required reservations and the hotels were already booked? It was summer, after all. I hadn't even thought to check.

It was unlike me to travel this way. I was a planner. I was responsible. I could turn a party boy who should have been a one-night stand into a year-long relationship. That was how pragmatic I was.

And because I was all those things, I'd had a firm talk with myself before the trip and told myself not to plan, maybe as one last token nod to the shift I wanted to experience when I'd started dating Johnny. I yearned to be more spontaneous, and at first, I'd hoped his lust for life and desire to live in the moment would rub off a tiny bit, at least to the extent that it could for someone like me.

Maybe that was a ridiculous idea. What if I ended up assaulted or lost or just... alone?

The waiter arrived with my coffee, a tiny espresso cup without an offer of milk or cream, which I normally required. It didn't matter. That valuable caffeine would have to fuel my next decision. It would have to help me come up with some kind of itinerary right there and then because the freedom I saw in front of me felt terrifying.

Fortunately, it was seven thirty in the morning back in California, and I could FaceTime Annie. She'd be at her job already because her firm had a New York office and she had to keep East Coast hours.

"Help! I mean, hello," I said when she picked up.

"Are you in France?"

"Yes."

"So, wouldn't that be *bonjour*?"

I could see the view of the San Francisco Bay through the window behind her. We'd always argued about it. I said she should turn her desk to face that view. She said she'd never get anything done if she could look at that view. She'd been calm and amused by the idea that I'd taken this trip alone, but she hadn't judged me. She never would.

"*Oui!*" I said.

"I'm envious. Working stiff here."

"Wish you were here," I said.

"Yeah, me too. I'd love to be lounging on the French Riviera instead of stuck in my office."

"You know that's not where I am, right?"

"Maybe you should be. You're a lot closer to it than I am."

"True, but it's still far," I said.

"So? That's the beauty of the European rail system. You can be anywhere by lunchtime."

"You sound like an ad."

"*People* magazine says all the French celebrities go to the beaches in the South in August. Saint-Tropez, Cannes. You should join them."

I'd read that too, thanks to Debra and her stack of magazines. But Annie hadn't gotten it completely right. The article I'd read had been about how some actor bought a house in a small town on the southern coast of France after he'd finished shooting a movie on location there. I couldn't remember his name. He'd been in the latest action movie, which meant by definition that I'd never seen him on the screen. Apparently, he'd been so taken with the charm of the town that bought a sprawling estate. "The people here are lovely," he'd said, as though he'd propped a lawn chair in their park, not purchased a bazillion dollar property.

Must be nice.

"Okay, well, if I suddenly find myself rubbing elbows with French celebrities, I'll send a selfie."

"Atta girl."

"I'm drinking coffee in a Paris café. Will keep you posted," I told Annie.

"Switch to wine. Jealous. Love you."

Since the waiter had been willing to speak to me in English, I took advantage of his fluency to ask a few questions. His initial frosty exterior dropped away once I gave up all pretense of trying to pass as anything other than a tourist.

"You're from America?" he asked.

"Yes. I live in California."

"Ah, *Californie*. I have always wanted to travel there."

"You should."

"Maybe next year. You can give me a tour?" He smiled and moved a little closer to let someone pass behind him. His teeth were a little crooked, but he had the confidence of a man who knew that didn't matter. The corners of his brown eyes crinkled, and he had a dimple on each cheek that dug in when he smiled. I understood suddenly what people meant when they said the French were openly affectionate. "And maybe I could give you a tour of Paris. Later?"

He asked my name told me his was Guillaume. "That is like William in America," he said. I had to admit, the French version sounded much prettier. "Your hotel is near here?"

"I don't have one yet," I told Guillaume. "Guess I'd better get that worked out." I looked up and down the street, trying to see if any of the buildings were obviously hotels. I really had no idea what part of town I'd landed in or whether it was a good place to find a hotel. I felt oddly calm about my zero prospects.

He looked at the sky, tapping his fingers on the table in front of me. "Ah. *Oui*. You will go to the Quartier Latin—the Latin Quarter. It is not far from here. Many students live near the Sorbonne. There are two hotels on Rue des Écoles that would be excellent for you. They have single rooms, not too big, but..." He looked under the table at my bags. "Maybe not big enough for you and your luggage, but you will try."

I couldn't tell if he was giving me a hard time. His smile provided the answer.

"Sounds perfect. Really." I took out my wallet. It was time to haul my bags down to his hotel picks on the Rue des Écoles. "Can I have... how do you say, 'the check?'"

"*L'addition.*"

"*L'addition,*" I repeated as he took a small piece of paper from his pocket and placed it on a tiny metal tray, like he'd done on the other table.

"You will pick up the language just by listening. If you're alone, it's easy because you can focus," he said. "If you came to Paris with friends, you'd all be speaking English to each other and you might not hear." I wasn't sure why he assumed I was in Paris by myself.

"You speak English very well."

"My mother was born Ireland. And I studied in school. But really, I learned the most quickly from listening to American music and watching TV."

That explained a lot. His English sounded very good, but I hadn't been able to place his accent. He spoke with a French accent on certain words and in a tone that almost sounded midwestern, a combination that left him with an intriguing but hard-to-place accent.

I downed the last of the coffee in my tiny cup and unwrapped a chocolate square that I'd found sitting in the saucer. It tasted especially delicious, chasing down the bitterness of the coffee. The coffee didn't need to be in an oversized Starbucks cup to be satisfying.

"Guillaume, *merci,*" I said, standing up and wrestling my bags from under the table. He turned from where he was talking with two women and shook my hand.

"*Merci,* Nikki." He pronounced it "Neek-y." He took a pencil from behind his ear and scribbled something on the check he'd put on the metal saucer. "Here's my number. If you have any problems at the hotels, maybe I can help."

I spun in a circle and took in the crisscross of streets near the Opéra Garnier, cars and mopeds zooming through the intersection then down the other way to another, equally busy corner. Guillaume was watching with an amused look on his face as though entertained by the dumb tourist who'd come to Paris without a map or a plan.

"The hotels you mentioned—are they within walking distance?" I asked.

He looked at me, then at my luggage, and shook his head. "If you didn't have those bags, maybe. But you'll get tired of walking after ten minutes, and you'll still be on this side of the Seine."

He pointed me to the nearest Metro station, Opéra, which was only one large city block away. Even then, he seemed skeptical about whether I could lug my stuff there, but I assured him I'd be fine. I left him five euros and, with the blue bag on one shoulder and my roller bag dragging behind me, waddled my way down the street.

CHAPTER FIVE

QUARTIER LATIN

WHEN I RESURFACED from the Metro station, the first thing I saw was Notre-Dame, and it absolutely lived up to its legend of grandeur. Its twin towers, rising above the ornate circle of stained glass, stood heroically like a grandmother who'd withstood wars, weather, and a fire and still managed to remind her grandkids that she knew more than they'd ever discover in a lifetime.

The second thing I saw was the Seine. It was narrower than I'd imagined and more grey-green than blue. But it was beautiful.

I took a deep breath, leaned on a stone rail facing the river and Notre-Dame, and took in the magical setting. This was Paris. My heart flooded with emotion at the view of the river and the fact that I was looking at it for the first time. I knew I had to push through and stay awake as long as possible so I'd have the best chance of acclimating to the new time zone.

I'd read about fighting jet lag, and one key strategy was

spending time outside. From where I stood, my phone GPS showed that I was less than a five-minute walk from both hotels recommended by Guillaume. Even though I didn't want to tear myself away from the view, I desperately wanted to ditch my luggage, so I made the short walk and found success at the Hotel des Écoles. The rooms were affordable, and there was a vacancy.

"You are lucky to be single," the young woman behind the desk told me. If she said I was also brave, I was going to be concerned about international conspiracy.

It turned out she was talking about the hotel room for one. "It's the only room we have left." She looked to be about my age and had the effortless flair for dressing that I'd only heard about when people described French women. She wore a printed scarf tied around her neck and a long linen dress with a leather belt and sandals. Hair in a high ponytail and only a sweep of lip gloss on her lips. There was no way I could pull off that level of *insouciance*.

"Come with me," she said, telling me her name was Sylvie.

I was impressed that everyone I'd encountered so far spoke English so well, and I kicked myself for not at least studying Spanish for a couple more years in high school.

Sylvie took an antique-looking key attached to a rectangle of wood the length of a shoebox from a hook and had me follow her up four winding flights of narrow steps to a door marked with the number nine. She turned the key twice in the lock and pushed open the door. She wasn't kidding about being single. A twin bed was wedged into the space next to a tiny painted bedside table. There was room for exactly one person in the room, and because it was on the top floor, the ceiling slanted under the pitched roof. Unless I stood right next to the wall in the doorway, I'd have to bend down to avoid hitting my head.

She pointed to the opposite side of the bed, where there was a narrow slit of space and a door. "*La toilette.* You will stay for how many nights?"

"Oh, probably a week?" I wasn't sure. Maybe I'd take a side trip. "Can I let you know tomorrow, once I get settled?"

"*Oui. Bien sûr.*" She smiled and headed back down the winding stairs, her strappy sandals clicking on the stone steps. "You are always welcome here. This room is small, so it's usually available."

I closed the door and surveyed my tiny room. I could only imagine how tiny the "toilette" would be, based on the size of the room. Likely the size of the lavatory on the plane, I figured. When I pushed the door open, my jaw dropped in shock. The bathroom was larger than the room itself. It had a full-sized claw-foot tub, a pedestal sink, and a toilet with a chain hanging above it for flushing. And there was a bidet.

I dragged both my bags into the bathroom so I'd have the most space left over in the actual bedroom. I couldn't believe how lovely this bathroom was. It even had a window.

The beginnings of a plan were forming in my mind. I could picture myself a bit later, stretched out in this tub with a glass of wine in my hand and maybe some pastries or a hunk of cheese on a fresh baguette.

I'd need to roam around my new neighborhood to figure out where to buy those things, but I could make something of this bathroom. No problem.

I DECIDED TO WANDER. Notre-Dame was crowded with tourists taking photos in front of it from all angles and waiting in line to go inside. I decided to save the site for a later time and walked along a path behind it through a small gated park with benches and across a bridge back into the Latin Quarter.

I walked up the Boulevard Saint-Michel, which took me past clothing stores, bookstores, a McDonald's, and a Starbucks. Of course, those places had planted a flag in Paris, even with its reputation as a gastronomic capital. By early evening, the street was jammed with people walking after work to meet up with friends or buy groceries at small shops and pick up fresh bread for dinner at the *boulangeries*. I wanted to be part of the thrum of activity around me, but I didn't fit in anywhere yet.

I kept going until I reached the Luxembourg Gardens, an organized, manicured series of pathways around and across a glorious expanse of flowers and greenery. People jogged on the path, one man wearing T-shirt, shorts, and a sweater tied around his neck. The flowers lining the paths were in full bloom, hot pinks and yellows and whites reaching up into the sunlight.

In the middle of the garden, a circular fountain was surrounded by green lawn chairs, many of them in a reclining position and every one of them occupied. People sat with their eyes closed, enjoying the late-afternoon sun or chatting with friends. Small kids pushed sailboats with wooden sticks, watched them sail from one side of the fountain to the other, then ran around to give them another push. I sat in my own green chair, mesmerized by the fact that everyone seemed to be outside, enjoying the late sun of summer. It was past seven in the evening, and the sun was still high over the horizon. Paris was far enough north that it stayed light much later than at home.

My phone dinged with a text message. It was Annie. *You meet a French prince yet?* she texted.

Ha ha. Not likely. You busy right now? Facetime? You can ogle French delicacies with me, I wrote.

Ugh, sorry. Running into a meeting. Just saying hi. Will check in later.

It was just as well. I had to get over needing a crutch, and being alone would give me a chance to learn the language. Guillaume had said the only way to really learn French was to sit alone and observe.

I started walking again, and as I passed restaurants with outdoor tables, I could see that everyone was gathered in groups. Debra's words came back to me, "You'll be eating dinner alone. I've never done that."

Neither had I.

As comfortable as I was my own company, I didn't think I was ready to sit alone in a restaurant. I passed a Monoprix grocery store and debated buying some food to eat in my hotel room. Then I felt even more depressed at that thought. Maybe I could eat in a restaurant alone. I'd just bring a book or something to occupy myself while I ate. Or I could text someone and have a conversation that way. I psyched myself up for the adventure of solo dining.

Pommes frites for one!

I walked back down Boulevard Saint-Michel and bought a magazine from a kiosk. Fashion was a universal language even if the articles were in French. Then I looked for a place to eat that didn't seem too fancy or too gross. Men stood outside the restaurants down one small pedestrian-only road, holding out menus and pointing at signs that showed three-course and four-course dinners at different prices.

"Come, you want to come?" one man asked. I shook my head.

The next one held up a menu. "Excellent price for three courses."

Somehow, I doubted this was the height of French cuisine. The *crêperie* a couple of doors down had inside seating and a window open to the street. A sugary smell like a waffle cone drifted my way, and I was done. I could buy a crepe and eat it while walking. No solo dining. No sad picnic on my twin hotel bed.

I chose a savory crepe, pointing to a picture on the menu. The man in the window took my money, poured batter from a pitcher onto a large circular griddle, and chased it around with a wooden stick that looked like the rake for the Zen sand garden I used to have on my desk. After a minute, he flipped the crepe over and loaded it with cheese and spinach. He let the cheese melt a little before folding the crepe up into a triangle and wrapping it in a napkin.

Oh my God.

I had no idea anything could taste so good. Forget about eating in restaurants. I would eat crepes every day. Done.

I took another turn and ended up back at the Seine, looking down at the large night cruise boats—which were called Bateaux Mouches, according to the writing on the sides— passing through the channel. Below the bridge where I stood, a large group of people congregated down by the river's edge, some sitting on a strip of grass no more than five feet wide, right up against the stone wall.

There were other people on chairs or benches under bright-blue umbrellas and even more people walking or roller-skating past a few tables where people sat with drinks. A sign said Paris Plages. I used a translation app to figure out that the sign said that temporary beaches were being set up all along the Seine in honor of summer. There would be music and a beach cabana with cocktails.

I wanted to be down there.

A staircase wrapped around on the other side of the bridge, and within minutes, I was on the "beach," standing in line at the cabana and ordering a glass of rosé. The bartender handed me a plastic cup of pink wine, and I found a spot on the grass between two couples and in front of a loud group of friends who were playing music from an iPhone.

This was it, the Paris I'd imagined when Johnny and I had talked about taking this trip together. Sitting on the grass, drinking rosé—without his sneering comments—made me happy. I was only a little wistful that I was doing it alone.

I mean, sure, I'd probably be having more fun if Johnny were with me. Johnny was built for vacations.

Each sip of wine lowered my resistance to picking up my phone and calling him. All around me, couples were nuzzling each other and sitting arm in arm. The French were openly affectionate, holding hands as they walked along or kissing by the water. By the time I was halfway through the second glass of wine, all I wanted to do was call Johnny. The sun had set, leaving the clouds pink with leftover sunlight and the air warm and still. If he were here, I'd be resting my head against his chest as we looked out over the reflections on the water. He'd lean down and kiss me, and I'd have the feeling I first had when we were together—that I couldn't imagine wanting to be anywhere else.

I took out my phone, which still had Johnny on speed dial. I looked at the number and his name, which sent a pang of longing through my heart. What would he say if I bought him a new ticket and asked him to come meet me? And how would I feel about myself if I backslid and went back to our relationship, which had no future?

Maybe I could get over the cheating. Maybe I wasn't ready to be done.

"Pardon," someone next to me said. It was a guy with close-cropped brown hair, rolled-up jeans, and a pale-blue button-up shirt. He was trying to wedge himself into a small space on the grass between me and the couple sitting next to me.

There was barely room for another person, but I scooted over, grateful for the distraction from my phone and the call I was about to make. The guy was drinking from a bottle of sparkling water, and I was debating whether I could broker some kind of conversation in English with a few French words thrown in when he moved even closer to me. I was taken aback until I realized he was making room for a pretty blond woman in a short black-and-white plaid skirt and dark sandals. She came armed with a bottle of rosé and two glasses.

I looked back at my phone. Paris seemed made for couples. Seeing everyone paired up like they were getting ready to board an ark for a ride down the Seine just made me miss my old plus-one and second-guess the decision to break up.

The sun had fully set, and the sky took on a warm royal-blue cast that made the lights from passing boats shimmer on water that had turned the same color. The sweeping lights from the boats shone onto the buildings that lined the riverbanks, and multilingual descriptions of the Paris sites came through the speakers on the upper decks. It was really beautiful. No one should experience it alone.

I looked at my phone again. Am I crazy, I wondered? *Probably*. Then I dialed.

CHAPTER SIX

La Palette

"I WAS A LITTLE NERVOUS TO CALL," I said to Guillaume, who was sitting across from me at La Palette, a café not far from where I'd been sitting by the river. The place was packed, and everyone looked fashionable and hip.

"I'm so glad you did. I assume you're not still looking for a hotel, though?"

"No, I'm all set with that. Thank you." I fished out the key from my purse and held it up, the large wooden rectangle dangling from it. "Hotel des Écoles."

Guillaume started to laugh. "You're not supposed to take those."

"What?"

"*La clef*. The key. That's why they have such a big piece of wood hanging from it. You return it to the desk when you leave the hotel."

"Seriously?" I asked, realizing I should have known as much.

No one would expect a person to carry around keychain this big. "Well, that makes sense now. It's kind of awkward. And heavy."

"I don't doubt that. It's how they know who is in the room. For housekeeping."

Housekeeping was okay, but I had to push down my paranoia that someone would be creeping around my room when I wasn't there for some reason other than to clean it. Then I reminded myself its shoebox size prevented standing upright, much less creeping.

He signaled to a waiter who was dressed in an outfit very similar to the black-and-white clothes he'd been wearing earlier. I wondered if that was a standard uniform for waiters here. "What would you like?" Guillaume asked.

"I've already had two plastic cups of wine at the little beach-front down by the river. I'm not sure I should have more." It was another side-effect of dating Johnny: I was always the designated driver and the level-headed yin to his carefree drunken yang. I didn't explain any of this to Guillaume, who was folding his reading glasses into a leather pouch.

"Ah, you found the Paris Plages. I love that. Well, the French pour small glasses, so you can have a few." Before I could object or even think about what else I might like, he told the waiter, "*Deux verres de vin rouge et une carafe d'eau.*" He turned to me. "Always ask for water," he said, gesturing to a carafe and two glasses on the table next to ours. "Otherwise, you'll end up spending all your money on bottled water. And our normal water tastes good."

"Good to know. Thanks," I said.

"Anything else I can tell you?" he asked.

A sigh escaped my chest before I could stop it. I wanted to be self-sufficient and independent, but exhaustion and disorganization were prevailing. "I don't know why this is so hard. I'm on vacation and I'm stressed out because I feel like I don't know how to do that."

"Do what?"

"Have fun." I filled him in on some details of what brought me on my solo trip, feeling whiny and pathetic.

"I think you'll find your way back to fun," he said quietly. "It sounds like he was just the wrong person for you." He was sweet. I felt guilty that I was boring him.

"Ugh, I'm so sorry, Guillaume. I dragged you out of your house, when you were probably perfectly happy to spend a relaxing evening at home, because I'm scared to be alone with my thoughts."

He placed a hand on mine. The gesture of intimacy caught me by surprise. I worried that he thought this—the lost-American routine, calling him at night—was all a big flirtatious come-on. Oh no. Did he think I was going to invite him back to the Hotel des Écoles? He'd be in for a rude awakening since he wouldn't fit in the room.

I looked up at him, but I couldn't decipher his expression. I'd felt like he'd taken a fatherly interest in my well-being back at his café, but I couldn't be sure anymore. He was at least ten years older than me, but that didn't mean anything. I realized I might have given him entirely the wrong impression. And here he was, ordering wine for us both.

I was an idiot. I realized he'd come out expecting a *menage à moi*, and I'd have to extract myself without angering a man I didn't know at all and who knew where I was staying. *Shit. Or the language app instructed, merde.*

"I did not mind getting out of the house. My husband is working at home tonight, and he can be... irritable when I'm there because our apartment isn't big and I like to sing."

Okay... I was wrong.

I broke out laughing—about the fact that I'd so misjudged

the moment as well as about the idea of Guillaume, so buttoned-up and quiet, bursting into song to such a degree that it would annoy another person. The situation—calling my new gay friend to listen to me whine about my love life—was almost a cliché. I myself was a cliché. The whiny breakup victim. The thought was enough to smack some sense into me.

"Oh, I'm so glad. I guess it worked out well for both of us." I took out my phone. "Please witness what I'm about to do," I said, swiping to my favorites list and deleting Johnny's number. Then I went to my contact list and did the same. That was it. He was gone.

Timed perfectly, the waiter returned with our glasses of wine and our carafe of water. Guillaume held his glass up to make a toast. "*À santé*. To health and to your next love. And there will be a next one. Maybe here in Paris."

I waved that thought away. I couldn't think about another relationship. But I felt good to have closure on this one.

"Don't worry—they will come looking for you," Guillaume said.

I took a sip of the wine. It was chilled, which seemed unusual for red.

"Not strange here," he told me. "There are many summer reds that are good to drink a little cold." He swirled his wine in the glass and sniffed it, eyes crinkling again when he held it to the light and squinted at the garnet color.

"How did you and your husband meet?" I asked.

He smiled in a way that said he was smitten. "Dance class. My friend used to teach a jazz class, and I signed up on the first day." Again, this surprised me. I could no more picture him dancing than I could singing. "I had hoped once to perform in musicals, but it turned out I'm not as talented as I thought. But I'm perfect for a jazz class. Jean-Yves is another story, however." He laughed at some memory. "The first day of class, he danced like an elephant. And I say this to you because there's no other way to describe him. He dances like he's trying to make a hole in the ground with each step. He's completely uncoordinated."

"Does he know that's how you feel about his dancing?" I asked.

"Oh, yes. I said it to him the first day he came to class. He didn't like me much because of it, but he really liked our instructor. It resulted in a little healthy competition between us. We both wanted the teacher's attention but for different reasons. Fortunately for me, our instructor was happily married to a woman."

"What made Jean-Yves sign up for a dance class in the first place if he's not coordinated?"

"He did it on a dare. He's competitive that way. He'd never turn down a chance to prove someone wrong."

"Worked out well for you."

"Yes," he said, gazing down at a silver band on his finger. I hadn't noticed it before, partly because he wore it on the right hand.

The café was growing noisier and more packed the later it got. The waiter who'd served us was balancing a tray with a bottle of wine, six glasses, two coffees, and a couple of beers for the table two down from ours, where a group of six had just sat down, squeezing into a space I wouldn't have thought could hold them. They lit up cigarettes and talked loudly and quickly.

Maybe they weren't speaking as fast as it seemed, but to my ears, it sounded like melodic patter mixed with laughter. Mopeds came buzzing by, and about half the people who were walking on Rue de Seine stopped at La Palette to talk with the waiter, who seemed to know them all. I'd thought the place I lived was semi-urban—the city of Santa Monica, which had lots of restaurants and foot traffic —but this scene made my home seem like the distant suburbs.

Everything was happening right here in the streets, with people living upstairs in historic architectural works of art, convening in the cafés, and spending as much time as possible in the warm summer night outside. I suddenly felt exhausted amid all the invigorating action. The need to close my eyes was real and immediate. I had sympathy for people who had kids and always walked around sleep deprived.

Guillaume must have seen the sudden shift in my eyes. "You've had a long day. I think you'll sleep well tonight."

"I know I will."

"Everything will look different in the morning. And if you can't sleep, go outside. Paris is beautiful in the early hours of the day. Take a walk, take a nap, let yourself be on vacation."

I nodded, feeling the weight of my head and the sudden difficulty of holding it upright. Guillaume dropped a couple of ten-euro notes on the table, not letting me pay for the drinks. "But I dragged you here," I said. "It should be my treat."

"There is no 'should.' It is my pleasure to buy you your first glass of chilled red wine. I hope it will prove memorable."

"Already proven. Merci, Guillaume."

He wouldn't let me walk back to my hotel alone, which was lucky for me because I might not have found it on my own through the haze of fatigue and wine. I followed him without paying attention to the route or to any of the shops along the way. I had one destination in mind—that tiny twin bed under the slanting roof.

We walked toward the water then stayed on the quai, which ran alongside the buildings, across the busy street from the river. At the intersection on Boulevard Saint-Michel, I froze, trying to decipher when it would be okay for us to cross the street. Cars seemed to be coming from all directions, and I couldn't see clearly which traffic lights they were following.

"How do people know when it's their turn to drive or walk?" I asked.

Guillaume pointed to a small post, no higher than a stop sign, with a light on it. "Traffic lights."

"I didn't see it. It's so small."

He shook his head. "Americans do everything bigger. But when you're used to it, you see that a small light is just as good. We don't have large kitchens with big refrigerators, so we shop for fresh food. There would not be a use for a place like Costco here."

I was surprised he knew about Costco, but I was too tired to ask him about it. A few minutes later, I could see the now-familiar towers of Notre-Dame, which signaled that we were close to my hotel.

When Guillaume left me in front of the hotel, he kissed me on both cheeks like I'd seen him do with other people earlier. I passed right by a new woman at the front desk, who looked at me quizzically, like she was ready to retrieve my key from one of the hooks. But I held mine up. "Sorry," I said. "Tomorrow, I'll turn it in when I leave." She smiled and nodded.

When my head hit the pillow, I slept without dreaming.

CHAPTER SEVEN

A MODESTLY-PRICED HOTEL IN PARIS
The Next Morning, Sort Of

I COULDN'T BELIEVE it when I looked at the glowing screen of my phone. It was three a.m., and I'd only slept for a couple of hours. Yet I was wide awake. It was six in the evening at home. I spent the next few hours trying to force myself back to sleep because I knew I needed to sleep at night and stay awake during the day. It would be hard to function on only two hours of sleep.

Drifting off and waking up for the next few hours brought me to morning, at least. The sun shone through the window and I was awake for good.

Paris looked even more beautiful in the early-morning light. Guillaume had been right. The streets had gotten magically scrubbed of trash as if by tidy vacuumers who worked through the dawn hours. A few boulangeries had opened their doors, and a framework of metal stalls indicated where a farmer's market would soon be open for business, but otherwise it was quiet.

I walked back down to the Seine, which was flat and blue. It was too early for the boats to begin their tours. I still couldn't wrap my brain around how it would feel to live and work every day in a city with gorgeous Haussmann-era architecture and picturesque monuments with hundreds of years of history behind them. It wasn't like I expected everyone in Paris to resemble Marie Antoinette, but the young, hip French looked a lot like the people who lived in my neighborhood, and I felt envious that they got to work and live in such a beautiful place. I doubted that I'd ever get tired of the view, even if I moved to Paris and lived there for years.

From where I stood, I saw at least four cafés, none that stood out or called to me in a special way. So I chose the nearest one and took a seat outside, facing the street. I fumbled through an attempt to order coffee and a pastry, ultimately asking for what I wanted in English because the kind waiter sensed my struggle and told me he could understand me without having to pull out my translator app.

The café was empty, and the seat I'd chosen was far away from the only other people outside having coffee. I inhaled a deep breath, smelling diesel fumes mixed with fresh air and cigarette smoke. The smells comingled into a city perfume that felt uniquely Paris, and I had a pinch-me moment. I was really sitting at a French café. I was really a trans-Atlantic adventurer.

Moving efficiently between tables, the waiter came back with my coffee and a croissant. He tilted his head at me like he could sense I have some questions, but I did my best to offer up enough of a smile that he seemed reassured. I couldn't spend my entire time relying on the kindness of waiters to get me through the days. I needed to put on my big girl panties and come up with a plan. I was in France. On vacation, for crying out loud.

The coffee helped. Like a magic bullet, the first couple sips woke my brain up and started me thinking more clearly about what I wanted to do all day in the city of love. My first thought— shopping. Even if it was only window shopping at stores I couldn't afford, I could grant myself a little retail therapy.

It turned out I'd picked a good café because I could see up and down a couple of streets right from my table, so I could come up with a plan just by looking around. The bright red sign of something called Monoprix caught my eye. I had no idea what it was, but my loose translation of the name made it sound like maybe everything at the store was one price. I felt a surge of excitement, thinking that I'd found the French equivalent of a Dollar Store. That had to be worth a visit.

A few minutes later, coffee drained and croissant devoured, I paid my check and walked down the block to Monoprix, my mind zinging with glee over the cheap Parisian finds that were certain to be waiting inside. I figure that even a tiny travel-sized deodorant would be exciting if it was French.

The automatic doors zipped open and I stepped inside.

Monoprix was a supermarket. A big one. And nothing was cheap or the same price. But Monoprix was nothing short of awesome.

In addition to regular groceries, it had a huge department of clothes, a lot of which were on sale at crazy-cheap prices. Though I didn't really need leggings and T-shirts printed with English-language sayings like "Surf's up" and "It's all good," I took comfort knowing they were there if I needed them. I debated buying some underwear, just because. French underwear, even from a supermarket, still seemed glamorous.

I spent a good half hour browsing up and down the aisles, where whole sections were devoted to colorful pens and notebooks, makeup, baby clothes, towels... I was fascinated by the French versions of all the things I'd seen at home, as though they were more exotic and interesting. Eventually, it dawned on me that I'd yet to see any food.

That was because Monoprix had a whole second floor below ground and all the food—plus a zillion kinds of bottled water, some with gas, some without—was on the other level. I had to look at everything—the dairy cases with high-fat butter and more varieties of cheese than I knew existed, the aisles of chocolate bars and cookies. I immediately appreciated the brilliance of Monoprix when I realized I could buy a piece of luggage upstairs and fill it with cookies and chocolate downstairs to take home at the end of my trip. There didn't appear to be a consumer problem for which Monoprix wouldn't have a solution.

My day had already done a one-eighty. I was giddy with excitement over an entire aisle of mustard varieties. I also felt myself getting sucked into an epicurean vortex that threatened to derail my sightseeing, so I collected my wits. I grabbed a bottle of water, a package of butter biscuits, and a few peaches and got in line at the cash registers. I had a long day of sightseeing ahead and who knew if I'd have time for lunch? Or dinner? And yes, I realized I was already making up reasons why I couldn't possibly dine alone.

When it was my turn, I handed the cashier my items and waited for her to ring them up. She took the peaches and gave me a strange look. She turned them over and examined them, then shook her head and said something I didn't understand in French, handing them back to me.

"I... I'm sorry, what?" I stammered.

She repeated what she'd said, throwing her hands up like she had no idea what to do with someone as inept at grocery shopping as me. She had to know I wouldn't understand because I didn't get it the first time. I examined the peaches like she had, but I didn't see anything wrong with them.

I could hear rumblings from the people in the line behind me and next to me. A couple of them were looking my way, and one was pointing. They all seemed to be mocking me for something I didn't even know I'd done.

"You're supposed to weigh them first," came a voice from behind me. I turned and caught a quick glimpse of a guy under a baseball cap. I couldn't really see his face but he was probably annoyed, and I realized I was holding up the whole line with my mistake.

I still didn't know what he meant. *Where was I supposed to weigh them?*

Overwhelmed and embarrassed, I dropped the peaches and dumped the cookies and the water on the counter before backing away. "Never mind. I don't need it." I left the cashier to figure out what to do with my aborted purchase and hurried up the stairs and out of the store.

My heart was pounding and I felt a rivulet of sweat drip down from my temple. At a grocery store at home, I'd just have apologized and fixed my mistake, but here, in a different language, nothing felt manageable. I was a little shocked at myself that I bolted without trying harder.

The strong independent self I was counting on seemed to be on her own vacation someplace else.

I thought about going back to my hotel and asking Sylvie at the desk to give me a download on everything I needed to know if I wasn't going to embarrass myself several times a day. I clearly hadn't done my homework. It was so unlike me to come to a foreign country unprepared, but because it was supposed to be a trip for two, I'd decided to be more spontaneous. The two of us didn't need a plan. We'd have each other.

In the month since our breakup, I'd been too busy uncoupling our possessions and my emotions to read up on how to properly buy fruit.

I had no idea where I was going, but I'd walked the better part of a block before jet lag and emotions got the better of me. I leaned into the doorway of a bakery that had a sign saying it was closed for summer vacation and would reopen August 15. I hoped someone wouldn't yell at me for loitering, and as I imagined being scolded yet again, I felt the tears well up in my eyes.

I desperately didn't want to be the kind of person who was afraid to eat dinner alone or who couldn't make a mistake without crying. I also hadn't slept very much and that could make a person tearful, I reminded myself, working hard to add *sympathetic self* to my independent self.

People walked by, oblivious to me, happily talking to one another in fast bursts of French that I wasn't going to pick up just by sitting around cafés and listening. And definitely not in a matter of hours. No one expected that, so I needed to chill the heck out.

"Thank God you slowed down. I didn't want to chase you all over the city to give you these," I heard from a male voice to my left. The English was a salve to my aching Anglophile ears.

I looked up and saw the guy in the baseball hat, the one who'd seemed irritated in line behind me. He held out the three peaches I'd attempted to buy, only now they were in a plastic bag with a sticker on them, properly weighed and priced. "The cashier was going to wait and let you go back and weigh them, but I guess you didn't understand what she was telling you... anyway, no one should be without peaches."

I felt so overwhelmed by this act of kindness that a new wave of tears formed, ready to spring forth. I fought them back, trying to maintain my composure, because crying over peaches wasn't something I was prepared to explain to a stranger. After a couple seconds of hard swallowing and blinking, I croaked out my gratitude.

"Oh. Wow. That's so nice. Thank you." I took the peaches

and awkwardly stuffed them into my bag. He handed me the cookies and water too. "You bought all my stuff?" I was shocked that a stranger could be so nice to me. And, once I took a closer look at him, an exceptionally great-looking stranger. My heart started beating a little faster and I felt a blush creep over my cheeks.

"Well... yeah. A person's gotta stay hydrated. And you seemed like you were having a rough day."

"Yeah, that's an understatement." I stopped myself before I unloaded my tale of two warring selves, because I doubted he was super interested. "Anyway, thank you. I don't usually fall apart at the checkout counter... but I panicked in the face of angry shoppers."

He nodded, his lips tugging to the side and relaxing into a smile. Yes, he was definitely attractive. I didn't want to stare, mainly because I wasn't sure where I wanted to look first; his high cheekbones, his sharp jawline or his pretty, plush lips, which were still parted in a smile which revealed some very straight, very white teeth.

But what really got me was his eyes. They were a different shade of brown than I'd seen before, almost deep grey and impossibly dark and bottomless, like they possessed a magic power to prevent a person from looking away. I had a feeling they could make women bend to his will, not that I had any intention of proving that theory. Ugh, it almost hurt to look at him directly, like staring at the sun.

I did my best to cast my eyes down, not wanting to stare, and a little frightened that I might fall under a spell of some kind.

At the same time, despite the astounding face, he seemed like a regular person, touring around Paris grocery stores and buying peaches for wayward female travelers. He seemed so comfortable—the polar opposite of how I felt, trying to acclimate and understand street signs and snippets of conversation on no sleep.

I snuck another look at him, trying to avoid the eyes. In his baseball cap, he looked like the guys I was used to seeing in Santa Monica, right down to his beige linen shorts and crazy-expensive trendy sneakers. He was definitely American.

"First time in Paris?" he asked.

"Is it that obvious?"

He laughed. "Not at all. But jet lag and a new city will kick anyone's ass."

"I appreciate the sympathy."

"And look at it this way—you'll never make that mistake again in a grocery store. You can check that off your list of life lessons." He swung a dark-green backpack off his shoulder, unzipped it, pulled out his own bottle of water, and unscrewed the top to take a drink.

"You got that right, because I'm never going in a grocery store again."

"Oh, come on. You scare that easily?" His eyes—those eyes—were challenging but playful. I willed myself to adopt his attitude.

"Yeah, I guess you're right. It's true—I'm really jet-lagged. And I kinda hit the ground running here without looking at a guidebook or figuring anything out," I said.

"Trust me, there are lots of bigger ways you can offend people here. Don't try to pick your own fruit at an open market. The produce sellers'll have your head. You tell them what you want and let them pick for you. Unless they invite you to touch the produce."

"Thank you. Offending the fruit vendors was next on my list of ways to make a crappy impression with the French."

He smiled then fished in his backpack and extracted a pair of sunglasses, which he put on. Now I could barely see any of his face, but I was protected from the magic eyes. He put out his hand and introduced himself. "Chris."

"Nikki," I said, shaking his hand, noting that the gesture seemed oddly formal here. I'd already seen so many French people leaning in to hug and kiss each other on both cheeks that the handshake felt like we were doing business. And then I stopped myself because I realized I was unconsciously wishing for more of a connection than a mere exchange of stone fruit for gratitude.

It felt so nice to talk to an American, who wouldn't judge me for speaking English in a French-speaking country. I found myself wanting to linger with him a bit longer before I went back out on my own. Maybe he was alone and looking for someone to hang with. Maybe we could tackle Paris together.

While the scenarios for how the rest of the day might go unfurled in my head, I realized he'd been speaking, and I hadn't heard a word of it. I mentally chastised myself for thinking he was interested in anything other than doing a good deed. I needed to let him say goodbye like a normal person.

That was what he was saying, right?

"I'm sorry, what did you say?" I asked.

"I said... have dinner with me," he repeated. But it still didn't sink in.

"I'm sorry, what? I zoned out for a second. Jet lag. It's killing me."

"It's my last night here in town, and I've got no plans. Have dinner with me. I know the city pretty well. I can give you my download on stuff you shouldn't miss while you're here..."

I raised one eyebrow and tried to sound mysterious. "You're assuming I have no plans." I think I just sounded confused about the situation.

He looked sideways at me, his skepticism clear in the way his mouth hooked to the side. "You said you just got here, so I figured... Do you have plans?"

"No. I don't know why I said that. I have no plans... and yes. Dinner would be great," I said, inwardly gleeful that I'd forestalled dining alone for one more night. He seemed nice. And there was certainly nothing wrong with looking at him over a plate of snails for a couple hours. "Do you have a place you like? Or should we meet somewhere and figure it out?"

He looked down at his backpack and stalled, suddenly seeming uncomfortable. "Can I get back to you on that? I need to check a couple of things." It felt like maybe he was rethinking his invitation.

"I mean, only if it works for you. Whatever you want," I said. Trying to be chill. Possibly failing.

"No, it's not that. I just don't know where we should go. Can I...?" he asked, gesturing to my phone. I obediently handed it over, and he tapped in his phone number and sent himself a text. "Great. Now you have my number. I'll get my act together and text you a time and a place. Sound good?"

"Sounds great. Yep. Great," I said, immediately thinking I sounded idiotic. But I was gleeful that Monoprix had, in fact, delivered a solution to all my wants and needs. "And thank you. For the fruit save."

He nodded. "Happy to help out a fellow expat." His phone beeped, and he looked down at it. "Okay, so, good," he said, seeming consumed by the contents of his text message.

"Yes. Good."

Still looking down at his phone, he said, "I gotta run. I'll text you later." Then he was moving off down the street practically at a jog. It was then that I noticed he also had broad shoulders and a nice ass, which was receding in the distance with the rest of him.

I felt like jogging, too, because for the first time since I'd arrived in Paris, I had a plan. Despite my yearning to fly by the seat of my pants and be a little more carefree, the plan made me comfortable and happy. I fished one of the peaches out of the plastic bag and rubbed it on my shirt to clean it. When I took a bite, the juice dribbled down my chin. It tasted delicious and French.

CHAPTER EIGHT

Rive Gauche

I WALKED for the next two hours. Over bridges, around gardens, beneath stunning stone architecture.

Then I was hungry again. I crossed the large Boulevard Saint-Germain and finding a seat under the awning of Café Napoléon, where I ordered a café au lait and a *chèvre chaud*, my mouth watering in anticipation of the two circles of goat cheese, each melted atop a toasted piece of bread, with some salad greens on the side. That's how it was described on the menu, the English translated version, which I was grateful to have.

From my seat outside, I could see the Saint-Germain church and the Les Deux Magots down the block, which had been a favorite hangout of Ernest Hemingway when he was writing novels in cafés and drinking absinthe.

The area felt touristy. A family walked past me, the husband wearing a Yankees cap, a camera bag strapped across his chest, and the wife in big sunglasses, carrying a Gucci purse, and speaking in a thick drawl. "I'm gonna smack you if you don't stop messin' around," she told her kids, two girls who looked about ten years old and who were trying to trip each other by flat-tiring the other's flip-flops.

When they stopped to look at the menu at Café Napoléon, I was worried that they'd sit right next to me and I'd overhear their family drama rather than work on absorbing a word or two of French from the people around me. But they kept moving down the street.

A forty-something impeccably dressed woman, her hair hanging down over her shoulders, pulled out a chair and spread a napkin on it before lifting her small dog—who I could tell was a boy from his navy blue collar emblazoned with boats—and setting him down on it. She sat down in the chair next to him and ran a hand over his fur and then took a cigarette out and lit it with the other. She ordered a glass of wine and a plate of pâté, from what I could discern. I only caught a couple of words, but I was pretty sure "*vin*," and "*fois gras*" were in the mix.

The waiter appeared with my hot goat cheese, which smelled amazing and dripped with butter. I'd decided to fully embrace France, eating real butter and full-fat cheese and drinking wine. *Why not start with a glass right now?*

I felt inspired by the woman next to me though not inspired to smoke. I had yet to toast myself and launch the beginning of my solo adventure. I tried not to think that my change of mood and attitude had anything to do with my dinner plans, later, but a small part of me knew it had helped push me along. Some-times a girl just needed a push. The independent spirit was there, waiting to be unleashed.

I cut through the cheese and bread and brought the first bite to my lips, knowing the impending food coma would be a theme of my time in France. The cheese and buttered bread tasted decadent and delicious, and the vinegary salad greens cut through that taste perfectly. The wine was a mistake, however, because no sooner did I scarf down the last bite of lunch than I felt a wave of exhaustion overtake me with a force I hadn't experienced before. I had no choice but to race back to my hotel and turn in for a two-hour nap and dream of butter and cheese.

The rest of the day disappeared in a blur because I couldn't pull myself out of the groggy nap. I knew all the rules about getting past jet lag, and the middle of the day was the worst possible time to give in to fatigue. But working so hard to stay awake and function like a normal human had made this feel like anything but a vacation. If it took me another day or so to get my body clock on track, so be it. I'd preferred not to push through the afternoon only to be a basket case by dinner.

By the time I woke up, it was almost four o'clock. I scrambled off the bed and into the shower. I wanted to have time for my hair to dry before I met Chris for dinner. He hadn't confirmed we were even meeting yet, but I needed a shower desperately, so technically I wasn't doing it for him.

When I dried off and checked my phone, I found a text message with a time and a place, along with a couple of emojis —a fist bump and a smiley face. *See you then?* he'd typed.

I had no idea where the place was, but I typed back a thumbs-up and *Looking forward.*

And I was. He'd seemed kind, and there was nothing wrong with having a table for two instead of a table for one. Plus, he seemed to know his way around, so I'd have a safety net to keep me from skirting more French customs.

The restaurant was not too far from my hotel. I looked on the map to see what might be between here and there so I could do some sightseeing on the way. The Musée d'Orsay, with its world-renowned impressionist collection, was open until seven in the evening, so I could get there and have at least a little bit of time to look at a couple of floors of art before finding the restaurant. It seemed like the perfect plan because the museum was a place I wanted to visit and the timing worked perfectly.

The walk along the Rue de l'Université took me past some art galleries and a lot of large closed double doors, some of which had interesting doorknobs. I started snapping photos of the best ones, a couple that looked like lions with door knockers in their mouths and a few round decorative knobs on red or blue doors. The best was a claw holding a ball that hung down as a knocker on a maroon door.

As I passed by, I heard the buzz of an electronic lock, and one of the doors swung open as a man in a long coat stepped over the transom and exited the building. Before the door shut, I caught a glimpse of an adorable cobblestoned courtyard entrance to the apartments in the back part of the building. After that, as I passed the painted doors, I imagined the court-yards that lay behind them and the lives of the people who lived in those buildings. I realized I could probably find an Airbnb rental instead of my hotel, and if I could afford it, maybe I could stay in a cool apartment off a pretty courtyard like one of these.

It didn't take long before I was walking up the steps outside the museum and paying my entry fee. Once inside, I looked up at the high ceiling of the atrium, admiring the ornate design of the glass ceiling and the carved arches of the building. It had once been a train station, its outer facade recognizable by the large clock faces that looked over the Seine. Arrows pointed to the restaurant on the top floor. Never one to pass up a good view, I headed up there first.

A large clock, backed by glass, took up one whole wall of the restaurant, and I could see through it all the way across the city to the white-domed church, Sacré-Coeur, which sat atop Mont-martre—another place on my long list of sites I wanted to see. For the moment, I settled for seeing it through the clock face, which made for a cool photo. The open doors of the restaurant urged me outside to the balcony, and from there, I could see across the Seine to the right bank and the Tuileries Garden.

I was already lovestruck by the Musée d'Orsay for its view of the sites of Paris, and I hadn't seen a single piece of art. After swooning for a few more minutes, I headed back inside and went floor by floor, artist by artist, taking in as many impressionists as I could before the alarm on my phone reminded me to meet Chris. I saw whole rooms filled with Monets and Manets, water lilies, ladies with parasols, and lakeside scenes. I ogled dancers painted by Degas and fields and portraits by Van Gogh. I'd never seen so much stunning art in one place.

For the first time since the plane had landed, I felt fully alive as if in the beginnings of a great love affair. With masters of art. With centuries-old architecture. With Paris. As I looked at room after room of gorgeous paintings, a wave of emotions washed over me and left me with a rosy aura of calm and appreciation for being here.

This was why I'd traveled so far—to be in Paris, staring at paintings of the masters. All residual worry over traveling alone fell away. I could easily look at art and architecture for two weeks. And I felt firm in my conviction that I was done worrying about being alone, done thinking about Johnny. He had no place in my life anymore.

Lower floors of the museum had sculpture and furnishings, but it was the impressionist paintings that I couldn't stop gazing at. When my phone alarm pulled me from a love fest with Van Gogh's *Starry Night Over the Rhône*, I kind of didn't want to leave and meet a guy I'd talked to for five minutes in a doorway, even if he'd been exceptionally nice to me. I debated texting him and apologizing that I couldn't make it. The museum would be closing soon, but I could spend the last twenty minutes staring at more paintings. I hadn't realized how much I loved the art.

And Chris was leaving in the morning. He'd never see me

again and probably wouldn't think anything of it. Maybe he could still meet up with his friends.

I took out my phone, prepared to send him a *thanks anyway* text, but then I fast-forwarded a couple of hours to the evening, picturing myself back where I'd sat the night before, alone with my plastic cup of wine, looking at all the couples around me. After a little wine, I'd start feeling lonely again, and I couldn't keep running back to Guillaume, as nice as he was. He did have his own life.

Once I fully admitted to myself I was using Chris so I wouldn't have to face an empty dinner table, I turned my back on the beautiful Renoir paintings of children's faces and happy crowds and headed back down the stairs and out of the museum. I wasn't proud of my motives, not at all. But I gave myself a half a point for being honest.

There were worse things than meeting a good-looking guy for dinner, and I reminded myself that I'd be in Paris for two weeks. There would still be plenty of time to return to the museum and ogle the impressionist paintings.

CHAPTER NINE

La Fontaine de Mars

IT WAS about a ten-minute walk from the museum to Rue Saint-Dominique, where Chris had said to meet him. The street was packed with restaurants, cafés, and people. Everyone seemed like they had somewhere to go.

At first, I didn't see Chris outside La Fontaine de Mars, because he had his head down, looking at a menu. He also had his back to me and I barely knew him. But I recognized the trendy sneakers, which he was wearing with light-colored cotton pants and a dark grey T-shirt—casual, and necessary in this heat. Anything with more fabric or weight would just soak up sweat.

I exhaled a small sigh of relief that I wasn't underdressed in my navy-blue wrap dress and the leather sandals that my feet would tolerate even if I walked several miles. Walking was a given in Paris. It was still pretty warm out, and the sun was high in the sky, reflecting brightly off Chris's sunglasses when he turned, his face half-hidden by the menu.

I caught his eye and he put up a hand to wave me over. He continued to hold the menu up in front of both of us like we were reading it, but he was talking instead. "How're you doing?"

"So much better than this morning. I slept, I showered..."

"It looks good on you," he said, his gaze moving from my eyes to my lips and back with a look of appreciation. I couldn't process the meaning behind his look because he was already rattling off instructions. "I thought we could grab a drink here then find someplace else for dinner. There are a bunch of great places that don't take reservations, so it's good to go either early or late. We've already missed early... Does that work for you?"

"Um, sure. Sounds good," I said, a little surprised that he'd already decided on the course of our whole evening but equally pleased that he'd relieved me of having to come up with a plan. "A plan that I don't have to make is a good plan."

"Especially in a new city, right?"

"Exactly."

He spoke in French to the waiter, who led us to a table at one end of a patio. Chris gestured for me to take the seat facing the street, and he took the one opposite. "So you can people watch if you want."

"Thanks." I scooted into my seat, which was wedged against the wall, and Chris said something I couldn't understand to the waiter. I took the opportunity to get a better look at him. I'd been too overwhelmed by exhaustion and embarrassment when I met him that morning to really take in his features. Well, that's not true. I took them in then, and I allowed myself the bonus of taking them in again.

Now that I sat facing him, there was little stopping me from noticing the strong curve of his jaw and the two days' growth of beard that looked good on him even though half his face was still hidden by his sunglasses.

"Do you like red wine? There's one I liked when I was here

once before and they still have it. I checked the menu while I was waiting."

"Sure. Red is good," I said, fighting my feminist instinct to be offended that he was taking control again. I kind of liked it, and he seemed to have a preference, whereas I had none. Guillaume had done the exact same thing the night before, and it hadn't bothered me at all. But he was French. It was a cultural thing. This guy was American, so I questioned his motives.

Did he just think I was a clueless tourist who couldn't order her own drink, or was he trying to show me that he knew his way around a wine menu? Or was he just trying to make things easier because I was new here and he was nice, and I needed to chill the hell out?

I had to go with the odds, which were stacked in favor of the latter. I needed to chill.

He explained what he wanted to the waiter, who was nodding and smiling like he was downright charmed by Chris and his pretty face. "I hope you like it," he said to me. "The wine."

"I'm a big wine aficionado. Hard to impress. I won't even drink wine unless it comes in a cardboard box," I said, my self-deprecating attempt at humor masking my discomfort at what felt like an awkward date. He looked at me like he wasn't sure I was kidding.

I could be looking at a few more Renoirs right now.

"So... you speak French well," I said, searching for a topic.

"I'm really trying to learn. Definitely better now than the first time I came here, when all I could say was 'I'd like a beer' and 'Where's the bathroom?'"

"Both useful." I smiled, but I was terrible at small talk. "So when was that—the first time you came here?"

"College. I did a semester in Spain, and my friends and I

traveled every chance we got on weekends. France was an easy trip over the border."

"So you speak Spanish too?" I wasn't about to test him with my leftover Spanish skills from high school.

"Yeah. I grew up with it. My mom's from Madrid. She raised us bilingual." In my foggy brain, something about that sounded familiar. Did I know someone else whose mom was from Madrid? I couldn't remember.

As I was puzzling this out, the waiter returned with a small bowl of olives and another bowl of potato chips, along with the wine, which was chilled, as it had been the night before. He showed the bottle to Chris, who nodded. As he uncorked the bottle, he spoke to Chris, rattling on so quickly I couldn't make out a single familiar-sounding word.

Chris smiled and said, "*Merci*" a couple of times. That, I recognized. I wondered what he was thanking him for. The waiter patted Chris on the shoulder a couple times and grinned at him some more.

After Chris had sampled and approved the wine, he offered me a taste. "I shouldn't be the only one who decides."

I appreciated being considered even though I didn't know squat about wine. I was pretty sure red wine came from red grapes and white wine came from green grapes, but I wasn't about to share my pseudo knowledge with Chris. I took a sip. It was cool and had a nice dry fruit taste. "It's yummy. Does that qualify as an official wine rating?"

"Works for me." He nodded at the waiter, who filled both our glasses and, with a regretful last glance at Chris, left us alone. He held up his glass for a toast. "*À santé.*" We clinked and sipped. I didn't want to be rude, but it was tempting to look over his shoulder and watch the people walking past. Everyone seemed to be a study in fashion or relationships or the marvel of contemporary people living in a historic place.

"Fun to watch, huh?" he said. But he didn't turn his head to see what I was seeing. Since we were seated at the end of the row of tables, there was room on the side if he wanted to move his chair around for at least a partial view.

"Do you want to sit there?" I asked, gesturing to the seat with the better view.

"Nah, this works for me." I liked that he wasn't fussy.

"So how long have you been in Paris? You said you came with friends?"

"Sort of. I have friends who live here. I've been in the city off and on for a couple months."

"Nice gig if you can get it," I said.

"I'm not complaining. It's been an interesting time to be here, politically."

I wasn't sure what to say to that. I followed the news as much as the next person, but I wouldn't have jumped all over a trip to France just for arguments between socialist and far-right politicians. "Are you involved in politics?" Maybe he was a diplomat or something.

"No, I'm just an armchair policy wonk. I studied it in school, and I can't tear myself away from politics no matter where I am. It's an election year, so it's been particularly brutal here."

"I haven't been following French politics, though it would have been a good thing to do before coming, I guess."

He shrugged. "Not necessarily. I'm happy to fill you in on what I know, but be honest. Does it really interest you ore are you just being nice?"

I laughed. "I'm interested. But I'm afraid you'd have to back way up to the Napoleon era because I haven't taken a history class in a while."

He took me at my word, and for the next forty-five minutes, I got an in-depth tutorial on protests by city workers, socialist economics, and the fragile political détente that held the whole system in place. It was fascinating, and I slowly found myself tuning out the passers-by behind Chris and all the chatter around us and soaking up his wealth of knowledge.

He went deep on issues in parliament and the complexities that came after the Brexit vote in neighboring England. I'd studied math and computer science, so most of my political knowledge came from a freshman year poli sci survey class and whatever was on my phone's news feed. His knowledge came from reading Politico, reading books, and asking questions. "Okay," he said, finally, shaking his head. "I'm stopping now before your eyes glaze over."

"I wasn't glazing."

"I'm still stopping." He grabbed the wine bottle and refilled our glasses. Then he gazed quietly into my eyes again and I got uncomfortable. I had a hunch he could see right through to my brain and read my thoughts, which were about him. Who was this gorgeous poli sci nerd?

"So are you here for work?" I asked, wondering if I was being too nosy. But he'd invited a complete stranger to dinner and had to know there would be some getting-to-know-you questions. Like I said, I'm terrible at small talk. I didn't know how else to fill the quiet void.

"Yeah, pretty much. I finished up a week ago, and now I'm taking a break, kind of still getting daily emails that are keeping me from leaving anything at the office, so to speak. How about you? Work or play?"

I opted not to pour out my whole saga about the breakup and the trip that was supposed to be for two. "Vacation. I was supposed to come with a friend, but it didn't work out." Much as I tried, I'd stumbled a bit on the word *friend*.

"Got it," Chris said. I had the feeling he'd caught my meaning. "Well, your friend's loss, because look at this place. Have you gotten to see much outside of the fluorescent lights in

Monoprix?" He was smiling. What I saw in Chris's expression was genuine contentment in being in the moment. The feeling was contagious. I felt myself relax, aided a little bit by the wine, which tasted just fruity enough and was perfectly chilled as it rolled over my tongue.

"I spent a great couple hours at the Musée d'Orsay. I might have to go back."

"It's amazing, isn't it? The first couple times I went, I didn't know you could get out on to the roof, but then I saw a photo in a travel magazine taken through the clock with a view of Sacré-Coeur."

I nodded and produced my phone to show him I'd taken that exact photo. "I guess I'm not that original."

"Hey, at least you figured it out on your first trip there. I had to go back three times and read about it on a plane."

"Do you travel here a lot for work?" I asked. I was curious to know what he did that allowed him to be in Paris for two months. He'd made a reference to an office. I knew management consultants who traveled most of the year, moving from one city to the next so they could help companies downsize or evaluate their growth plans. One friend had been gone so often he'd given up his apartment in LA and just stayed in a hotel when he was home, which he referred to as being "on the beach."

"Sometimes. At least a couple times a year." The wheels in my mind chugged along, determining what I thought he might do for a living, purely based on surface impressions. He seemed bright, so business or law felt like logical assumptions. I tried to think of other reasons a person would come to Europe for work. Of course, I could have come right out and asked, but this way was more fun.

"Sounds like nice work if you can get it. Right?" I asked.

He looked at me quizzically, like he was evaluating whether it was a trick question. Maybe it was inappropriate to ask. Maybe he was in the CIA, and I just hadn't picked up on the signs. I studied his face again. He'd taken off his sunglasses, and I noticed he had long lashes shielding the brown-grey almost protectively.

But there was no hiding the fire in those eyes. The color was mesmerizing, so much so that I had to force myself to look away. I knew my eyes weren't mesmerizing. They couldn't be more ordinary and pale brown. Until that moment, I'd never thought of eye color as an asset. For him, it definitely was.

"I mean, yeah. It's all good. Of course, not all the travel takes me to Europe. Depends on the project. The next one shoots in Georgia, which doesn't thrill me only because it'll still be hot as hell, but most of the work'll be done on a set," he said like it was an addendum to a conversation we'd already had.

My brain was churning through the new information. Shooting, sets... He clearly worked in entertainment. As he continued to talk, I started to get the feeling I should know who he was. Director, model, actor... living in LA had made everyone with good looks seem similar to me, and I'd long since stopped wondering if someone was in the entertainment business, because so many of them were or wanted to be. It didn't impress me one way or the other.

I started to sweat as I realized Chris was still talking, answering a question I couldn't remember asking. "But I've been lucky. France... it's kind of become a home away from home for me over the past few years. I actually bought a little place here."

I stole a glance down the row of other tables. Maybe it was my imagination, but I thought I saw a couple of people trying to furtively get a look at him as if even here, away from the American film industry, people might know who he was, which made me realize I'd better figure it out pretty damn quickly.

"So how did you get into it? What made you go into the field?" I asked, being as vaguely specific as I could. I knew that if he really did have some kind of notoriety, people probably asked him this all the time, and he might not want to talk about it.

But he leaned back and took a sip of his wine, seemingly unbothered. "Drama class. When I was eight. I went to this Catholic school, and we did this winter sing every year at school, and one year, the teacher needed a few kids to act out little parts with lines. I got picked, and I was terrified. But my mom forced me to do it. 'You don't say no to the nuns.' So I did it, and it was really fun. So I signed up for the play the next year and every year after that."

So he was an actor. Of course, he'd assume I knew that. Actors had big egos. I felt a little dumb for not recognizing him, but I wasn't a big moviegoer, and there were a lot of actors out there. Half of them didn't really do much acting other than going to auditions and booking tiny television roles or commercials. I had no idea where he fell on the spectrum. Plus, we were nowhere near LA, where actors were a dime a dozen. I needed context clues if I was expected to draw the right conclusions.

"That's a great story. I wish I'd known what I wanted to do when I was eight. I'm not sure I know now."

I told him about my job at the public-relations firm and how I'd had to write press releases on a daily basis for companies that wanted to gin up news stories about things that didn't always seem like big news. "I had to learn what news reporters were looking for. It's not enough to write a press release saying, 'Gap has a new line of jeans.' Saying something's new isn't a story, at least not for a big news outlet. Reporters don't want to work that hard to figure out how to turn my press release into a story. If I can do that for them, I have a better chance of them running a news piece." I realized I'd been going on and on. "Is this boring?"

"Not at all. Tell me more. What would you do to sell a story on jeans?"

"Well, it's about making the jeans part of a larger trend—like teenagers bringing back the preppy look. Or about a company making a big financial bet on these jeans to turn things around after a mistake."

"So you're giving the reporter the headline and then making sure the company you work for gets a good mention in the story."

"Exactly."

"Smart," he said. "Sounds like you're good at your job."

The waiter returned and poured the last from our bottle of wine. I couldn't believe we'd almost finished the bottle. I barely felt its effects. He lingered a moment longer, asking Chris a couple of questions. Chris shook his head in answer to each one and gave a polite, "*Non, merci.*" Then finally, he said "*Oui, d'accord.*"

The waiter seemed elated and practically skipped away. Chris didn't explain, but he seemed a little perturbed.

"Everything okay?" I asked.

"Oh, yeah. It's fine. He was saying the wine is on the house, but he wants me to take a photo with him before I leave."

"Do you not like the whole photo thing?" I was starting to realize this guy might be a bigger celebrity than I'd realized. Not too many people got their checks comped in exchange for a photo. I was desperate to pull out my phone and do a Google search to figure it out, but I wouldn't even know where to begin. *Actors named Chris* would yield a few too many results to casually page through under the table.

"I'm fine with the photo—it's not that. I just feel like I should pay for my own wine."

"Well, if it makes you feel better, some religions believe that taking a photo steals your soul, so if you think about it that way, you're paying a lot more than the price of the wine."

He laughed. "That's the best thing I've heard in a year. Okay, well, let's enjoy it, then, because it sounds like I've made a deal with the devil."

"Only according to certain religions. You'll have to ask the nuns how they feel about it."

He picked up his glass, clinked it against mine, and took a healthy sip. I could barely focus on anything except the urgent need to find out his last name. If I'd been back at home, I'd never have accepted a dinner invitation from someone without knowing his full name. Then again, maybe that was part of my problem. I was trying on something new, going with the flow. Right now, it didn't seem to fit too well.

The discomfort wasn't going to go away until I solved the puzzle of who was sitting across from me. I couldn't come out and ask. And if he wasn't going to pull out a credit card, I couldn't casually glance down at his name.

"So what's the name of your next project?" I asked casually, like I was just making conversation. Bad conversation. But at least knowing that would allow me to hunt down his identity once and for all so I'd feel like I was on even footing.

"It's the next *White Serpent*. Part four."

"Cool. Well, I guess you've got the part down by the fourth one, right? That's gotta be nice," I said, my voice sounding about an octave higher than usual. I was already getting up from the table because I'd heard of *White Serpent*. It was a multi-billion dollar franchise. On the scale of my moronic questions, asking about his next film had ranked right up there. "Sit tight a sec. I'm gonna run to the restroom."

"It's downstairs," he said, pointing.

Of course he knew where it was. He'd been here before. If my hunch was correct, he was a huge actor and probably went jet-setting all over the world, making movies and having dinner at fancy restaurants. I hadn't seen any of the *White Serpent* movies, but I'd seen the billboards. Everywhere.

On my way downstairs, I was looking up the movie on my phone to double-check that the guy who'd been nonchalantly sitting across from me for the past hour and a half was the guy behind the mask on those billboards. There'd been signs—him wanting to sit facing inward, away from potential gawkers, and just the fact that he was so comfortable with himself, worldly, like he'd been at a hundred restaurants in a hundred fabulous cities. Or maybe he was just pretending to be that way because he was an actor and was playing the role of pleasant companion.

But confusion aside, I'd liked him so far, and I was looking forward to checking out whatever no-reservations dinner place he had in mind. Nothing about him seemed arrogant or pretentious, and nothing needed to change if he was an actor, especially since I wasn't particularly worshipful of celebrities. I'd never seen him act, so I couldn't pretend to be a fangirl.

He'd have to take me as I was—clueless.

I pulled up Annie's number, knowing full well she was probably in the middle of a business lunch. She'd just have to deal with it, because I had a feeling my text was something she'd want to see: *I think I'm about to have dinner with Chris Conley.*

CHAPTER TEN

La Toilette à la Fontaine de Mars

THE FACETIME on my phone rang immediately. "What?" she said. In the background, I could see a conference room full of people she was clearly leaving in the lurch in order to talk to me.

Wedged into the tiniest bathroom I'd ever seen, I held up the phone close to my face because there wasn't room to extend my arm. There was only one square tile where I could stand without leaning on the toilet or injuring myself on the sink.

"He's sitting at a table, waiting for me to come back. I just wanted to tell you because I know you're into that stuff."

"Hang on. I'm still processing that you're not messing with me. What do you mean, you're having dinner with Chris Conley?"

I told her the whole story about forgetting to weigh the peaches and running out of the store and looking up to find a guy named Chris who'd taken pity on me. And then I'd agreed to have dinner and our waiter wanted a selfie and I put two and two together, eventually. It sounded unbelievable as I said it.

"I can't believe you don't know what Chris Conley looks like. Haven't you seen his movies?"

"You know I haven't."

"Right. You only go to art-house movies, where you sob for three hours because of the beautiful tracking shot or the beautiful lighting."

"Ha ha. Superhero stuff just isn't my thing. It just seems kind of stupid to me," I said.

"Um, I wouldn't tell him that."

I couldn't search the internet while I was on the phone, but I knew that Annie was way ahead of me. I could hear her tapping away on her laptop. "Okay, this is what I could find." She started reading, "'Chris Conley just wrapped sci-fi thriller *Last Moment Before Death*, which was shot on location in Ireland and France.' So I guess you're the beneficiary of his time in France. I could kill you right now."

"Don't do that. It's one dinner, one night. He leaves tomorrow for whatever he's doing next."

"Is he amazing, though? Seriously, those eyes are just crazy gorgeous."

Yes, we had consensus on that. But I was also controlled by my pragmatic ruling planet. This was one dinner. I saw it for what it was and couldn't get too worked up about Chris, actor or not. He'd be gone in a matter of hours.

"He's... he's quite pretty to look at." I felt like I was talking about a painting.

"Nothing wrong with looking. Or... what happens in Paris..."

"Oh, please. It's just dinner."

"Doesn't have to be," she said in a sing-song voice. "I mean, you're on vacation, he's only there one night? Kind of the definition of a one-night stand."

"Stop it. This is me. I'm not having a one-night stand. I've never done that."

"Again, the very reason to have a one night stand... And don't hate me, but I've got a conference call with Japan in five minutes, and I've gotta prepare. Can I call you later?"

"Oh, of course. So sorry I disrupted your meeting. I was just... I had to tell you."

"Damn straight, you had to tell me. Live your best life. Love you." And she was gone.

I knew I'd better get out of the bathroom before Chris started to think I'd come down with some intestinal virus, but I still had to satisfy one lingering question. Fortunately, there was Wi-Fi in this basement bathroom, so I was able to pull up the *People* magazine story I'd read on the plane. It took a few seconds to load, but sure enough, my eyes seized on the detail I'd remembered and forgotten in equal measure—the actor in the story mentioned that his new villa was much closer to Spain, where his mother's side of the family still had relatives.

Chris had mentioned his mother and Spain just a half hour earlier, and somehow, my brain had only vaguely connected the dots. I could continue to blame jet lag, but I needed to up my game right now.

I needed all brain cells firing if I had any hope of making it through dinner with a superhero.

CHAPTER ELEVEN

A Bridge in Paris
Later

WHEN I GOT BACK to the table, I saw that Chris was posing for a photo with the waiter and a man who I presumed was the restaurant owner. They were smiling and taking selfies, but when I got close enough, the phone was handed to me so they could back up for proper photos, all three men smiling. The two Frenchmen thanked Chris profusely and kissed him on both cheeks. They shook my hand and kissed me as well, then fanned the commotion they'd created by escorting us past the onlookers and out the back door of the restaurant.

"Thanks for going along with that," Chris said when we'd rounded the corner onto a quiet street.

"No problem. Does that happen a lot?"

He grimaced. "Sort of. Not so much here though, which is why I like it." He grabbed my hand and pulled me through a crowded pedestrian area toward a quieter street where we could walk without bumping into other humans. He let my hand go and I felt a small twinge of disappointment.

The sun had dropped, but there was still plenty of daylight left at nine in the evening.

"So this restaurant you have in mind, can we get to it by way of the river?"

"Sure. You want to catch the sunset?"

I nodded. "It was pretty last night, but with the high clouds right now, I bet it'll be even better."

"Perfect. A couple of the places I thought about checking out for dinner are on the other side, so we can watch the sunset from one of the bridges and then head across and pick out a place."

"Works for me," I said. I couldn't help comparing him to Johnny, who was my most recent frame of reference for how a guy should act. Chris acted like a grown-up. That wasn't to say he was dull, but as I reflected on Johnny, I fixed on his desperation to be happy and fun-loving all the time. I wondered if Johnny really was as carefree as he seemed. Maybe he had demons he'd never shared with me. Maybe he didn't even know he had them. With a little distance from the relationship, I saw more clearly that I'd been chasing something Johnny represented: freedom from myself, freedom from my planning. Then I realized how wrong it was to be thinking about Johnny at all when I was standing next to another guy.

"Where'd you just go?" Chris asked, looking at me instead of the sun setting over the water. We'd been standing there for a few minutes in silence.

"Sorry. Lost in thought," I said.

Stop doing that. Be in the present.

"You did that earlier. Outside the grocery store."

"Yeah. I was just working some stuff out in my head, and

sometimes I forget that I'm doing that in front of another person."

"Everything okay?" He looked concerned. It was sweet. He didn't know me at all, yet from the first words he said to me, I'd felt like he was looking out for me like a family friend, someone he'd grown up with and thought of as a sister.

"Yes. All good. Sorry."

We looked out at the sun, which was just dipping into the horizon, and I thought about how many times I'd seen this same sun hit the horizon in California. It felt different here but I couldn't articulate why.

"Where do you actually live when you're not on location filming?" I asked. I realized I knew nothing about him despite Annie's quick download of information in the bathroom.

"New York. You?"

"LA."

"Ah, been there. Many times. Never caught the bug."

"Which bug is that?" I asked.

"The beach, the surfing, the whole Hollywood thing."

"But you are the Hollywood thing, aren't you?"

"Not if I can help it."

He'd taken out his cell phone just as the sun hit the halfway point and sat in a half circle on the horizon line. He snapped a photo. "The light's perfect right now. You want a picture?"

That embarrassed me. I started to protest because I didn't want him to think I was like the waiter and the other gaping fans who just wanted a selfie with a movie star. Then I realized he was offering to take a picture of just me with the river behind me and the sun on my face.

"Oh, okay. Sure," I said, handing him my phone. He moved around to different angles and I felt suddenly self-conscious, having never mastered the art of looking social media cool in photos.

"I've spent a lot of time around directors. I know good lighting when I see it." He backed away and held the phone up. "You have really beautiful features, do you know that? High cheekbones... your face is like a porcelain doll." He said the words like he was admiring a piece of art.

"Thank you." The compliment made me uncomfortable because I felt his eyes on me, so I quickly changed the subject. "Want me to snap one of you?"

I took his phone, and we switched spots. Just as I snapped the photo, a Frenchman in grey slacks and a white button-up short-sleeved shirt asked us, in accented English, "You'd like me to take one of you together?"

Adding to the awkwardness of posing in front of someone who knew camera angles and lighting, now we were being mistaken for a couple. I felt like I needed to explain the error to the kind Frenchman so Chris would know that I knew we were not a couple.

I started to protest. "Oh, thank you. But no, it's okay." It didn't matter what I thought. The man was swept up in the kindness of his gesture, and before I knew it, he was taking my phone, and I was standing next to Chris on the bridge, with the perfect pink evening light on our faces and the Seine and its boats behind us.

A wave of emotion washed over me because I was in Paris. At sunset. I'd dreamed of coming here, and it was finally dawning on me that it had happened. It wasn't about meeting a guy, though I wasn't about to kick this one out of the picture. It was about spreading my wings and figuring out if I was flight-worthy.

Chris put an arm around me for the photo, and I felt an unexpected twinge in my belly. My cheeks flushed as my heart started beating faster. Just being that close to him made me feel a nervous glimmer of attraction. I worried he could feel it from where his arm rested across my shoulders, but his body language didn't betray anything. My physical reaction surprised me, partly because I was normally levelheaded and my head was clearly not calling the shots. We were playing the part of a couple on a bridge for one picture, and my body was buying right into it.

His touch felt like an electric jolt, running from his hand through my body and quickening my pulse. The physical attraction was beyond my power to control it and I struggled against its unwelcome intrusion into a pleasant dinner with a fellow traveler, albeit one with a stellar physical form. The fact that he had this effect on me had nothing to do with his fame or his place in the public eye. I hadn't felt it when we were just sitting and talking. Well, maybe I had felt it a little, but my rational brain had still been holding court, reminding me that it was just one dinner with someone I'd never see again.

But now... his hand across my shoulder burned like it would leave a mark, a hot, sweet reminder of the butterflies that were massing in a storm as I tried to breathe evenly and slow my heartbeat.

"Merci, *bonne soirée*," Chris said as the man handed back my phone and he leaned in to look at the photo.

"Not bad," Chris said. "See what I mean about the lighting? Perfect, right? You'll have to send that to me."

That surprised me. He wanted a copy of the forced photo with the girl who cries over groceries and doesn't watch super-hero movies? Well, he didn't know about that second part yet. Maybe it didn't need to come up.

"I have to tell you," I couldn't help saying, "you don't seem actor-y." I looked him over, up and down. He certainly looked like a person throngs of female humans would want to watch on a screen in the dark, but I wasn't talking about his appearance. He was just... real. And kind and normal. He was the kind of person I would want to be friends with... or date... or spend much more than one evening with, if we weren't in a foreign city with pre-set parameters and limits. So I stuffed those thoughts away, because... what was the point?

"Well, thanks. I think. Was that a compliment?" The corners of his mouth edged up into a grin and he looked pleased, but a little confused.

"Yes. Totally. Absolutely. And I don't know a lot of actors, or any actors other than my neighbor who does the voice in Burger King commercials. So I know I shouldn't generalize. But like I said, I work for a PR firm, and we have some actor clients, and my colleagues kind of complain that they're a handful. Demanding and arrogant. You just seem really... nice."

"Thanks," he said again. "I strive for nice. And normalcy. And sorry your clients are like that. Some actors are, I guess. I mean, I certainly know a few..." He got a strange look on his face that I couldn't decipher.

"I'm sure."

"And I should say, you're chill compared to most women I meet. I'm glad our paths crossed this morning."

I grew suddenly tongue-tied. Was I chill? I had no idea. I decided not to admit I'd had no idea he was any kind of a big deal until a half hour earlier. Let him think I was chill. "Thanks," I said, eager to change the subject. "Um, I guess we should go to dinner?"

Chris didn't move. He kept his back against the rail of the bridge as I moved to start walking. He grabbed my hand and pulled me back, so I turned to face him. He didn't say anything for a moment. He tilted his head and looked at me like something about me confused him.

"Everything okay?" I asked.

He nodded, his gaze shifting to my eyes. "You didn't know, did you? That I'm an actor. You didn't recognize me?"

Caught. I felt the heat creep over my cheeks again. He didn't seem bothered, just curious. "I... I mean... no. I'm sorry. I don't see a lot of popular movies."

"Please. No apologies," he said, looking from my eyes to my lips like he had earlier. "I like it."

"You like that I live under a rock?"

"I don't think you live under a rock. I think you probably have better things to do with your time than watch action films."

"You don't find it insulting?"

He shook his head. I was acutely aware that he was still holding onto my hand and like every other part of me he'd touched so far, it was melting. "Not at all. The types of movies I do aren't for everyone. It's not a thing for me."

"But it's your job. And you're obviously good at it. I just happen to be the one person in the world who doesn't like caped crusaders."

That made him laugh. "I don't wear a cape."

"Maybe you should. I think you'd look fetching in a cape."

His smile opened up a little more. "Noted."

I was relieved to hear that he really didn't seem to mind that I was oblivious to his clearly-successful career. I'd be able to relax during dinner and not worry about that secret coming out. I'd have enough to worry about just trying to keep my pulse from skyrocketing and my face from turning the shade of a beet if his hand happened to graze an exposed inch of my skin.

The sun was down, and the clouds were reflecting even more beautiful shades of pink and orange. "Look. Gorgeous, right?" I pointed to make him turn around and take in the last moments of the sunset and see the astounding color spectrum. He gave it the sunset a passing glance and nodded.

"Gorgeous," he agreed.

But he wasn't looking at the clouds. He was looking at me.

CHAPTER TWELVE

Frenchie Bar au Vins

IT WAS ALMOST as if that Frenchman on the bridge had decided we were a couple, so we started acting like a couple. Or maybe it had nothing to do with him and everything to do with the insane molten heat that erupted every time Chris touched me. After walking a half dozen blocks and crossing over the Les Halles mall, Chris put a hand on my back to point me toward a set of stairs. Just for a moment. But I swear his hand left its own heat signature, a mark on my back that I felt radiating warmth for blocks. I started to wonder if he really had superpowers. I also started to wonder if I'd be able to relax at all during dinner, between his arrestingly deep, dark eyes and this new mysterious heat element.

We made our way down a lively street which was dotted with dozens of cafés and bars, all spilling over with people who congregated in the street. Chris grabbed my hand as we wove in between groups of people milling and hanging outside the bars. It felt completely natural, like Paris had cast a spell over the evening, except for the flames licking my palm and snare drum in my heart. I needed to get a grip.

I decided not to clutter my brain with analysis. Actor, super-hero, whatever. One night dinner, one-night stand. I didn't feel the need to put nouns and descriptions to the night ahead. Chris was leaving in the morning, which was a huge relief. It allowed me to let down my guard for the night and just enjoy being there with him. There would be no awkward questions at the end of the night—*what are you doing tomorrow? Should we try to meet up again? No? Too awkward?*

Annie's words came back to me: "It's the definition of a one-night stand." It felt good not to think too much.

The restaurant Chris liked was down a small street, where I saw that every table was filled at Frenchie, the fixed-menu restaurant I'd seen written up on countless food blogs when I initially researched the trip. I looked longingly through the window at the perfectly presented dishes on the diners' plates. Johnny would've hated it. Chris said he'd been there twice and loved it.

"It's great, but honestly, I like the wine bar better. It's more casual, and the food is incredible," he said, pointing at the sister restaurant across the street. "But if you come too early, people are crowded three deep at the bar and hanging out the door. The wait can be an hour. We timed it perfectly."

I didn't bother to point out that he could probably get a table instantly anywhere he wanted. If people recognized him as easily as the waiter had at La Fontaine de Mars, they'd roll out the red carpet and give him the best seat in the house. But he didn't seem like he had the kind of ego that would exploit that.

Even though the crowd was thinner, every seat in the wine bar was still full. We waited about ten minutes, sipping glasses of Sancerre wine by the bar. The bartender, who looked a little younger than me and a lot prettier in that French-chic way, was eyeing Chris the whole time we stood there. I almost felt protective of him, annoyed that people didn't just leave him alone and let him come to a restaurant in peace. But he seemed unbothered or even oblivious to the attention, so I wasn't going to be the one to make a big deal of it. His eyes never wavered from mine, a bit to the irritation of the bartender, who tried a couple of times to interrupt our conversation to ask if we needed anything else. We didn't.

Dinner was a blur of wine and small plates, which we shared at a tiny high-top table, perched on barstools in the window. Something about being in France allowed me to drink coffee and wine and barely feel their effects. What I did feel was the effect of Chris.

He lightly touched my hand while I was telling him a story about my dad, interlacing his fingers with mine like we'd known each other much longer than a few hours. Maybe he was always like this with people—comfortable in casual intimacy. Maybe he was just acting like a good dinner date. But I was falling for it.

With every touch of his hand, I felt another magnetic urge of wanting to be closer to him. It was loud in the restaurant, where every table was still occupied an hour after we'd arrived, so I had to lean in to hear him talking. When he moved his barstool closer to mine, I wasn't sure whether he was just making it easier for us to talk or feeling the same attraction to me.

We talked about mundane things, telling each other stories that gave a small window into parts of ourselves. I learned that Chris's mother met his dad when she was a visiting professor at the university where he was finishing up graduate school. "She was a few years older than him, and he was very impressed with how smart she was," he said. "She's definitely smarter than him."

"What does she teach?"

"Art history. And he's an accountant. He always says he has

to work hard to keep up with her when she's talking about her work, and she has to work hard not to fall asleep when he's talking about his."

"Cute."

"They are pathologically cute. It's almost annoying. It's the kind of relationship people write about in timeless classics like Jane Eyre."

"Except Rochester was tricked into marrying Jane's sister and she goes mad."

"Okay, maybe not the best example."

I put my hands up. "Hey, I'm not judging. They're your parents. If you say your dad is Rochester, I believe you."

He laughed, but then his expression changed suddenly, like he'd gotten distracted by a thought that bothered him. He swirled the wine in his glass and looked away. If I'd known him better, I might have understood the meaning behind look or whether it was one of his personality traits. But this was a guy I'd met only hours ago and would never see again after tonight, I reminded myself. And while I cared that he seemed unhappy, it didn't seem like my place to dissect his expressions and offer analysis.

Instead, I focused on drinking my entire glass of water, and by the time I was finished, he pivoted and asked me about my family. I gladly talked his ear off to fill the void.

"I'm an introvert in a family of extroverts... I focused on school and my grades because I knew it was a way to win points with adults, teachers, and my parents... My best friend from college lives near San Francisco, which is hard because I have more fun with her than with anyone and I don't get to see her much..."

He listened quietly, and eventually, his mood shifted back, and he was asking me questions. "Was your dad always into cooking?"

"It was kind of a phase. Not a good one. Every Sunday night, we'd have some new dish he'd learned to make because he'd taken a Chinese cooking class with some chef he found on YouTube. He dragged me to a market that had some kind of black eggs that smelled like Sulphur and chicken head and feet and I swore to him I was never going to eat anything he made with those ingredients."

"Was that what he bought?"

"No, he bought noodles and a wok and a lot of soy sauce. The cooking was fine. I just wasn't a big fan of hot and sour soup or fish sauce, and truthfully, most of what he made was awful. And my mom was worried I'd offend him if I didn't eat what he made..."

"Kids don't have a palate for those kinds of flavors unless you start them young. My mom made Spanish food my whole life," he said.

"Sounds delish."

"To me, it was. I was a kid who was used to squid and pork belly and saffron, but after one or two tries, my friends wouldn't come for dinner at my house unless I promised we could order pizza."

"Ah, now it's sounding like my childhood."

"Good old American junk food. Nothing better," he said.

"Hey, pizza doesn't have to be junk food. It has at least three food groups if you count the sauce."

"I see we're dealing with a low nutritional bar here," he said, smiling.

"I'm actually a pretty healthy eater, but I do have a soft spot for pizza. And anything involving cheese."

"Well, you picked the right country for that."

As if on cue, three more small plates were dropped on our table, one of them a cheese plate with three selections, a small ramekin of marmalade, and two dried apricots. We'd just finished a dish of tomato and cherry salad and fried zucchini in an amazing sauce. I couldn't tell what was on the other two new plates, but I trusted anything that came out of the kitchen. Every dish had been perfection, and I'd long ago lost count of how many plates had been delivered to our table.

Despite my rocky start at Monoprix, my day had turned out well. I snuck a glance at Chris and noticed once again how attractive he was. His eyes did that crazy sparkling thing and when he smiled, it actually made me feel a little breathless. I could see why people would want to watch him on a big screen.

At the same time, I was having a hard time reconciling the calm, solicitous, regular-seeming guy across from me with the mega-star I now knew him to be. So I chose not to think about it. What was the point? We were just two people having dinner and tomorrow I'd be back on my own to gawk at more art.

Six more plates and two glasses of cold wine later, we were outside on the street, reversing our path back toward the river. I'd already come to think of it as my anchor in the city, with everything I wanted to do in Paris having some relation to the water. I knew the Seine bifurcated the city, giving it its character-istic right bank or left bank, but I hadn't anticipated its magic. The water, which at nighttime reflected the lights of the build-ings, exerted a magnetic pull. As we walked, I felt more ener-gized as we got closer to the river, eager to see the lights of the Eiffel Tower looming over the water.

Or maybe I just wanted to go back to the bridge where I'd first felt my surprising physical response to being touched by Chris. During dinner, he'd been one hundred percent focused on our conversation and our food, but as we walked back toward the bridge, he grabbed my hand again and brushed the back of it against his lips. It was a sweet gesture, but the small fire that ignited every time he'd touched me caused a small inferno in my belly that I had to work hard to quell. I struggled to control my heart, which was racing and causing a flush in my cheeks.

Get a grip on yourself. He's just being nice.

When we got back to the spot where we'd stood hours earlier, we stopped and looked out over the water. This time, we didn't need the eager Frenchman to suggest that we stand close to each other. I rested my elbows on the rough stone wall of the bridge, looking at how the lights shimmered in the current of the river. He reached an arm around me and pulled me nearer. I felt the breath go out of me again with the closer contact.

Just to be clear, I was not a person who went all jelly-like over contact with a guy. It never happened. So this was something new, this feeling that merely having his hand on me made it hard to breathe normally, this sense that I was falling into an abyss of unreal pleasure. I couldn't rationally understand how one individual person could have this kind of effect on me. It was a little unnerving. And I didn't want it to stop.

"Different in the dark, huh?" he said, gazing out. It snapped me out of my rapture. A boat was passing under the bridge, shining its lights on the riverbank while the passengers gasped at the beautiful buildings reflected in the water. Everything about this place was picturesque. "Equally amazing though. There's no such thing as a bad view here."

He moved behind me so I was leaning against his chest and he had his arms wrapped around me. "It's perfect," I said, feeling my heart rev up another notch as his arms folded me in.

"You're perfect," he whispered near my ear, sending a shiver along my skin. When I turned to look at him, his mesmerizing gaze made my breath hitch. From just inches away, I took in his face, all his features gently chiseled as if Michelangelo had deftly sculpted them from soft marble. I could imagine him playing the role of swoony best friend in a rom-com and leaving throngs of women moaning his name, but at that moment, we were alone. And he was running a finger over my cheek, staring into my eyes.

Then he leaned in, and his lips brushed mine, slowly finding their way until he gently sank in deeper, claiming more of my mouth. I felt myself respond instinctively, melding with his delicious lips. When we drew back, he traced a line over the contour of my face. "I've been wanting to kiss you for hours," he said.

"That must've been distracting," I said, putting my hand on his chest and tilting my head to look at him.

He laughed quietly. "It *was* distracting. And it was worth the wait."

"Then, maybe you should do it again."

He cupped my jaw in his hand and leaned in again, sweeping his tongue into my mouth and kissing me in a way I wouldn't forget anytime soon. His kiss was sweet and hot, and it gave me a hint of what I might feel if we gave in to the feeling completely. I instinctively knew I wanted that. I also didn't want to shortchange the kissing, the sweet beginning part.

I felt myself press into him, lifting my hand to the back of his head and running my fingers lightly through his hair. He had good hair—well-conditioned, it seemed, and soft against my hand. And his lips were also soft, exploring mine and breathing heat against my neck. My insides churned and I felt a small moan escape my lips. Sounds were possible; words were not.

The warm summer air held us in its grasp as Chris turned so his back was against the railing and pulled me in tight. He tilted his head back a couple inches to look at me. His eyes roamed over my features like he was memorizing them. I understood the urge to commit the moment to memory. We had the one photo, but I wanted the feeling etched in my brain and my body so I could return to it after tonight.

His look didn't require a response, at least not a verbal one. So his lips were on mine once more, more certain and insistent and hot. Now there was no question that he was capable of setting my whole body on fire with one kiss and two very capable hands, which he wove into my hair. I didn't want to question it. Or to think. I just wanted to kiss him on that bridge, holding onto the moments that I knew would end by morning.

When our lips parted and we looked at each other, it felt like I'd known him for longer than a day. I was at a loss for words, my heart pounding and my brain suddenly empty of anything but sweet thoughts about how much I liked him.

And then fear. And realization—that this was an everyday thing for an actor.

He could kiss any woman he wanted and probably did. And because he did, he'd gotten good at it, and I'd been naive enough to fall for it and think it was anything more than the fun nightcap to a nice dinner. Maybe he even thought I owed him because he'd insisted on paying and I'd finally stopped protesting. He was an actor, a player. And I was an idiot.

My brain tried to reel my emotions in, but they were already down in the abyss. I needed to leave right away before I fell in any deeper. I was tipsy from the wine and attracted to his nice face and pleasant conversation and definitely out of my depth. Before I could speak, Chris was looking embarrassed and saying something I hadn't expected.

"Um... this isn't something I do often. I... just so you know, I wasn't planning it."

"By 'this' you mean, kissing me on a bridge, this?" I asked.

"Yeah. I was just expecting we'd have some dinner. A couple of Americans in Paris." It was a line. It had to be a line. Of course he was planning it, of course he expected we'd do more than have dinner, but protesting such a plan was just the kind of thing a person like him did. It was the right thing to say, so a person like him didn't sound like a player.

"But you're a big actor. Don't you—by definition—do this?

It's got to be in the movie star manual or something, making out with willing participants, of which there are certain to be many."

He laughed softly and his face settled into an amused expression. "I haven't read the manual. You'll have to share your copy. But no, I don't go around kissing women on bridges. Or in tunnels. Or at railroad crossings."

"So no transportation-related kissing," I said, feeling another shiver when he cupped my cheek with his hand and gave it a soft caress. Chris shook his head.

He brushed a few strands of hair off my shoulder and bent to kiss a trail from my collarbone to my ear, where he whispered, "But I'm making an exception for you because I like you."

"So you don't just think I'm a starstruck groupie who you're obligated to kiss so I can Tweet about it?"

"Not the way I'd describe you, no."

I smiled, wanting to believe that he wasn't an actor-player. He brushed the few strands of hair off my face that had been taken up by the breeze. "I've been staying in an apartment not too far from here. I don't want to sound like I'm making a move, but if you felt like coming back there with me, I could fix us a drink. Or some coffee."

I had to laugh. "I appreciate the disclaimer. But what if I want you to be making a move?"

"Then consider the move made." He had his arms around me and he leaned in and kissed me again. I wasn't sure if he knew how persuasive his kisses were. His lips tasted like Sancerre and cherries. "Come back with me," he whispered. He was running a hand through my hair and pulling me closer as I inhaled the smell of rosemary and mint from some sort of body product. I couldn't do anything but nod like a zombie.

It was the second time he'd suggested doing something by saying it like it was a command, the first being when he told me to have dinner with him, earlier outside the market. I normally didn't like being ordered around, but coming from him, it didn't feel that way. And I definitely liked it. "Um, okay, yes."

He kissed me once more by my ear before promising quietly, "No strings. I'll be a perfect gentleman."

It made me burst out laughing. "Ha. I have no doubt," I said, imagining his gentlemanly hands just might have their way with me as soon as we had some privacy. I didn't think I minded.

But I knew what he meant. He was telling me I was safe. I wasn't nervous about being alone in an apartment with him. I trusted my gut, and it told me he was one of the good guys. He didn't seem like he was playing me to get me into bed just to prove something to himself. I already knew he was leaving, so if I wanted to hook up, it was my choice to make. It was a built-in assumption that whatever happened next would be a fun Paris one-nighter.

We both knew how it would end, either late that night or early the next morning—with him leaving for the airport and me spending the balance of my two weeks here alone. I was fine with that. The whole point of my trip was to push boundaries and have adventures. It made me game for whatever happened with him.

He took my hand, and we walked back the way we'd come, to the right bank and farther than he'd implied when he said his apartment was not too far. We covered at least a mile, if not more, winding our way into the eighth arrondissement, but I didn't care. We talked just as intently as we had in the restaurant as the world fell away, and the only thing I could see was Chris.

Every so often, while waiting for a light to turn green, he'd turn to me and we'd kiss some more, like so many couples I'd seen the night before at the little fake beach on the riverbank.

Johnny who? Yeah, over it.

CHAPTER THIRTEEN

A Crazy-Beautiful Apartment in Paris

THE APARTMENT WAS GORGEOUS. Calling it an *apartment* made it sound like a one-bedroom efficiency, a small box on top of another small box. Chris's place spread out over the entire story of a building that was several hundred years old. The wood floor of the foyer went on for yards and yards in a burnt-brown herringbone pattern, leading through an entryway that held a baby grand piano and had several doors leading in different directions, each doorway framed by triple molding and each door its own work of art.

Chris led me by the hand into the living room, which had a chandelier hanging from a ceiling decorated with swirls of floral designs sculpted into the plaster. Paned windows that reached almost to the ceiling were flanked by heavy drapes pulled back with metal tiebacks that were festooned with the faces of lions.

"Wow," said. "This is incredible."

He looked around as though seeing it anew. "It's really something, isn't it?"

"I just... wow. It's like the setting of a classic French film. I almost feel like everything should be in black and white."

He laughed. Above the fireplace, Chris lit two candles on the mantle, still not letting go of my hand. The flames danced in the breeze from the open window, doubling their light in the large mirror reaching from the mantel to the ceiling. A pair of footed sofas covered in pale-beige velvet flanked a yellow upholstered settee that conjured an image of someone lying on it being fanned with a palm frond. The term *fainting couch* came to mind, but I had no idea why. The coffee table in the middle was an antique rectangle inlaid with a woven top.

I knew Chris hadn't selected all the furniture himself because he'd made it sound like he didn't own the apartment, but I couldn't help complimenting its splendor. "This is what I always imagined French royals would have in their living rooms."

"I have no idea who owns this place. My assistant rented it for me," he said.

His assistant. Of course he'd have an assistant. The actors on the PR firm's roster had them for all kinds of reasons, and some of those actors were definitely abusive. They had their assistants take their dogs to the vet or pick up their dry-cleaning or buy their wives birthday gifts. I'd always rolled my eyes at the entitlement and what I perceived as pure laziness on the part of those actors who had so much money and months off between films, yet they thought nothing of paying other people to cart around their laundry.

Chris seemed different, yet here we stood. In a place sourced and procured by his assistant. He hadn't had a hand in deciding where to stay in Paris.

Then again, neither had I. I'd taken the suggestion of a kind waiter and never questioned it. I didn't want to be a hypocrite.

"Nik?" he asked. "Did I lose you again?" His voice shook me

out of my reverie, as did the fact that he'd called me Nik. Only my closest friends did that. I'd always been highly annoyed by people who reverted too quickly to nicknames for people they barely knew. But it didn't bother me when he did it. Maybe that was because I'd stood on a bridge kissing him for an hour. I liked him. I knew I should squash those feelings, but I couldn't.

"Yeah. Sorry. So... you have an assistant?"

He nodded, starting to clue in. "Is that weird?"

"I mean, I'm sure you're really busy, so it's probably necessary, right?"

"Depends. When I'm on a project—or sometimes two at once—I don't even have time to read the newspaper, let alone answer letters."

"Letters? Like fan mail?" I still hadn't grasped what it meant to be Chris Conley. In our few hours together, he'd seemed so normal—spectacular looking, but normal. It was hard to picture him surrounded by piles of fan mail and walking red carpets with paparazzi screaming his name. Thinking about him that way made me uncomfortable and intimidated. I decided I didn't need to picture that. I liked the live version standing in front of me better. And after one night, that was all I'd be left with.

I shook my head. "Never mind. I don't care about your assistant. I care about the view from that window. Does it open?"

"Oh yeah, wait till you see." He led me to the tall dormer windows, undid the latch, swung the doors open, and stepped with me onto a small balcony. He stood behind me, his hands on either side of my hips and his head tipped down toward my shoulder, which he grazed with his tongue and a series of light kisses. There it was again, the Eiffel Tower, guarding the city with its sparkly lights. The view didn't disappoint. Neither did he.

"Hang on," he said, looking at his watch. "Oh, good. Five minutes."

"Wow, you wear a watch?"

"I find it's handy for knowing the time," he said with a wry grin.

"Well sure, but don't you just use your phone for that?"

"No, I use my watch." Forget about not seeming actor-y. He was different from most people I knew. In a really good way. Confident, matter-of-fact, wholesome.

"Oh. Okay." I shrugged. I liked that he wasn't obsessively checking his phone. The watch passed scrutiny. "What's happening in five minutes?" I asked.

"Were you outside last night on the hour?"

"I don't think so. Why?"

"You'll see." We waited, staring off at the lights together. That was too long to stand in a small space without feeling an intense need to kiss him, so I turned to Chris and put my arms around his neck. The feeling of desire and heat was fueled by the fact that I knew my time with him was fleeting. He kissed me like he was oblivious to time, as if each time his lips met mine was a new chance to start the clock on forever. He pulled me to him tighter, more urgently. I wasn't sure that whatever was supposed to happen when the hour struck even mattered anymore.

Then he pulled a few inches away, still holding me close. "Look."

I turned and was awestruck. The Eiffel Tower had started glittering like a Fourth of July sparkler, lit up with a thousand tiny bulbs that flickered over its surface, like jewels glinting in the sun. Except that it was popping white lights against a black sky. So beautiful. "It does that every hour?" I asked, mesmerized by the sight. I knew I'd be outside each night, every hour, on the hour for the rest of my time in Paris.

"Yes, then at one in the morning, there's a grand finale that lasts a few minutes longer. When it's done, the tower goes dark for the rest of the night. It's kind of sad when that happens, but maybe if it didn't, no one here would ever go to bed."

"We'll have to stay up and watch it."

"Oh, I had every intention of staying awake." His voice came out as a sultry growl and he dropped his lips again to the soft spot beneath my ear. I felt the effects of him on the skin of my neck, in the depths of my chest, down in my core. Then he was walking me back inside and over to the couch.

The velvet was surprisingly soft as he guided me into a reclining position and hovered above me. We kissed like that for a long time—an hour, maybe more—our lips like liquid molding into each other. He never suggested we move to the bedroom, which was fine by me. I was happy on the fainting couch with my brains scrambled by his touch.

I wasn't a one night stand kind of girl. In fact, I'd never had one. I always needed a little time with a guy—a few dates, a sense we might be headed somewhere—before I took the plunge. I didn't know how I'd feel about myself tomorrow if let my body take over and make my decisions for me.

Did I need to know?

The Eiffel Tower saved me from having to make a decision. By one in the morning, we were back on the tiny balcony. The light show finale left us silent, a soft blanket wrapped around us on the terrace, staring into the night. The tower sparkled with vigor, on and on, until it seemed like it had spent its final diamond sparkle. Then it went dark.

In the sudden darkness, it was as though the night shifted into a different, more intimate phase. Chris's lips brushed over mine, making me shudder with every pass. He cupped my cheek with his hand and his tongue swept across my bottom lip, causing my breath to hitch and my eyes to lull closed. I parted my lips and felt the swish of his tongue over mine, lazily drawing me in.

We still didn't know each other all that well, but our bodies didn't seem to feel inhibited by it. For the first time in a long while, I felt good about myself and my desirability.

I pressed a hand against his chest, feeling the taut muscle under his shirt and wrapping my other hand around his neck. His hands moved down my back and over my hips to where he tugged up the hem of my dress. The minute I felt his hands against the skin of my thighs, the impossible heat ignited again and I think I let out a sigh. Those hands, his lips, that spark. He melted me like a pat of butter in the sun.

We stayed on the balcony for what felt like an hour. But what did I know about time? I was lost in the aura of him.

When I finally opened my eyes, something felt different. Without the sparkling tower, it was like the light that had propelled our dinner forward into the magic of kissing on the bridge and coming back to his apartment had been extinguished with the lights. *Time for bed*, the tower seemed to say.

It was late. I fought a feeling of sadness. I didn't want to go back to my tiny room in my sensible hotel. Not if it meant saying goodbye. I wasn't ready to do that yet.

But I didn't want to overstay my welcome. More than that, I didn't want anything like an awkward goodbye to ruin the memory of this night. So I had to make it quick, a thank you and a farewell, the finale after the finale.

"So... I should get back to my hotel. I'm sure you have some packing to do before you head out," I said, trying to be logical about the Eiffel Tower's implied curfew.

He looked surprised. Maybe he'd just expected me to fall into bed with him like every other fangirl he'd met. Or maybe he didn't know what it was like to be with someone who wasn't a fangirl. "Really? The old 'I should pack' line?"

"It wasn't a line. I just thought..." I didn't know what I thought. All reasonable thinking had gone out the window a long time ago. I felt flustered and suddenly unsure what was the right thing to do. And I *always* knew the right thing to do. He was confusing everything.

"Stay here with me tonight," he said. "I'm not trying to get you into bed. Though I'm not gonna turn you down, just to be clear. But"—he put his hands up in surrender—"we can just hang out here and talk. Whatever makes you happy. I don't care. I'm just not ready to let go of you yet."

I smiled at him. He was so genuine, so real. Except that I still couldn't fully accept that he was for real. Because he was an actor and he was good at saying believable things in a way that melted hearts. He got paid millions to do it, so I had a hard time taking him at his word. There had to be a catch.

"You want to... talk?" I felt sure it was a euphemism for fucking each other's brains out, but what did I know?

"I have to leave in, like, seven hours. Just hang with me till then?" he implored.

I could already feel myself liking him more than I wanted to, more than made sense for a one-night fling. After breaking up with Johnny just over a month before, my heart was still in pieces, ripped up because I'd finally accepted that we needed different things from life and hurt because he hadn't even waited until we broke up to find it. I hadn't begun to put myself back together, and I wasn't sure if the best remedy for that was a hot fling with an even hotter actor. I needed to protect myself a little, making sure I didn't add new salt to my wounds and give myself a new guy to feel sad about after he was gone. Maybe it would be smarter to cut and run.

I reached out and ran a hand down his arm, noting despite myself that his arm was frightfully strong and muscular. "It's not that you aren't extremely tempting..." I said, not really knowing how to turn him down because I didn't want to do it.

"Then give in to temptation. I won't stop you."

"It just doesn't seem smart," I said.

He smiled. "Do you always do what's smart?" he asked softly. He dipped down and placed a row of kisses under my jaw.

I nodded vigorously, even though he was making me doubt the wisdom of prior mandates. "I do. I make good decisions."

He kissed me harder, pulling my body flush against his, and being smart didn't really enter the picture. Every thought fled from my brain. Well, almost every thought. The only ones that were left demanded that I pull his shirt off and let him do whatever he wanted to my body. There was no wrong answer when it came to full contact with his skin.

I reached for the hem of his shirt, edging it up and feeling his muscles jump when I ran my fingernails along the taut skin over his abs. He pushed the hem of my dress higher and his hands claimed more of my skin, leaving his characteristic heat signature everywhere he touched.

I could feel us heading in only one direction and my lust brain decided in a momentary about-face that merciless fucking was back on the table. In fact, it was a mandatory meal. I ran my hands lower on his abs, inching toward the waistband of his pants. His hands were roaming over my ribs and into the cup of my bra, when he abruptly pulled them away and moved back.

"Sorry," he said. He hadn't done anything wrong, so I was confused.

"You're sorry?"

He slowly brushed the hair out of my face and curled it behind my ear. "I had the feeling earlier you wanted to keep things... light. I realized I was getting carried away."

"It wasn't just you," I admitted. Now that we'd stopped, I felt a little more able to think. "You're hard to resist."

His mouth tugged to the side in a semi-smile. It was a perfect response. I wondered if he had to practice his expressions in the mirror as part of his acting work. "I don't want you to do anything you don't want to do."

"Ugh. I suck," I said, shaking my head vigorously. Why was I such a mess? Why couldn't I have a no-holds-barred sex-fest with a hot actor?

"Not at all. I like you. I like talking to you. We can just do that."

"It's so lame. I've just... I've never had a one-night thing where I knew there was no future."

He took my hand and looked me in the eye. "That's not lame. It's awesome."

"I'm not sure awesome is really the word for it..."

"C'mere." He turned so his back was against the arm of the couch and pulled me toward him so my back rested on his chest. "Let's just hang out. Tell me more about the Sunday dinners your dad used to cook."

So I did. I did it without a plan for how I'd feel in the morning when he was gone. I'd have the rest of my time in Paris to work that out. I followed my gut, which so far hadn't been wrong about Chris.

We spent the rest of the night snuggled up on the couch, sipping coffee he made with the Nespresso machine in the kitchen and talking. Our endless conversation was punctuated by twenty-minute interruptions to kiss until we were breathless and on the verge of removing clothing.

"You're leaving in the morning," I reminded him more than once.

"I know, I know. Stop reminding me," he said more than once.

Then we would both regain our composure and settle back into conversation. At least for a couple minutes. We did that for the rest of the night.

CHAPTER FOURTEEN

A Minuscule Balcony

I LEARNED something that night in Paris that should have occurred to me earlier in life—sunrise is really beautiful. I'd never seen such a thing at home because my rule was never to wake up before it was light outside, even during the winter. That made for some rushed mornings getting to work on time, especially if I opted to fit in a workout, but my rule was ironclad. Having stayed up all night, Chris and I stood on the balcony again, watching as night gave way to early-morning light. It felt optimistic, that shade of pale blue opening up to pinks and yellows like it was heralding good things the day might bring.

"I wish we could sit out here. My legs are starting to feel tired," I said, wanting a chair.

"I know. These balconies aren't really made for doing much besides casting a glance and going back inside."

The term *balcony* was generous. In reality, we stood on a two-by-four-foot ledge with an iron railing around it and hanging plants attached to the outside. But then, most things in France, I was discovering, didn't need to be overstated to be lovely and useful. The small space made it necessary for us to huddle together, which I didn't mind at all.

We'd been talking all night, and Chris had been especially interested in how I got into the public-relations field. The truth was, I'd studied English in college and I was a decent writer. PR didn't require much more than that, other than people skills. I wasn't passionate about it. I was still looking for something that moved me and made me want to work at it because I had no other choice. I believed I'd find that something eventually. For now, the daily demands of the job suited my need for consistency along with the occasional stressful challenge to keep things interesting.

"So are you doing publicity for these companies?" he asked, wanting to know the difference between public relations and publicity. He knew what publicists did.

"Either publicity if they have news they want to get out into the market or damage control if they need to manage bad news like a quarter when their earnings are down. It's basic spin. Talking up stuff that isn't such a big deal to keep them in the news, then telling the story another way to minimize fallout when the CEO is accused of sexual misconduct."

"So it's exactly the same as what publicity firms do for actors."

"Yes. I told you, some of our clients are actors. I just don't happen to work on those accounts."

"By choice?" he asked.

I had to be careful how I explained it. The truth was, I did avoid working on the accounts of actors because I was bored by the egos and I'd been scared off by my colleagues' stories about how their clients felt like they were more important than anyone else. "Corporate executives are just a better fit for me. I like business." The executives could be dramatic, too, but in a different way. They were captains of industry, and their egos were real, but they had a lot at stake with huge companies to run, so they followed advice when I gave it.

Then Chris turned the conversation in a direction I wasn't expecting. "You know I'm doing everything in my power not to roll you onto the carpet and make love you right now, don't you?" he said, smiling like he was being a saint. "I just... I thought you should be aware it's... testing my resolve."

"Um, I appreciate that. Because I'm not sure I could resist."

"And remind me again... you'd need to resist because... I'm leaving a few hours?"

"Because I don't want to have to get over you after sleeping with you."

He ruffled a hand through his hair. "It's funny. There have been times in my life when a one-night fling was all I wanted out of a woman."

"Not sure I need to hear about all your flings," I said.

"What I mean is, there have been times when that was all it was ever going to be. I knew that sex was just sex and a one-night thing was blissfully over by morning. And I think... part of the reason I'm... I don't know, enjoying *not* having sex... I guess I like you more than that. Which seems counterintuitive, I know..."

My heart started beating faster. He wanted this to mean more? Or maybe he was saying that because he liked me, he wasn't dying to have sex—that I was more like a friend. "Thank you?" I said, unsure if he had more to say. "So then... no sex. Cool."

He pulled me closer. "No, definitely not cool." He ran a hand lightly down my arm. It gave me chills. I could tell he was wrestling with something, but I didn't know him well enough to read him. Maybe he felt guilty that I'd have to get over him even just after kissing for six hours.

"This may be insane, and feel free to tell me if it is..." He stared off, still thinking.

"What?" I asked, reaching for him and turning his face so I could look at him.

"I was just going through everything and thinking maybe it could work. I tend to be a planner, so I'm throwing myself off a little bit—"

I had to laugh. "Okay, you're talking to a planner. I get it. It's hard to pivot when you're set on one direction. What is it you're trying to work out?"

"I don't want you to go. I know we just met but... I want to see what tomorrow looks like with you." Wow. It was the nicest thing anyone had ever said to me and it couldn't have sounded better if it had been scripted in a movie. I was so completely bowled over, I said nothing. "Why don't you come with me?"

My brain had a hard time forming words. "Come with you where? When?"

"Tomorrow. Today, actually. You'd have to grab your stuff from your hotel, but we could do that on the way to the airport. I could have the car come a little earlier so we could make a stop..."

"Chris, hold on. Where? I don't even know where you're going."

"Did I not tell you?"

"No, and I didn't ask. Probably because I was in denial that you were leaving. General avoidance works for me most of the time."

"So come. To Antibes. It's beautiful there. There's a boat, there's the beach, the most charming little town, and the people are—"

"Lovely," I finished.

As told to *People* magazine.

How had I not put it together before now?

Maybe because I'd been nervous on the plane, oblivious to superhero actors and on a cloud since the first sip of cold wine, sitting across from Chris. And now he was inviting me to accompany him to the lovely town I'd gawked at for a moment on a plane. How crazy was it that I was considering it? It would mean this wouldn't be our last night together. We'd have almost two weeks together, before we went our separate ways to our separate coasts and separate lives.

And that could mean my one-night stand issue would be solved by many nights when we could do whatever superheroes did with their lady friends. Phenomenal sex was my thought, to be clear.

"Nik...?"

I looked at him and realized I'd spaced out on him again. But yes, I wanted to do this. It would be on the spontaneous side for me, but unlike all the times when being spontaneous felt like a dare, this decision felt thrilling. "I'm so sorry. Yes. I'd love to go with you. Please and thank you. Yes!"

He kissed me differently this time, more insistent and conclusive, a kiss so full of promise that I felt in a torrent of wild heat and emotion that left me dizzy and breathless.

Then he called his assistant.

CHAPTER FIFTEEN

A Black Town Car
Early Morning

I COULD ALREADY TELL I was in over my head. The feeling set in when the black Mercedes arrived at the apartment an hour later and the driver carried Chris's three pieces of matching luggage down to the car. When it came time to retrieve my two bags from the Hotel des Écoles, my face grew hot at the sight of the ordinary hotel where my ordinary twin bed had made me perfectly happy for the one night I'd slept in it. There was no bellhop to roll my bags to the curb.

I asked Chris to stay in the car while I checked out, but he insisted on helping me lug the bags down the four flights of stairs. He said nothing about the room or my choice of hotel. Still, I felt uncomfortable, and I worried that it might be a mistake to go with Chris after having known him for all of one day. *What are his expectations? What are mine?*

Realizing that my breathing was bordering on hyperventilating, I knew I had to talk myself down. This would be okay.

Trains left every day for other cities, and I could just get on one of them if things didn't work out. What was the worst that could happen? We could end up annoying each other, and I'd just come back to Paris.

Or... maybe it would go really well. I knew it could only be a summer fling at best, but I was just a month past a breakup. Could my tender heart recover if I started to fall for him?

Yes, I decided. *It can. It will.* I needed to launch myself head-long into this adventure, wherever it landed me. That was why I'd come to Paris by myself—to eat and drink and feel things and live. So I'd do just that. I'd live the next handful of days to the fullest, feel everything, and if I had to, I'd patch my sad little heart up when I got home.

I handed the woman behind the desk a stack of euros to pay for my room and raced out the door before her curious expression led to actual questions. The driver stowed my bags in the trunk, and I lumbered into the air-conditioned car. The sweat that had gathered on my brow began to cool. Chris was looking at me the way he'd done numerous times by that point, and I realized I hadn't spoken in a while. I tried to cover with a levity I didn't feel.

"News flash: I'm just a normal person who stays in one-star hotels."

He looked at me, surprised. And a little offended. "Do you think I care about any of that?"

"I... I don't know. Look, I don't travel by Uber Black or whatever this is. I don't stay in fabulous apartments with views of the city. So before I spend any more time with you, I just want to make sure you know I'm just... average."

His expression softened. He picked up my hand, and I felt the familiar surge of attraction that had gotten me here in the first place. "First of all, you're a far cry from average. But why are you worried all of a sudden that I expect you to be some socialite?"

"I figured that's what you're used to."

"Not necessarily. Or what I mean is, of course it's great to stay in nice places—"

"No, incredible places. That apartment was amazing."

"Yes. And a lot of the time, the studio pays for it. Because a lot of my travel is for press. But that's why I bought my own place in the South. It allows me to feel normal when I'm there. Away from the madness."

I felt a shred of relief, bolstered by the comfort of his hand intertwined with mine. I was looking forward to normal. I could do normal. "Okay. I just wanted to make sure. And to warn you, it may not be the last time I freak out."

"Okay, I'll be prepared." He kissed me on the cheek, and I settled in for at least fifteen minutes before I freaked out again, when the car drove us straight onto the tarmac at a small airport so we could walk the few yards to a private plane.

CHAPTER SIXTEEN

A Private Jet

WE WALKED RIGHT onto the tarmac. It was crazy. "So there's no security?" I asked for the third time. I couldn't get over the fact that we didn't have to stand in a line.

"They checked our passports when we walked past, remember?"

"And that's it? Now we just... fly?"

He laughed. "Pretty much."

I tried not to like it too much when the plane lifted off less than a half hour later, after the lone flight attendant had poured us champagne and opened a tin of caviar to put on top of smoked salmon and tiny crackers. I was a little nervous about the luxury of the plane. "I don't want to get too comfortable traveling in plush leather armchairs," I told him.

Chris tried to nudge me into acceptance. "You aren't insulting all other forms of travel just because you enjoy this for now." He was right. I could at least enjoy the fact that I didn't have to stay in my seat if I didn't feel like sitting.

By way of example, Chris pulled me out of my seat and onto his lap. He wrapped his arms around me and nuzzled my neck. "It would be too easy to get used to this. All of it," I said, not referring to the plane.

"Enjoy it."

Chris was quiet after that. Which made me quiet. Which meant I started thinking and also worrying. "Hey," I asked, looking up at him. "Is this crazy? I mean, we barely know each other and we're flying to your vacation home."

He smiled. "It sure as hell seems crazy, doesn't it? But, I don't know... it doesn't feel wrong."

It didn't feel wrong at all. So I kissed him. And I didn't worry for a few whole minutes. Then he added, "Besides, what the worst that could happen? If we don't get along, my house is big enough for us to coexist without getting in each other's way."

"Hmmm... I'm not sure what disturbs me more, the idea that you've got a plan for us not getting along or that your house is *that* big."

He smiled, which turned into a laugh, which turned into another hot kiss. "I think we'll get along just fine. I like you. I can tell you're a good person."

"I'm okay," I said, shrugging. "I don't murder kittens or put ketchup on mac and cheese or anything."

"You have no idea the kind of people I deal with. I'd take kitten murderer over some of them."

I held up a finger. "No one should murder kittens. What do your people do that's so bad?"

"Just the usual celebrity-fucking. People who like being around actors because of what it might do for their careers, their image, their bank accounts."

"That's gross."

"I agree.

I thought about that for a minute. What must it be like to

always wonder if a person liked Chris for Chris or because he was famous? His earlier comments about how I made him feel normal made more sense now that I was starting to understand the demands of his celebrity. "What makes you think I'm not a celebrity-fucker?"

"Well for one thing, you didn't know who I was."

"You got me there. So I guess I'm just a regular fucker," I said. I meant it as a joke, but he looked like his brain might explode. "Sorry, I'm a little nervous."

He took my face in his hands and kissed me. "Don't be nervous. We're going to have a good time. You're the first person I've met in a long time who's so normal you're making me feel normal."

"You're welcome, I guess?" I wasn't sure if being normal was such a great thing. But what was great was this plane. It had leather armchairs and stellar views of the landscape below since it could fly lower than other planes. Chris wasn't even looking at the view. "I guess you're used to the views?" I asked.

"I do a lot of flying," he said. He was looking at me instead of checking out the landscape.

"Doesn't matter how much flying you do, you should still see the view. Look out there—the farms are beautiful." He looked and he smiled.

"Thanks. You're right."

The flight was quick. Forty-five minutes and we were circling the private airport. "I'm almost sad to arrive because I really like this plane," I said. It was like its own luxury hotel, with armchairs and couches in the main cabin and a bedroom in the back. On a longer flight, we might have made use of that.

"I'm glad you like the plane, but I think you'll like the house more. It's on the beach."

I nodded. Something told me I had no concept of what a

multi-million dollar house on a beach really was. But I had a feeling I'd like it.

CHAPTER SEVENTEEN

Juan-les-Pins – Antibes, the French Riviera

THE CÔTE D'AZUR city of Antibes was nothing like I pictured. I'd expected a few sunny beaches and clear blue water, but my imagination didn't take me far beyond that. I lived in California. I thought I knew what a coastline looked like, even a French one.

Antibes, however, was a postcard-perfect swath of white sand, with the most picturesque view of the bluest water I'd ever seen. Built onto a promontory, the warm-beige stone buildings arose from a wraparound fortified wall that had been built during the Roman occupation of the area more than two thousand years earlier. A château rising at the point served as the Picasso Museum, which I was dying to visit. The private car that took us from the airport drove through the town on the way to Chris's recently purchased villa, and I tried my best to stay calm at the sight of the exclusive hotels we passed on the road through Cap d'Antibes.

"Are you following the politics of this place too?" I asked, trying to connect a little with his interests and also keep my mind off what he'd look like without his clothes. The nervous anticipation of feeling his hands and tongue on my skin made me tremble a little now that it felt like we were hurtling headlong toward it.

"Actually, yes. Leonetti, the mayor, is president of the Republicans, but he's also part of the Radical Party. He was a doctor before he got into politics. So, interesting guy," he said, and I nodded, intentionally not meeting his eye. I knew if I did, I'd feel all kinds of things and I was trying to maintain a little perspective and keep my nerves at bay. I could tell he was watching me, but I glanced around the car, trying to land on anything but him. The flapping wings of butterflies were making a playground out of my belly and I knew if I looked at him, I'd collapse with wanting.

He gently reached a hand out and turned my face to look at him. His eyes were clouded with sudden desire. "I don't want to talk about goddamn politics."

His lips met mine with crushing intensity that matched what I felt and I was so swept up I forgot to breathe. Within seconds he'd unhooked my seatbelt and pulled me toward him, angling so we were half-reclining. Normally, my cautious self would be all about automobile safety, but my physical need put a muzzle on my cautious self.

We were a tangle of lips and limbs. Chris pushed his hands into my hair, and I ran my hands under his shirt and over his tight muscles, grateful to whatever on-set trainer forced him to do eight-bazillion crunches. I continued to be convinced he had special superhero powers. How else could he be that good at kissing and instinctively knowing the route to every pleasure center on my body?

He snapped his own seatbelt off and we fell the rest of the way to fully reclining on the seat. "You okay?" he asked.

"I'm very okay." I pushed up onto my hands as our hips circled and pressed against each other. We were dry-humping in the back of the town car like a couple of teenagers on prom night.

An unconscious groan escaped my lips as Chris trailed his fingers under my shirt and gently massaged one breast through the lacy fabric of my bra. He kissed down my throat to my collarbone before using his tongue to set my skin aflame again.

I still had the wherewithal to find it amusing that for all the self-restraint we'd shown for hours last night, we were seconds away from banging it out in this car. And in the light of day, I was very okay with that.

I felt breathless and light-headed when he slowed the pace of his assault, my hazy, lusty thoughts starting to come back into focus. I pushed away and did my best to put a little space between us so I could look at him. I watched his face as he smoothed out my hair and reached to kiss me lightly on the lips.

"We're almost at my house," he said, gesturing out the window with a nod of his head.

"You timed that well. Or maybe you've practiced," I said, wondering if he had a set series of moves he knew he could get in between the airport and the house.

He returned my suspicious look with a smirk. "Just lucky, I assure you."

I was aware that the air had changed even in the temperature-controlled car. I inhaled the smell of sea air and sat up a little straighter, needing to look out at the magnificent view of the coastline. It was blue water and bluer water.

NO SOONER HAD the town car delivered us to the circular driveway of Chris's villa than he put a key in the lock, thanked the driver, and scooped me up in his arms and carried me upstairs like Scarlett O'Hara. I had a momentary thought of wondering what happened to our luggage, but that thought escaped me as he planted a soft kiss on my lips and I lost myself in lust again.

The master bedroom was down at the end of the hallway. I didn't see much else along the way. "What, no house tour?" I asked.

He didn't even smile. "Fuck the tour. I want you. Now," he said, laying me down gently on the cool white expensive Egyptian cotton. His eyes ran over me with an appreciative gaze that made me feel wanted for the first time in a while.

"That might hurt your Airbnb rating," I said, my nerves giving way to an attempt at humor. But I wanted him too, and it felt like my pounding heart was tearing through my chest. I'd spent most of the flight thinking about this moment and most of the car ride building up to it. I took in a slow calming breath to quiet my nerves and give in to the moment.

Chris slid next to me on the bed and pulled me toward him, running a finger over the contour of my cheek. "So beautiful," he said, his eyes moving over my face. Normally, my self-conscious inner voice would force me to say something self-deprecating like, "Well, you haven't seen me in the morning" or "I'm so happy to be with someone who's nearsighted," but that voice was drowned out in the chorus of goodness he evoked. It shut up my inner critic, and that had never happened before.

Then his lips were on mine, hard and demanding, like the ride in the car had been amateur hour. He tasted like mint and all kinds of delicious, and I felt myself pressing harder against him, wanting to feel his body flush against mine.

I craved him more than seemed logical for someone I'd only met the day before. I couldn't explain my overwhelming desire for this man. The vacation infatuation factor had to be at play.

Or he was just that seductive. When I was good and dizzy-brained, he sucked on my bottom lip and I was done for.

"You're good at that," I practically panted. He took my meaning as intended—as encouragement to do it again.

"And you're delectable."

His hands brushed over the sides of my face and he edged my lips apart with the tip of his tongue. I responded to every subtle searching stroke, wrapping my arms around his neck and feeling my semi-collected wits scramble even more under his influence. What was he doing to me?

I felt breathless, dizzy, and a little nervous that I was fully committing to sex with him. Even though it was the next morning, it still felt crazy fast. I was going to be naked in front of a guy I'd met one day earlier, and I wasn't brimming with confidence about my body. I'd always been fit and active, but I'd also always been curvy and soft in places where other people had angles.

And he was an actor, so he was used to perfect faces and bodies being directed into camera-perfect performances.

I didn't know how I could possibly measure up.

Almost like he knew where my thoughts had wandered, he ran a hand over me from my thigh, over my hip and along my waist. "You're just so sexy, I hope you know that."

No, I didn't know that, and I had no response. So I kissed him instead.

When I saw his eyes flashing a more intense shade and his smile that lit up only for me, I started to settle into the idea that he wasn't judging me like I was on an audition. He was enthusiastically appreciating the curves and I slowly started to believe I had nothing to worry about.

"Do you mind taking this off?" I asked, tugging the hem of his shirt up and marveling at the six-pack I'd felt earlier but not seen in all its glory. He raised himself up to his knees, pulling me up with him.

"Only if you do the same," he said, mouth crooking into a grin. He threw his shirt across the room and I ran my hands over his chest, appreciating the hard muscles under hot skin. He was tanned as if he'd already come back from two weeks at the beach. And those abs—they could have starred in their own movie.

Chris pulled my T-shirt over my head and lowered the straps on my bra. He paused and looked me over, hungrily. "It's really not fair," he said, running his fingers over the lacy cups.

"What's not?"

"This looks so good on you and yet, I'd really prefer to take it off." He reached around and unclasped the back and it fell to the bed. Chris's appreciative gaze never strayed, but his hands did, covering every inch of my hips, waist, and then cupping my breasts. We stayed on our knees, facing each other, and kissed some more, hands everywhere on each other's bodies.

Then he lowered his mouth to one breast and slowly began running his tongue over every contour. I inhaled sharply, feeling a rush of need for him and everything his tongue could do. He circled the taut peaks with the tip of his tongue and I felt a rush of heat to my center. And with every graze of his hands and every word he said to me, I felt my nerves settle and my second-guessing cease.

I let my hands work their way lower to his taut hipbones that led down below his belt. I reached one hand below the waistband and felt how hard he was. And how thick and perfect in my hand. He let out a low groan before shifting us so we were lying facing each other.

"Let's not rush," he said.

"I have no other pressing plans." I titled my face to kiss him, my hands running over the smooth skin of his back and coming around to rest on his rippling abs.

Things slowed down as our earlier desperation settled into

the rhythm of longer, deeper kisses and the reality that we didn't have anywhere else to be. His hands caressed different parts of me, working their way lower. Then he moved me again, so I was lying on my back and he was sliding my shorts down my legs.

"I want to taste you," he said, kissing a path over my hip and down my inner thigh. "Can I?"

I was amused and impressed with his politeness. Would any woman ever say no to him? I desperately wanted to ask if anyone ever had, but it was *not* the time. "Um, yes... yes, that's... sure."

He let out a low laugh and ran his tongue up the opposite inner thigh, spreading my legs a little wider when he got back to the apex of my thighs. My breath caught when I felt the melt of his tongue sweep up my center and lavish the sweet spot with circles of endless attention. His merciless tongue took me farther and farther from control until I was moaning with pleasure and begging him not to stop.

I heard him chuckle. "I don't plan to."

I grabbed onto the expensive linens and tried to hold back, but the dam that held my desire was no match for Chris. I felt myself come undone in one more instance of never having experienced anything like him.

I was barely conversant in my native tongue when he crawled up my body and I guided his lips to mine, needing to express my gratitude without words because I had none.

"Ah, I'm just... that was..." I just couldn't. He smiled and kissed a trail between my breasts to my throat.

"I want you to feel that again," he whispered, and I could see the strain in his pants.

"Yes. But..." In a very ungraceful way, my hands fluttered around, as though gesturing at his hard-on, but not really, but needing to make sure he understood that I was concerned about the ever-present issue of a condom. I'd thrown caution to the wind in coming to Chris's villa, but that didn't mean I'd lost all sense of reason.

"Covered." He rolled away and pulled open a drawer in his bedside table, digging around and grabbing a foil packet. "I don't want you to think I have these because I have tons of women here all the time."

"I didn't until you said that."

"Well, then, I'm going to do my best to make you forget I ever opened my damned mouth," he said, rolling back toward me and kissing my neck and exhaling his hot seduction behind my ear. I heard the rip of foil and reached to take the condom from his so I could roll it on. Then I savored the feeling of his hard length in my hand while Chris gently reached down and slipped a finger inside me, sliding easily through the wetness that was so ready for him.

Then he was inside me, moving slowly, watching me to make sure I was okay with each movement, wanting me to feel the longing I could see in his face. I did. And then I was flooded with exquisite joy, exploding each time he moved an inch.

We moved against each other and with each other. None of the awkward first-time bumping and apologizing. It was all sighs and moans and mounting levels of passion. We fit together like our bodies were made to do only this.

It didn't take long before he'd coaxed yet another orgasm from me. I was barely hanging onto my senses when I felt him start to thrust and quiver with his own. We lay under a ceiling fan, wrapped up in each other and silent for a while, both of us regaining control over our breathing.

"Thanks for making the trip with me," he said finally. He smiled a boyish grin of having gotten what he wanted.

"Thanks for having me," I returned. "I'm really glad we got the awkward sexing out of the way to we can just hang out now."

He let out a surprised choke of laughter, then stroked my

cheek with his finger. "That was the only reason I rushed us up here."

"I could tell you were feeling awkward," I said.

He laughed again and kissed the tip of my nose. "I can't decide whether I'm exhausted or hungry. Or whether I just want to lie here with you," he said.

"Can it be all three?"

"It can be whatever you want."

"Okay, I want to see this place. You forgot to give me a tour."

"I did. I forgot. I was... distracted."

"I forgive you, but I still want the tour."

He shrugged. "I still want my five star Airbnb rating."

"It'll take more than a tour. I'm rating your hostessing skills as well."

"My hostessing?"

"Yes. I'd like you to wear an apron and serve scones."

"We're in France. We eat croissants here." Chris rolled off the bed, went to an antique chest of drawers, and pulled out a bathing suit. It hadn't occurred to me he'd have the place fully stocked with his things, but course he did. This was his house. I thought about my duffel bag and roller bag full of stuff. I'd packed for heat and thrown in a bathing suit because it was summer, but now that we were in a beach town, I realized I probably didn't have the right clothes. I pulled my T-shirt back on and mentally went through my luggage, trying to recall what I'd brought.

He came back over and waited for me to finish my mental discourse with myself. "Sorry," I said.

"It's fine. It's your process. I'm not trying to change it, just trying to figure out how to work within it."

Could a person be this nice and easygoing for real? I didn't fully trust it. I couldn't help feeling like he was acting like the perfect guy, channeling parts of scripts he'd memorized. Then I chastised myself for my cynicism.

"So do you have any quirks or weird habits?" I asked. "Maybe a stormy dark side?"

He laughed. "I have weird habits, trust me. And even a dark side."

"Care to share?"

"Not looking to spoil your quirk-free perception of me yet. But eventually, sure."

"I'm holding you to it," I said.

"From what I know so far, I'd expect nothing less."

The house tour took longer than I expected. Chris had stories to tell about different parts of the house, like a professional docent, and the place was enormous. The house was a pale-pink two-story colonial with a red-clay-tiled roof and white shutters and balconies. Every west-facing window had a view of the ocean below the cliff on which the house was perched.

Inside, someone had fully equipped the white marble chef's kitchen with every necessary modern appliance and stocked the open shelves with floral-painted dishes and delicate glassware. I couldn't imagine Chris handpicking everything in the kitchen, or in the house, for that matter. Not when he traveled for work and lived in New York.

"Who furnished this place?"

He looked sheepish. "I had to hire someone. I knew I couldn't be here to do all of that. Does that seem... bougie?"

"No, and please don't feel self-conscious for having money. I know you work hard. I have a job too. I just don't happen to get paid as much at mine."

"Which is unfair."

"Well, you don't know that," I said. "I could be shitty at what I do."

"I somehow doubt that."

There were at least five bedrooms if you didn't count the small second house on the property, which had one more, along with its own living room, kitchen, and bathroom. I'd have been happy with that place, let alone the impeccably furnished main house. Every room had stylish but comfortable overstuffed sofas and chairs and was decorated with patterned throw pillows, glass lamps, and blue-green rugs that matched the Mediterranean Sea.

The grounds spread out for several acres, lush green grass rolling toward a rectangular pool and surrounding deck with lounge chairs under wide umbrellas and a cabana in the corner. All the cushions were white and pristine, which meant someone must have been there ahead of us to clean everything and make sure not a speck of dirt or dust marred any surface.

I had no idea whether that was according to Chris's instructions or those of his assistant, but I couldn't help feeling acutely aware of a level of privilege no one else I knew had experienced. And at the same time, all I wanted to do was jump into that pool and lounge on a chair in that yard. The setting was entirely too inviting.

Every moment since our dinner the night before had been dusted with the glow of movie romance that turned my questionable travel choice into a vacation dream I never could have pictured. It scared me.

I knew I was living a fantasy, one that would end in a matter of days when I flew home and Chris went back to New York or wherever he had to go next. Of course, it would end. A big part of the wild attraction we felt was knowing our time together was fleeting. The ticking clock made every moment precious and romantic.

That's why I knew I had to keep my emotions in check. *This is just a fling*, I almost said out loud. I'd known him for one day, and we'd already proven that we couldn't go an hour without our hands all over each other. As good as it felt, it was almost too much. I hadn't planned for any of this, and I couldn't be certain if I was carefree enough not to get attached. Chris seemed lost in his own thoughts, but I couldn't worry about that.

Breathe, I told myself. I had a habit of getting overwhelmed when I didn't have a plan, and nothing about being in a new city, secreted away behind the walls of a stunning beach house with a man I barely knew, spelled *plan*. With my mind spinning off in directions that were only going to take me to a meltdown, I had to get a grip.

"Hey," Chris yelled from the other side of the grass, where he'd been typing on his phone while I explored. "You hungry? There's a cute place in town that opens at twelve."

I nodded. Cute was comfortable. Cute was something I could manage. The house, on the other hand, was overwhelming. "I'm in."

CHAPTER EIGHTEEN

I INSISTED ON WALKING. Chris said he hadn't walked into town once since he'd bought the house. To me, that seemed like all the more reason to do it.

But he had bikes and mopeds and even a skateboard and I'm sure he figured they were fun and a lot faster.

"The bikes are fun. We could ride into town," he said, hinting once more. I could tell he'd prefer that, but I smiled and took his hand, leading him away from the storage shed where he kept his toys.

"Can we do that next time? I'm kind of excited about the walk," I said.

"You're adorable. There's no way I'm going to say no to you."

"I think it will help me get the lay of the land if I'm on my feet, and I don't want to get lost here."

"It's a lot harder to get lost here than in Paris. And what makes you think I'm going to abandon you all of a sudden and you'll lose your way?"

"I assumed you've got stuff to do here. Isn't that why you came? I figured I'm not going to be with you twenty-four seven, so I'll need to find my way around."

"Sounds like you're working on a plan."

"It helps me sleep at night if I plan things," I said, which reminded me we hadn't slept all night and I was still reeling from jet lag. I couldn't recall the last time I'd actually slept for eight hours straight. It had to have been three days earlier in LA. No wonder I felt light-headed. It couldn't all be because of the guy. I wasn't that easily bowled over.

"I'm fine walking, but you should know that the place I had in mind is about an hour away if we walk. On bikes, it will take us twenty minutes max," he said. "That'll leave us time for other activities."

"Ha. What kind of activities?" I asked, smirking. Maybe he meant things like paddle ball on the beach, but that's not how it sounded. He grabbed my hand and interlaced his fingers with mine.

"Whatever you want," he said.

"Four-hour Scrabble tournament?"

"If that's what you want."

"I don't want that, but you've convinced me. Let's take the bikes."

"Are you always this easy and pleasant?"

"Not always. But a morning of orgasms has made me very agreeable," I said.

"Well then, I'll make sure you're agreeable the whole time we're here." He went back to the shed to pull out the beach cruisers. I opted for the green one, which left him with the purple.

He scowled and I laughed. "Why do you have a purple bike if you don't like the color?"

"I didn't pick out the bikes. And I'm fine with the purple."

"Lemme guess. Your assistant picked them out?"

"They came with the house. How long are you going to give me shit about having an assistant?"

I laughed and started to pedal. "As long as you have an assistant."

I was hungry. Bikes were the right call. After we'd ridden for a while, the air changed as we got farther away from the water. I could see what he loved about this place. As small and quaint is it was, it had nuances. Like the cobble stones that appeared every so often and shuddered under our bike tires.

We cycled to the small road that led from the coast. It was flanked by bushes and palm trees and a wall that every couple hundred yards had a gate leading to a private home. I liked how one second we were on a side street and the next we were on a larger street with taller trees, no longer palms but Mediterranean in feel, with agave and lavender growing outside some of the properties. It was the perfect road to travel on bikes.

The restaurant Chris chose was a vine-covered country farmhouse with white tablecloths on small round tables nestled against an ancient cement wall. It had so much charm. Concentric circles of pebbles spread out below our feet, creating a rock floor with grapevines forming a trellis above our heads.

"It's perfect," I said.

I loved its simplicity. I had no interest in dining in a Michelin-starred restaurant, mostly because I was wearing shorts and I might not know what to order. Fortunately, Chris knew better than to go overboard with a crazy-fancy venue. The place was casual, though the people around us were clearly of an elite set.

Across from us at another table, a woman in a large straw sunhat and tortoise-shell glasses sipped wine. Her floor-length white caftan would have been as appropriate at a wedding as by the pool at an expensive hotel. She and her companion, a man in pressed navy shorts and a sweater tied around the neck of his polo shirt, looked like they'd just stepped off their yacht. They were sharing a bottle of white wine, with drips of condensation glistening in the sun.

"Should we have wine?" Chris asked.

"Oh, yes. I think we should," I said, deciding that if I was going to be on vacation in the South of France, I would go for it one thousand percent. I'd started my day with caviar, and I saw no reason to veer off course now.

He handed me the wine list, and I carefully looked it over before passing it back. "I have no knowledge of French wines, or anything that isn't in the cheap reds section at Trader Joe's. But thanks for the option."

"I don't know that much about wine either. I usually just order something in the middle of the price range and hope for the best. It mostly works out."

"Sounds good to me."

Chris knew the restaurant owner pretty well, and he came over with a warm greeting and a kiss on both cheeks. He kissed me as well, welcoming me like a guest in his home.

The menu was simple—cheese, salads, foie gras for starters, fish and meat as entrées, and a bunch of desserts. We had the option of choosing a salad and dessert, a main course and dessert, or a main course and salad. I didn't think long before deciding. "A salad, no question because it's hot and I can't imagine eating hot food. And a cheese plate for dessert. You can share it with me."

"Works for me," he said.

I looked again at the woman in the caftan and the big hat. She was tanned, chic, and fabulous in the way that a third-generation baroness who was born into a certain way of life would be—casual and comfortable around caviar and good French wine. Chris caught me stealing another glimpse of her and turned to check out the object of my fascination. He looked back at me and shrugged.

"That woman is the image of the French dream, swanning through the Côte d'Azure, dipping her toes into the Mediterranean—but not going farther because she doesn't want her silk caftan to get wet—then lounging on a mega-yacht and sipping champagne."

"Sounds nice," he said before shaking his head. "You realize, of course, that she could be meeting with her divorce attorney, who's picking up the tab for lunch, and planning whether to use her Crock-Pot or the microwave to cook dinner for one later."

"You really know how to spoil an image."

Chris ordered grilled fish and a chocolate tart with Tahitian vanilla cream. "You will be having a bite of that. I insist."

"I *will* be having a bite."

Chris was looking at me like he has something on his mind, and once we were finished with our first glass of wine, I discovered why. "You mentioned you were supposed to have a friend come with you on this trip," he said. I did mention it, but I was surprised he was mentioning it now.

I froze while lifting my class to my lips. "Um, yeah. I was."

"What happened? Why couldn't your friend come? Is it okay if I ask?"

I put my glass down without taking a sip. "Um, sure. You can ask."

He didn't say anything, maybe because he'd already asked. I wasn't sure whether I wanted to answer or what I should say. I looked at my glass like I might find the answer in its depths.

"Hey, forget I asked. It's not important. I don't want to make you uncomfortable," he said.

"No, it's okay. He was my boyfriend. He cheated on me, we broke up, so I came alone." I looked up at him, relieved to have gotten the words out.

"Ah, I'm sorry."

"Don't be. He's not worth it. I was momentarily heartbroken, but I'm over it. Really."

"Are you really over him?"

I smiled. "Are you worried I'm on the rebound? I might be on the rebound. I don't feel like I am, but I don't really know."

He nodded slowly. "I'm not sure that matters."

"You mean because we're just here having a fun vacation fling?"

"I mean because I like you and I don't care what brought you here." He seemed to reconsider what he'd said. "I just mean, I'm happy you're here. And for the record, your ex-boyfriend is an idiot."

"He is an idiot. And thank you. I'm happy to be here with you too. So can we not talk about my idiot ex now?"

He reached for my hand. "Not now or ever."

Lunch unfolded over an hour and a half of sipping wine and talking about why Chris had been so taken with this place. I confessed that I'd read Debra's magazine article about the house, though I hadn't focused enough on it to notice who bought it.

"It's not pretentious in the South, not at all. A lot of farms spread throughout Provence and farther south, just humble, normal," he said.

"Even with Saint-Tropez and all the fancy beaches?"

"Those are different. That's why I like it here."

"I still feel like a student traveler who should be squatting in a hostel. Nothing's going to make me feel like I have anything in common with that woman in the caftan and the hat. Even a caftan and a hat."

"Well, I didn't buy a house in one of those places. This town is very low-key. Unless you stay at one of the resorts. They can feel a little more chichi, but that's because they cost a fortune.

Still, that doesn't mean we can't have a nice dinner by the pool at one of them. Maybe later in the week." He relaxed in his chair and closed his eyes as the sun hit his face.

I took the opportunity to take a good look at him, understanding for the first time what people meant when they described a person as having "movie-star good looks." It wasn't just that he was conventionally attractive. His face had character, subtle expressiveness, and lines that had to have come from experience. Or pain.

So far, he seemed so easy and comfortable. I couldn't imagine what his dark side could be. Then I worried that it was only a matter of time before I would find out.

CHAPTER NINETEEN

The Old City, Antibes

I COULDN'T GO into the Old Town without venturing to the Picasso Museum. After seeing the art at the Musée d'Orsay, my expectations were high.

"You know, there's an incredible Picasso museum in Paris. It was redone a few years ago, and it's in this really cool hotel *particulier*," Chris said.

"In English, *señor, por favor.*"

"A mansion, basically. Built for a guy who made his money collecting taxes on salt."

"Like, table salt?"

"Yeah, you know, back in the 1600s when salt was worth more than gold."

He'd done his homework. I remembered the salt tax from a class I took in college, but back then, the words I'd read in my textbooks had felt far removed from reality. Seeing the places where history unfolded, where the Romans built aqueducts and tax collectors built mansions, brought the events to life as if someone had just painted colors on my black-and-white text-book world.

"Got it," I said. "Well, if you've noticed, I'm no longer in Paris. So it's gonna have to be this Picasso Museum."

"I'm game," he said, starting to walk in the direction of the museum. I stopped walking, and he turned around. "What's up?"

"You've been here before, haven't you?"

He shrugged. "A couple times."

"So, like, what—five or six?"

"I have no idea. Does it matter?"

"Well, kind of. I don't want to drag you someplace you've been a million times."

"You're not dragging me. Will you stop?"

"Stop what?" I asked.

"Worrying about everything. If I don't want to do something, I'll tell you. Okay? But only if you promise to do the same."

I studied him to discern whether he wanted to go to the museum again or not. I couldn't tell. He grabbed my hand and pulled me toward him, walking backward in the direction of the museum, leading me like a small unwilling child he had to walk into her first day of school.

"Okay, I promise," I said, picking up the pace. I really did want to see whatever works of art this Picasso museum had on its walls. I anticipated the same joy I'd felt in front of all those impressionist pieces. Picasso did not disappoint. Neither did Chris.

AN HOUR LATER, we were done with the museum and back outside. I assumed we'd ride back to his house, but Chris had other plans. "I have an event later this week. Will you be my date?" he asked, kissing me sweetly on the lips.

I felt like he was asking me to the prom. "Will you bring me a wrist corsage or a nosegay?"

"Um, whichever you'd like?" he said, casting a side glance at me as though he wasn't sure if I was joking.

"No, no corsage. Kidding. What kind of event?"

"A movie premiere. I'm asking you to be my date at the movies."

"So, popcorn and making out in the balcony? Sure. I'm in."

"Definitely popcorn, and making out at anyplace else of your choosing, but not in the theater. Will you go with me?" he asked, rubbing his hands together like a nervous schoolboy.

I knew enough to know what movie premieres entailed. I'd seen plenty of red carpets outside of movie theaters, where the streets had been blocked off and sometimes fans lined up behind barricades, trying to get a look at the stars when they walked in. There were often lights sweeping across the sky to announce the film's opening. I was just not a starstruck kind of person, so I'd never gone to a premiere, even when a client set aside a handful of tickets for our office. People were always jockeying to go, mainly for the after-parties, where they could eat catered food next to actors and production crew and bring home souvenirs they could put on their desks. None of it interested me.

"You're making it sound really quaint. I just have one question. Is it your movie?" The *no making out in the theater* part kind of clued me in. I imagined there'd be gawkers.

He looked uncomfortable, but a tiny shred of pride couldn't help escaping in the guilty smile on his face. "Yes."

"That's amazing. Congratulations."

"Thanks," he said quietly. He folded his arms. I could see him shutting down. I didn't want to crush his buzz, as it were, and I had a feeling I had somehow already done that. Maybe my comments about the fancy hotels and my shock at the private jet had made him feel like he had to hide the trappings of his life.

"No, seriously. I'm excited to go. Yes, I'll be your date. And please don't feel like this is weird for me, because it definitely... is... but I'll get used to it. I promise."

"They're actually kind of fun. The movie itself can be a little stressful because I'm wondering what the audience is thinking the whole time but not this one. The studio packs it with supporters and throws in a few film critics. So the group is basically pro-*White Serpent*, so it's just a thing for the photos. You know—publicity—your area."

He was assuming that some part of my everyday life was remotely similar to attending a premiere for my own movie. It was not. What I couldn't decide was whether it mattered. A lot of people would give their right arm to be in my shoes—on vacation with Chris Conley, staying at his sprawling beach house, and going to his movie premiere as his date.

Then I realized why I couldn't be his date. "Wait. I don't have anything I could wear to a premiere."

"I can help with that." He pulled me down a small street, stopping when we'd gotten away from the people, and bent to kiss me. His lips covered mine and he looped a hand through my hair and curled it around his fingers, pulling gently on it while his tongue did magical things that made me dizzy. He pulled back and smiled at me. "I couldn't wait any longer."

"I feel fortunate you lack self-control," I said on a breath, wondering how it was possible he had such a mind-scrambling effect on me.

"Come on, we're almost there."

I was too caught up in him to wonder where *there* was, so I went. He led me to a tiny store where designer beachwear was on sale, next to an ice cream shop. He opened a green door between them and showed me inside. The room had a box on the floor and a mirror on the wall—that was all.

If I'd had a really active imagination, this is where I'd freak out that I was being led to my death. Instead, I only freaked out a teeny tiny bit.

From behind a curtain, an older French woman came out, squinting in the sunlight that beamed through the window in the door. Then her eyes grew wide. "Ah, Christophe, *mon cheri!*" She hugged him like her own son. For all I knew, he actually was her son.

"Marguerite, this is Nikki."

She hugged me. "*Bonjour*, Nikki. *Bienvenue à Antibes.*" She pronounced an extra syllable for the *e* at the end of the word so it sounded like, "An-teeb-uh," something I'd heard other people do here.

Before I could even begin to depress the woman with my paltry French, Chris said, "Nikki needs a dress for next Saturday night. What do you think?"

She looked me up and down, turning me to examine my backside. Then she hugged me again and winked at Chris. "I think you are a very lucky man, as I have said to you before. I can make her *une robe magnifique.* I think... *bleu, oui?*"

Chris was smiling, nodding. "She'd look amazing in blue."

I felt strange that they were discussing me like I wasn't even there, and I wondered what Marguerite meant about Chris being lucky. Did he bring his last flavor of the week here too? When was that—a week ago? A month ago? I fought to silence cynic inside. Worrying about imaginary problems wasn't going to get me anywhere.

"Hang on, do I get a say?" I asked.

"Sure. Do you think you'd look amazing in blue?" Chris asked.

"That's not what I meant."

He asked Marguerite something in French, and she reached behind the curtain and brought out a large black notebook. When she opened it and started turning the pages, I was expecting to see measurements or payment information, but what she showed me instead were colored-in line drawings of jaw-dropping couture-quality dresses and page after page of long, sweeping hemlines, empire waists, and strapless bustiers.

"Marguerite used to work for Halston. She's designed dresses for anybody you've ever heard of in one royal family or another."

"In the old days. Now I enjoy the beach and wait for my friends to come visit me at the shop, and if they don't come, I paint." She moved the curtain aside to give me a glimpse of her real purpose. Behind the nondescript empty room with a mirror, she'd hidden a three-hundred-square-foot art studio, where paintings—mostly portraits of women—sat on easels. "They are my loves," she explained. "Past and present."

"You finished the Julia portrait," Chris said, walking to the far corner to inspect a painting of a blond woman twirling on the beach, carefree, in a sundress. She looked about Marguerite's age.

I looked at the painting, which was, in fact, as beautiful as anything I'd seen at the Musée d'Orsay.

"It's really something." When I turned back toward Chris, I saw he had that same look on his face that I'd seen at the restaurant the previous night when he talked about his parents—sadness and regret. Maybe he missed his parents. Maybe Marguerite was about their age, and she made him wish he could see them. I had no idea what to say to him. Fortunately, Marguerite filled the void, and her talking seemed to distract him from whatever was bothering him.

"*Merci, cheri.* For her birthday, though really it's been a gift for me to paint it."

He nodded at her, admiring the painting again. "When's her birthday?"

"*Septembre*. Soon."

"And she has no idea you did this?" he asked.

"Not so far. But she's so nosy. It's been almost impossible to keep her away from here. I've had to come up with every excuse."

I didn't dare speak. I was fascinated by the relationship between them. Marguerite looked to be in her sixties, with a grey pile of hair on her head, bright lipstick, and reading glasses around her neck. She clearly loved Chris but not because of his movies. She seemed to understand him on a deeper level, and she clearly had his back.

Chris came to stand next to me and look through the designs in the book. He put an arm across my shoulders and rubbed the back of my neck lightly with his fingers while he paged through the book with the other hand. I caught Marguerite noticing. She made no comment.

"Is there one that calls out to you?" he asked me.

"Each one is more beautiful than the one before it. Though... I do like this drawing," I said, pointing to the barest of sketches, the least finished one, which showed a straight strapless neckline and a sweep of fabric that started at the bodice and flowed over the page. It was marine blue, slightly darker than the water we'd seen when the plane flew low over the coastline.

Chris smiled and handed the book to Marguerite, who said, "She has an exquisite eye."

"No, it's you who have an eye. Every one of your designs is a work of art," I said.

But she had to know that. She'd designed for Halston. She didn't need me to wander in from Los Angeles to compliment her.

Marguerite hugged me gratefully. "I will get to work."

I turned to Chris, about to ask if he wanted to walk around the town a little more. From his expression, I could tell he was already picturing me in that dress. And out of it.

"Feel like hitting the bikes?" he asked, the uneven tone of his voice betraying sudden desire. I nodded.

We rode back to his house. Fast. Tour de France fast.

CHAPTER TWENTY

The Villa

WE DITCHED our bikes on the driveway and walked hand in hand toward the backyard like we weren't in any hurry, as if we hadn't both been pedaling with a little extra effort, picturing the lounge chairs in the shade and the privacy of the space. Neither one of us spoke, but as though reading my mind, Chris stopped and looked at me. He pulled me toward him on the curving cobbled driveway before we'd even made it to the yard.

He ran a finger under my chin and tilted my face up toward his. "I hate your ex-boyfriend for cheating you."

"He's... not worth hating." I was surprised he was still thinking about that.

"He didn't deserve you. So maybe there's justice in the world because you're here with me," he said. I was bowled over and touched at his words.

"Maybe there is."

I wrapped my hands around him and ran my nails over the

skin under his shirt, which made his muscles jump at my touch. Kissing him made me want to do things to his body that weren't so soft and gentle. If we only had two weeks together, I wanted it to be everything.

We stayed on the driveway for a while, too lazy to move, losing part of the day in a kiss that went on and on. Then our hands were everywhere, pulling off clothing and lavishing skin and tangling in hair.

"Earlier, how you wanted to take it slow...?" I said, breathless.

"Yes...?" he said, looking like that might be a struggle.

"Not happening now."

"Good." He pulled me hard against him as his tongue swept my mouth like I was the dessert after his chocolate tart. Not breaking the kiss, we stumbled to the yard, where the chaise lounges were a huge improvement for my wobbly limbs. My legs were tired from the biking and weak from the effects of him. I was grateful when Chris laid us down on one of the fluffy terrycloth towels covering the double-wide lounge chair. He brushed the hair away from my face and kissed my neck, my jaw, the tender spot near my ear.

I was breathless, aroused. I was also intrigued by the pristine, luxury towels.

"Who does all this? Who fluffs the cushions and opens the umbrellas? Who put bottled water into an ice bucket while we were gone? Do you employ a team of minions?" I asked on an exhale.

"I can't talk to you about umbrellas when I want to hear that gorgeous moaning sound you make when you come."

It didn't even embarrass me that I'd let him know how good he felt. And was glad he had no problem telling my over-active brain to shut up. He was right. Sultry moaning on tap. He made me desperate for him and I knew he felt how wet and ready I was when his fingers slipped under the band of my thong and slowly stroked back and forth. I gave him the moaning he was looking for.

I reached down and raked my nails over the sensitive skin below his abs, wanting to drive him just as mad with desire. He grabbed my hands and pinned them with one hand above my head. "Don't move," he said.

Chris made quick work of ridding me of my bra and lavishing my breasts with the tongue action that made me go crazy earlier. I sucked in a rough breath while he kissed and licked the sweet spots on my skin that he seemed to know instinctively.

"That's so good," I said, as he sent me off into newer, better places. But I wanted my hands back. I needed to touch him. I tugged against his grip and he let go, so I started a slow descent along his chest, savoring every contour of his muscles and appreciating every inch of his hot skin.

His kisses were long and deep, claiming my mouth and my body and grinding his erection against my hot skin. I brushed my hand lower, dipping my fingers into his boxer-briefs, feeling him tremble when I touched his sensitive skin. But I wanted to feel his hard erection in my hand. I wanted to make him go crazy. So I pushed the fabric down until he helped kick it off his legs.

Then I took hold of his length, wrapping my hand around it and running my hand lightly up and down until I felt him tremble.

"You're gonna make me come like that," he warned, gritting his teeth.

"Good," I said, stroking him. I could take him all the way like this, let him come on my breasts or in my mouth. It was too good. I wanted him to lose control if he wanted to.

He shook his head. "Later. Right now I need to be inside you."

He pulled a condom from his shorts that were on the ground and tore open the foil. He didn't let me roll it on. He was going for efficiency. It was all need and desire and forward momentum.

I dug my nails into his back and sunk my teeth into his shoulder as he eased inside me. He started moving slowly, rhythmically. A tiny groan escaped from the back of my throat. "Oh God... yes... there." And he did. He hit the spot I needed over and over again until my body was begging for mercy.

I couldn't believe we'd only known each other a day. A very good, very long day. But still, one day. He'd invited me on a vacation after barely considering if for a second. And it felt right. Sex with Chris wasn't just sex. It was oxygen, necessary and basic. It was sweaty and all-hell sexy.

I wrapped my legs around him and grabbed his hair as I came, falling hard, cascading into him. Moments later, I felt him there too, whispering and swearing in my ear. Our bodies wore themselves out until we could barely hold onto each other in our blissed-out exhaustion.

We didn't move for a while. I kept my legs wrapped around his hips and he kissed my cheek and twirled a strand of my hair. Neither one of us had the wherewithal to stand.

I felt like I'd walked into a Hollywood film and seduced the leading man. Every moment since our dinner the night before had the glow of movie romance that turned my questionable travel choice into a vacation dream I never could have pictured. It scared me. I wondered whether any of it was real or if I was just going along with a fantasy, one that would end in a matter of days when I flew home and Chris went back to New York or wherever he had to go next. Of course, it would end. It had to, because part of the wild attraction was knowing our time together was fleeting.

I had to remind myself to keep my emotions in check. *This is just a fling*, I almost said out loud. I'd known him for one day, and we'd already proven that we couldn't go two hours without our hands all over each other. As good as it felt, it was almost too much. I hadn't planned for any of this, and I couldn't see where we were headed. Chris seemed lost in his own thoughts, but I couldn't worry about that.

Breathe, I told myself. I had a habit of getting overwhelmed when I didn't have a plan, and nothing about being in a new city, secreted away behind the walls of a villa with a man I barely knew, spelled *plan*. With my mind spinning off in directions that were only going to take me to a meltdown, I knew I had to get a grip.

Just as quickly, my mind slowed down because a wave of exhaustion descended and threatened to knock me out. I was so, so tired.

"I think I need sleep," I said, knowing my voice sounded soft and sleepy.

"Yeah. I'm running on fumes. Lemme show you a room upstairs where you can crash uninterrupted."

He led me into the house, up two flights of stairs, and out to a sunroom with open windows that let in a blissful breeze. In the middle of the room, a king-sized bed with crisp white sheets beckoned. He didn't suggest we sleep in it together, just kissed me on the forehead and closed the door quietly behind him when he left. I saw that my suitcases had been brought up to this room, not the master bedroom where we'd been earlier, and for a moment, I felt let down that I was being treated as just a houseguest.

Those thoughts were quickly replaced by the bliss of cool sheets, and I reasoned that Chris was just giving me some space in his house, maybe understanding that I'd strayed far and away from my comfort zone. At least, I hoped he was that intuitive. It didn't matter. All I wanted was to close my eyes, sink into the fat, downy mattress, and let my worries drift away.

He kissed me on the forehead and closed the door quietly.

CHAPTER TWENTY-ONE

I SLEPT for three glorious hours. I felt much better after the power nap, though by the time I woke up, I'd quashed any hope of getting over my jet lag and adjusting to European time. I'd be up in the middle of the night for sure. Oh, well. I'd take that over abject exhaustion. I felt so much better for having slept three hours straight.

Chris was in the kitchen on a phone call when I ventured downstairs, and he held up a finger in apology, so I went back outside to see if it was warm in Antibes in the evening. The air was dewy, the sun was gone, but it was still light out and I couldn't orient myself to figure out which way the house faced. I wandered out the back gate and found a dirt path that wound past some rocks, which gave way to a perfect beach, unmarred by footprints since the tide had last washed the sand. It really was spectacular—quiet and relaxing and perfect.

A few minutes later, Chris came out and found me sitting on a flat rock with my feet dangling in the surf below. There weren't any waves, but if I looked far enough out, I could see the lights on anchored sailboats and a few yachts on the water, though I couldn't tell whether they were moving. Chris looked relaxed, so I figured he must have slept too.

"Feel better?" he asked.

"So much," I said. It was amazing what a little sleep could do to restore a person's sanity. I no longer felt plagued by concerns about a plan or lack thereof, I wasn't worried about getting too attached, and I wasn't thinking about how I'd feel when I said goodbye.

Actually, that's not true. I was petrified about all of those things. A person couldn't change overnight. I couldn't instantly go from being a planner who liked to have a schedule to a carefree traveler who hopped on private jets with strangers and didn't worry about anything. But I was getting better.

Chris sat down on the rock and wrapped his arms around me. The universal thermal properties of being touched by Chris were at play once more against my skin. He leaned forward and lifted my hair to kiss the back of my neck. "Mmm, you taste sweet," he said, and I exhaled my calm contentment.

I relaxed into him, liking how easy it was between us.

"I've been trying to orient myself. Are we facing west?" I asked, turning to look at him.

He pointed at a sweep of coastline. "South, actually. Where it curves around there, it's west-facing." I followed his gaze to where the land curved, forming almost a protected bay. It explained why there weren't really any waves.

The house sat in a small private cove which was enclosed by high enough rocks that no one would dare try to climb them to get to where we were. Without having to ask, I knew Chris had picked this house for that reason—part of his effort to be normal, which was apparently easier when he wasn't around other people.

"It's beautiful. I can see why you like spending time here," I said.

"It's more beautiful with you." It was sweet, and it made me blush. "I'm usually here alone. This is... having you here is... a bonus."

Again, his eyes flashed with something I couldn't pinpoint, almost like sadness or regret. He stared off and seemed to lose track of time. I had to say something. "Is everything okay? I know we don't know each other that well, but I'm here. I'm a good listener."

"Oh," he said, his eyes reverting to normal as though he'd responded to a director giving him a note on his performance. "No, I'm okay. Sorry, I guess it's my turn to zone out."

"Did you sleep when I crashed upstairs?"

"I planned to, but I ended up talking to my manager, and it turned into a whole drama that I won't bore you with. Then I had to work. There's a hot script that's in turnaround, and I need to make a decision immediately. I doubt I'm gonna take the role, but I had to read the script to say for sure, and now I have to think it over."

"That's open-minded," I said, not knowing how else to respond. This was not my world at all, and he was talking to me like I'd have some idea what it meant to have a script in turnaround. "So, while I was zonked out, peacefully dreaming, you were working? That's a bummer."

"It's no big deal. It's just... if I say yes to the film, it would mean I'd go straight from promoting one movie to prepping for the next one. It's been like that for the past few projects I've done —back-to-back, no break. I'm frankly exhausted. That's why these few days here are such a welcome break."

"Lucky me. I caught you at a good time."

"The only time. I can't tell you the last time I had more than a few days off. Not that I can complain at all. I'm exceptionally lucky to have the opportunities to work like this. I've got to take the offers while I have momentum—at least, that's what my agent would have me believe. He always says, 'If you slow down, they forget.'"

"Well, he makes money if you're working, so it's kinda self-serving, no?" I said. I was pretty sure agents made ten percent of everything an actor brought in. Plus, some of the agencies got other percentages of projects. I'd read that somewhere. Agents weren't likely to tell their clients to sit around not working.

"True, it's just..." He trailed off, and I waited for him to continue. He seemed to lose his train of thought. "I'm an idiot to complain. I'm not complaining."

"Everyone needs a break sometimes."

He leaned back on the rock, resting on his elbows. "I don't, not really."

He stared off again at the ocean and the conversation hung, unfinished. I had no idea how to prompt him to go on. His problem was outside of my world, so I felt like I was grasping at straws, trying to relate. My job got intense sometimes, but I wasn't the face of the company. He had a whole different level of pressure when his name was on the marquee. "When was the last time you took real time off?"

"I just... I don't do that. I find little pockets here and there to escape. These two weeks are a total fluke."

"Again, lucky me."

He reached for me and pulled me back, so we were lying side by side on the rock, looking up at the darkening sky. He picked up my hand and grazed my knuckles with his lips. "No. Lucky me."

We were quiet for a while and at some point, I wondered if he'd fallen asleep, but when I looked over, he was gazing at me. "So tell me. I want to understand more about how your job works. If you're acting in one movie, are you already planning the next one?" I asked.

"It's a lot of everything all at once. Even if I'm not on a set or doing something to promote a film, I'm running lines in my head for the next project or thinking about a script or researching a character. And even now, during my supposed vacation, my reps have me loaded up with stuff. So if I drift off, it's not you. It's me trying to juggle. And I apologize in advance."

"Noted. You may recall, I disappear into my head as well. We can be distracted together." I thought about what the next handful of days had in store for me if he was busy working. Looking out at the view of the peaceful ocean, I realized I could be very happy with a book on a lounge chair and some swimming. "And if you have work to do, just tell me and I'll entertain myself."

"I'd rather be the one to entertain you. I owe you some hostessing," he said, pulling me in for a kiss. I wasn't about to stop him if he wanted to hostess that way. "Anyway, there you have it. My dark side. I'm a workaholic."

I rolled my lips between my teeth to stifle a smile because I wasn't sure if he was kidding. "Wait, the fact that you work a lot, that's your dark side? Because I hate to say it, but everybody works a lot. It's pretty common."

"I'm not sure it's so common to say I'll never do anything besides work and I'll never have a relationship because work comes first. It's a life of one."

I had to admit he took the idea of being a workaholic to a whole new level. I wondered if he was exaggerating. It didn't sound enviable to do it his way.

"Well, maybe that's not common. Do you really believe that?" I asked.

"Right now, I do. My job is everything. I can't slow down the pace, or I might not get it back, and that's okay. It works for me. I can still have a little fun on the side. But then I go back to work, shut the door on everything else, and I'm singularly focused."

It hit me that I was his 'fun on the side,' and I briefly thought of Johnny, who always wanted to have a good time. He was all about being in the moment and having fun and I'd never been able to make that mesh with my need to live in the real world.

But maybe with Chris, I could.

Because we only had two weeks.

I decided I could do *fun in the moment*. We both knew exactly how and when things would end, which was manna from heaven for a planner like me. It felt good to know at the outset.

"And she's gone again," he said, and I realized I'd retreated into my head.

"Sorry. I'm back."

"Did I scare you off?"

"Not at all," I told him, and I meant it. "I just think you may be selling yourself short. I'll bet you can get a little closer to a work-life balance than you think."

"Well, I can say that in the past twenty-four hours, you've done an excellent job of helping me with the life part. So thank you."

"I hardly think you should be thanking me. You've given me a bit of an upgrade over eating alone on my bed in a one-star hotel." I thought back to the Hotel des Écoles, which was so simple and charming, owned and run by a hardworking family who had been so welcoming to me when I had no idea how my trip would unfold. I almost felt like I'd sold them out by hopping on a private jet and leaving their native city.

"Please stop saying things like that. My job allows for all of this. I'm sure your job has perks."

"Yes, sometimes someone will send a basket of muffins to thank us for handling the fallout of some corporate misstep. I'm not gonna lie—muffin day is a good day," I said, trying to imagine how there could possibly be equivalency between perks.

"Okay, so think of this house like a giant muffin basket. And stop thanking me for sharing it."

I didn't want to ruin our time together with my incessant insecurity about how different my life was from his. What would be the point? We only had a finite amount of time together to begin with, so from that moment on, I vowed to shut up and just enjoy it.

"Okay, deal," I told him. I intended to keep my promise.

WE STAYED on the beach until the sky turned the perfect blue I remembered from that night I sat on the banks of the Seine with my plastic cup of rosé.

"It's blue hour," Chris said, watching me stare up at the sky.

"It has an official name?"

"*L'heure bleue*, they call it. That twilight color when all the lights in Paris look a little yellow before it really gets dark. Like Van Gogh's *Starry Night*. It's my favorite time to take pictures outside."

"I was kind of stunned when I saw the sky turn that color the other night when I sat outside. It figures I'm not exactly the first one to notice it's a special time to be outside."

"Especially in the summer, when it stays light out later. It's hard to feel as excited about twilight when it happens at four in the afternoon," he said.

"True."

I could tell the fatigue was setting in for him. He had the same dazed look in his eyes I'd seen in the mirror over the past two days. And even though I'd scratched the surface of feeling normal after my very long catnap, I could easily sleep some more. "Why don't we do something easy tonight? No big dinner at a hotel. No more bike riding. Just a quick something, and then we can both sleep."

He nodded, pushing himself up from the rock and brushing fine grains sand off his pants. Grabbing my hand, Chris pulled me to my feet, but he didn't let go of my hand. "That sounds perfect. The kitchen is stocked. We could have something here."

"Sure," I said, wondering again about the minions who must have scurried about before we got here, stocking the refrigerator and making sure every eventuality had been anticipated. I wondered whether they'd show up in the shadows and make dinner for us then disappear again without a trace.

We started walking back up the trail toward the yard, the ocean quietly lapping on the shore behind us. "Pasta okay? I'm a typical single guy who eats a lot of takeout, but I can make a pretty decent puttanesca."

"I'm kind of a typical single girl who eats a lot of salads. I can make that."

"Works for me," he said, his fingers squeezing mine. Small footlights lit the pathway between the beach and the backyard, which was aglow with tiny twinkle lights in olive trees and landscape lighting that showed off all the pretty plants.

"Did you do a lot of work on this place?" I asked, wondering whether he'd had a say in any of these details.

He shook his head. "It was pretty much turnkey. The previous owner bought it to sell, so it has every bell and whistle you can imagine."

"Yes, I've noticed some of them. Did it come with the mysterious elves who seem to have just been here right before us to make everything perfect?"

He laughed. "I do have elves. They know I like privacy, so they kind of do their work and disappear. It's a really nice couple, Henri and Clothilde. They live in the smaller house on the property year-round, so they keep an eye on everything when I'm not here. You'll meet them at some point."

It made sense that someone lived in the smaller house I'd noticed when we first arrived. But knowing the size of Chris's house, I wondered if it was weird for them to live in the lovely but smaller house that was a shack by comparison to Chris's villa. Probably not.

I'd started to understand that the French were different from Americans in many ways, especially the ability to be happy with work and accommodations that were sufficient without always wanting more. Guillaume had told me he'd waited tables at the same café for nine years and loved it.

Back home, people would be jockeying for a raise or a better job or something that gave them more trappings of upward mobility. But for what? So we could work harder to live in bigger homes that we'd see less of because work took up more of our time? I wanted to examine my life choices in this new light.

Henri and Clothilde had anticipated our needs perfectly. Fresh tomatoes, garlic, and goat cheese went into Chris's sauce along with Niçoise olives and capers. I had my pick of fresh vegetables to put in my salad, so I selected greens, tomatoes, corn, and avocado.

I could tell Chris was either tired or preoccupied because he prepared his dish with perfunctory precision, working quietly next to me. I didn't mind the quiet. Maybe we were past the phase in which someone always had to be talking. The plain fact was we were both exhausted, barely moved by the romance of eating outside at a stone table next to a fireplace that filled the air with a smoky, woodsy smell.

We ate and dropped into the bed upstairs. There was a bit of lazy kissing before he wrapped his arms around me and I fell asleep. I don't even think we said goodnight. But I know I dreamed about him.

CHAPTER TWENTY-TWO

A New Day

FOR THE FIRST time since I'd left Los Angeles, I felt awake. It made me realize what a blur the last several days had been, with people and drinks and planes all blending together. That part of the trip seemed like ages ago, the murky past. With a week left in France, I felt energized.

And maybe it was my newly wakeful state, but Chris was somehow even more attractive than I'd thought possible. He'd come downstairs in khaki shorts and a light-blue linen shirt with the sleeves rolled up over a white T-shirt. He'd already showered, and his hair was slicked back, a few pieces falling forward as it dried.

There was something special about his eyes. They were a different color that day, deeper brown, less grey. Fairy dust must have separated people who were born to be mega-actors like him from everyone else who could only wish.

"It's unbelievable out there," I said. I'd gone down to the

beach to look at the calm water while he was in the shower. I couldn't get enough of the placid blue.

"Well, then, I think you'll enjoy the day I've got planned. Figured we'd take the boat out. I hope you don't get seasick," he said, winking like he had a plan for that possibility.

"I'm not even sure. I've been on a few boats but not enough to really say if I get seasick."

"I was kidding," he said, and my heart sank with the realization we weren't going sailing. The idea of being on the water sounded glorious after gazing at it longingly since we'd arrived. My face must have fallen because he lifted my chin and kissed me sweetly. "What I meant was, put your sunscreen on, because we're going sailing. But you don't have to worry. No one gets seasick on this boat."

It was hard to wrap my mind around the drastic turn my week had taken, but for once, I chose not to think too hard about it. I took a sip of the coffee Chris handed me, from a Nespresso machine just the like one in the Paris apartment. It had a splash of soy milk, just the way I liked it. It might not be *that* hard to get used to living like this, with every fantastical whim anticipated and fulfilled before I had a chance to think.

He then produced a plate of warm croissants and a bowl of sliced peaches. "I recall you like a specific kind of fruit."

It was sweet. And he was correct. "They're my favorite. But only in summer. I never buy any of those hard peaches imported from the other side of the equator in the dead of winter."

"Farm to table. I get it. That's a very European concept. This region pretty much pioneered the idea of eating what's seasonal."

"Probably why I instinctively like it here. So when are we going on the boat?" I couldn't hide my excitement.

He looked at his phone for a confirmation of the time. "I told them we'd be down there in an hour. How long will it take you to be ready?"

"If all that's required is a bathing suit and some sunscreen, I'd say five minutes."

He nodded. "Low maintenance. I'm impressed."

Maybe I was missing something. I wondered how long it took most people to be ready to sit on a sailboat. Then I recalled my vow to stop worrying and enjoy my vacation, and I smiled. "Glad I can impress you."

He pulled me onto his lap and kissed me. It was a good kiss, ending with him nibbling on my lower lip. "You are impressive in many ways."

"Back atcha, sir... So tell me about this boat."

"Okay. She's a twenty-meter sailboat with a four-meter beam and nearly a two-meter draft. Her name is *Mary Celeste*." He looked at me with a crooked grin, knowing that would make zero sense but enjoying messing with me.

"Okay. I didn't really mean I wanted the boat's measurements," I said. My brain was still trying to calculate from the metric to figure out how many feet forty meters was. My rough calculation had it at over a hundred feet, which was a damned big boat. "So it's a sailboat. Cool. And just so you know, that's about all I know about sailing—that sailboats are cool."

"You'll learn. I promise."

"Does that mean I have to pull ropes and swab decks and stuff?"

"No to the deck swabbing. We have a crew at the marina that maintains the boats. But if you want, you can get a little experience with the ropes, which are called 'sheets,' by the way."

I didn't need to hear more. I would pull ropes—sheets—or whatever I needed to do if it meant getting out on the aqua Mediterranean Sea in a sailboat. I went upstairs to what had become my third-floor dressing area in the sunroom and dug through my bags for a bathing suit, just hoping my plain black bikini would cut it on the French Riviera.

Fortunately, I'd overpacked, and beneath the jeans and T-shirts were a couple of dresses, one of which could double as a beach cover-up. It was lightweight white cotton with huge blue swirls, which were actually flowers if you spread the whole thing out, and it tied at the waist. When I put it on with flip-flops and looked in the mirror, I realized I looked ridiculous, like I'd just come from a Mother's Day tea and needed to put on comfortable shoes because my high heels had hurt my feet.

I switched into a plain white cotton T-shirt and cutoff denim shorts. They weren't the nicest shorts I'd brought, but what did it matter? I wasn't destined to look glamorous on the high seas.

When I went downstairs, I found clothing I didn't recognize laid out on the white couch—a wide-brimmed straw hat, dark-brown sandals, and a cute pink knee-length beach cover-up alongside an expensive-looking high-cut black maillot swimsuit with cutouts on the sides and strings crisscrossing the back. Chris was reading through something on his computer and didn't seem to hear me at first.

"What's this?" I asked.

He turned around. "Oh, I asked Clothilde to grab some clothes when she was in town earlier. I know I turned your city vacation upside down when I invited you out to the beach, so I suspected you might not have brought anything."

It was a nice gesture, but it bothered me. "You could have asked." I realized it didn't sound particularly grateful, but I couldn't help it.

"I didn't think you'd have a problem with it. I apologize. Next time I'll ask," he said like that was the end of the discussion.

I wasn't sure I was satisfied, and I felt myself suddenly wanting to go back to Paris, back to a vacation I controlled. I wasn't accustomed to having things done for me, especially when they were being done on the assumption that I couldn't possibly do them right on my own. I knew he was just trying to be a good host, but I couldn't help feeling like a project, someone he was trying to mold into the kind of person he was used to entertaining.

"I just... I feel like you're anticipating all the ways I'm not going to be able to keep up with you and trying to cut me off at the pass before I embarrass myself. And you."

He turned around from the computer, where he was checking something, looking surprised. "Why would you think that?" He got up and moved in front of me. He gently tipped my chin up so I couldn't help but look at him, and the expression on his face was serious and caring. "Have I done something to make you think you embarrass me in any way?"

I thought about it. "I guess just the fact that you know I wouldn't have the right thing to wear to your movie premiere or the right clothes to go on a boat... it just makes me feel like you're doing everything you can—and it's really so nice—to make me fit into your world."

"Please stop calling it my world. I don't have a world. I live on planet earth just like you. But I do tend to move quickly and make decisions and push forward to the next thing, so this was a moment of thinking you might need a bathing suit. Then, I assure you, my mind was someplace else in very short order."

He ran a hand through his hair, which was slicked back and sexy. He was ruining it with each finger that loosened it and ruffled it up. I didn't want to be the cause of the ruin. "I just assumed you didn't bring a ball gown and resort wear. I apologize."

"No, I mean you're right that I didn't bring those things. I never in a million years imagined that I'd need them. It's more that you're anticipating everything I'm missing before I even realize it."

"Like I'm expecting you to come up short? Is that how you feel?"

I nodded. That was exactly it. So maybe this wasn't the first time he'd found himself overstepping on behalf of someone else. Or maybe he was just figuring out how it felt to live inside my head.

He sighed. "I'm sorry. I'm just... bad at this." It wasn't what I was expecting him to say.

"Bad at what?"

He closed his eyes for a moment, then let out a deep sigh. "Knowing the right thing to do for a woman I'm interested in." He looked at me like this was a big admission. The truth was, I'd had that impression. That morning, before Chris was awake, I'd done a little web surfing to learn more about this superhero man who I felt like I was getting to know but who was still a mystery.

He'd had his share of tabloid stories linking him to a long list of actresses, including photos of them on red carpets all over the world. And for each blurb suggesting he'd started dating someone, a week later there would be speculation that the real woman in his life was a different actress, based on a new set of photos. It seemed like always had dates, but he didn't really date any of them for long periods.

There were even a few murky images where it wasn't even clear who he was with or if in fact he was the one sneaking a kiss in the back booth of a restaurant, but it didn't seem to stop the tabloids from plastering the images all over their magazines with gossipy headlines about his "latest flame" or his trail of broken hearts.

I'd pushed away my initial instinct, which had me feeling jealous of those other women. After working in public relations, I knew better than to fall for the publicity machine fueled by the very film studios that made millions by keeping Chris's name in headlines. The articles were clearly there for the purpose of ginning up interest in the magazines or Chris or whomever he supposedly was linked with. It all felt fake and reminded me why I never took on actors as clients at the PR firm. I'd never been interested in that scene.

And here I was, dipping a toe into it. But not really. The time I'd spent with Chris—except for the luxury that surrounded me at his house—was about as removed from celebrity life as it could get.

It was my turn to take his hand and try to make him feel better. "Look, you're so sweet to think of me and worry about my vacationing needs. And I appreciate it, I really do. It just feels a little, I don't know... just not me. I don't wear caftans and expensive bathing suits," I said, picking up the maillot. I held it up, imagining how it might look on me.

"You don't have to. You can wear whatever you want. I just thought you might want to swan around like the jet set and drink champagne in your caftan."

I recalled our conversation at the restaurant, where I *had* been enthralled with the woman in the caftan. He was just trying to do what he thought I'd want. "How about if I swan around in my daisy dukes instead, but take you up on the champagne?"

"Deal." He pulled me in and kissed me, doing his best to undo all the effort I'd made to tuck my T-shirt into my belted shorts. Pulling my T-shirt over my head, he took in the black string bikini top. "I like this," he said, his eyes roaming over my cleavage like he was formulating an undressing-me plan.

"I'm glad."

He ran his hand along my waist and I shuddered. It was the heat of his hand combined with his whisper-soft touch on my skin. He kissed my breasts through the fabric of the bikini top, which was somehow hotter and sexier than had he taken it off.

His hot breath on the column of my throat made me moan and tilt my head back to give him better access. "You make me crazy," I breathed, feeling my brains sailing away without me on a boat of Chris's making.

"Good," he whispered. "Fair's fair."

He kissed my lips gently, then took my hand and led me back to the peaches and pastries. "Have some breakfast."

"Okay, but you'd better be right about the calm water. I don't want to eat all this, then toss my cookies."

"It's as calm as a lake. And I think you'll like the boat."

"I'm very interested in her four-meter beam," I said. He laughed and kissed me again.

CHAPTER TWENTY-THREE

The *Mary Celeste*, on the Mediterranean Sea

IT TURNED out four meters was the width of the boat. And she was one of the loveliest sea creatures I'd ever seen, spanning more than sixty-five feet from bow to stern. The *Mary Celeste* was white with polished wood trim and navy-blue seat cushions and its sails still furled while it sat bobbing in the slip. The mast loomed above us, with a tiny weathervane contraption on top that was spinning around.

The boat had a French flag mounted on the back, where a nice seating area had already been set up with navy cushions on all the benches and a tray of sliced bread and assorted cheeses on a wooden board.

Chris introduced me to Louis, the captain, and to the two crew members who would sail the boat while we lounged around like tourists. "I thought I was going to be working on this boat," I said.

"You want to work?" Louis asked in accented English. "I will put you to work." He winked. I wasn't sure whether I was scared of him or not. He seemed nice, but I'd heard captains could be mean if you didn't use boat terminology or respect the dangers of the sea.

"Later maybe. She can get a lesson once we're out of the harbor," Chris said, leading me to a seat on the bench. "I figured I'd get you started on your champagne drinking, but Louis loves to teach, so if you have questions, ask him. Or ask me, and I'll translate."

They got busy untying lines and talking to each other in a language I didn't understand, even though some of it was in English. "Can you secure the traveler?" Louis asked Chris after he'd returned from below deck with a bottle of champagne and two glasses. Chris did something with a rope then pressed down on something else.

We sat on our appointed bench, and I watched everything Louis was doing at his perch behind the large steering wheel. He was fiddling with dials, and it looked like he was checking readings of something.

"Is he making sure this thing is seaworthy?" I asked, trying to sound casual despite my nerves. The truth was, I had never been on a sailboat, and the sight of the giant mast made me think of pirate movies where boats were plundered and ended up at the bottom of the ocean. I knew that probably wasn't what Chris had in mind, but I couldn't fight the image.

"Oh, she's seaworthy."

"That's right, she's a female."

"She's my favorite one here. I don't go on any of the others," he said, looking out across the marina, where each boat was larger and more elegant than the last.

"So this isn't your boat?"

"Nope. Maybe someday, though."

Now that he had the house here, I felt certain the boat

wouldn't be far behind. I couldn't blame him. If I could afford the life he had, I'd be looking at boats too.

Louis and the crew began pulling the boat carefully out of the slip and motoring through the harbor while Chris and I hung out on the deck in back and drank cold champagne and tasted the cheeses. I couldn't stop until I'd tried every one. Once we'd made it out past the boat slips, Louis turned into the channel that would take us into open water. Then he turned off the motor, and they started unfurling the sails.

Louis was yelling orders, the two crew members were pulling on ropes and cranking levers, and moments later, a huge white sail flapped above our heads. Louis yelled some more, and they pulled and cranked again until the sail stopped fluttering and caught a bit of the wind. Then they unfurled the one in front, which I later learned was the jib, letting its triangular shape help the other sail gather wind that was beginning to guide the boat.

"Okay. We're sailing," Chris said, leaning back on the bench seat and putting an arm around me. Louis had stopped yelling, and the crew had settled into positions near the ropes they'd later work on. It was almost silent on the water, the wind pushing us along and the boat tipping to one side as we picked up speed.

Despite its enormous size, the boat moved with such quiet grace that I almost couldn't believe it was completely powered by wind. I'd been on a few motorboats pulling water skiers and associated the noise of the ripping motor with being on the water.

The boat tipped to almost a forty-five-degree angle to the water, and I tensed up, feeling like it could easily overturn. "Is it supposed to do that?"

"Yes. It's called heeling," Chris said. "The wind pushes the sails, and it takes the boat with it. If you can relax into it, it's like being in a recliner."

"I don't know if I can relax, because all I can think about is tipping over."

"It's impossible. The boat has a keel on the bottom."

"I'm not really a seafaring lass. What's a keel?" I asked.

"It's a huge iron counterweight that hangs down into the water. If the boat leans over too far, the keel will always right it. Trust me, no one's tipping over." He held my hand reassuringly.

I decided to trust him. I looked at the boats out on the water, some twice the size of this one, all well-appointed with leather seats and technical contraptions and polished wood. I doubted anybody would spend the kind of money it cost to own a boat if it could easily tip over. After a few sips of champagne and the breeze blowing on my face, I fully relaxed.

We were headed into pale-blue water more brilliant than any I'd ever seen on the California coast. The color grew only slightly deeper as we moved farther from land. As the French coastline receded behind us, I felt a sense of calm wash over me with the endless possibilities of an open sea.

"I could get used to this," I said, getting comfortable on the seat and feeling my shoulders unclench as I breathed in the salt air and absorbed the quiet.

"Aaah. Right?"

"Oh yeah. It's a good life if you can swing it."

"Finally, she gets it!" he said. "I knew something about this week would grab ahold of you."

"Are you kidding? Everything about this week has been incredible. But that was never the goal. I hope you haven't been trying to impress me, because the whole point was to spend time together. We could have done that anywhere."

He looked at me like he couldn't understand how it could be so simple. "Well, true. But this is a little more fun, isn't it?"

"It's a lot more fun." I curled up closer to him and looked at him from the side, this generous, mellow guy who'd swept me out of Paris on a private jet and who'd been the perfect companion for the past few days. Was he for real?

He brushed back a strand of hair that had blown loose from behind my ear then ran a hand down my arm. Each time his fingers grazed my skin, I felt the same shiver of attraction, the same destructive heat. While a small part of me felt like it was a good thing we had finite time together because he was awfully distracting, a bigger part of me wanted to stay next to him forever.

Whoa! Slow down, missy.

I had to remind my fantasizing brain that this was a summer fling. There would be no forever. Neither of us needed to say that out loud to know it was true. He'd go back to New York and the jets that took him to movie sets all over the world, and I'd go back to LA and the pretty decent life I'd built for myself there. Eventually, maybe I'd meet someone I liked half as much as I liked Chris. Better to calibrate expectations.

I looked up at Chris, who was staring out over the water as the boat skimmed along. He turned to look at me and smiled, because we were already becoming that couple—the ones who know what the other one is doing instinctively. So we shared a kiss and I tipped my head to rest it on his shoulder. The breeze coming off the ocean felt calming and I felt happy.

Louis and his crew seemed to have the same ability as Chris's elves to do their jobs and disappear. The boat drifted on, and the sails shifted from time to time, but the crew members were in their own space, doing their own thing.

"Thanks for understanding my thing about the caftan," I said. "I'm just more comfortable in shorts. And besides, I think it would have blown away by now and be off choking a dolphin somewhere."

"I like you in those shorts. And the bikini is something else."

An idea had been swirling in my brain and I had to know if there was merit to what I was thinking. "Were you a little bit worried someone would take pictures of you with a girl in cutoffs and the fashion police would put you in the dungeon by proxy?"

His lips twisted into a grin. "I'm learning so much from you. There are movie star manuals and fashion dungeons... you must think I lead a very dangerous life."

I shrugged. "You know what I mean. If you were spotted with me, is it a thing?"

"Not particularly." He looked like he was going to say more, but he stopped himself.

"But maybe a little?"

He shook his head. "More for you than for me. Paparazzi is annoying, but I'm used to it. And I don't read what they write in the rumor magazines, but I wouldn't want them invading your privacy."

He looked like the topic bored him, but I wanted to know more about his life. "What's it like, starring in movies? And seeing your face on billboards and buses?"

"Acting in movies is what I love more than anything. That's the reason for going along with all the other stuff. But I'll admit, the billboard part... was strange at first. Then it was cool for a minute. Then it was strange again. But then it just became part of life, and truthfully, I don't look up anymore. It's a job, and it's necessary for the promotion of movies, and I know that's all it is. I have to keep it separate from myself."

"It's your face, though. It's you."

"Exactly," he said. "If I bought into it being me on the billboard, I think I'd want to crawl under a rock and hide. But it's a character in a movie. And that's how we get people to come see the movie, so it's a necessary part of the machine." He seemed at peace with the concept. He wasn't that much older than me, and he already had an outsized sense of perspective and maturity about the whole thing.

"So you just think of it as a job?"

"Well, it's a job I'm lucky to have. I mean, I get to do what I love, I get paid well, and I get time off between projects, in theory. Which means never, I guess. And I get to travel. So whatever crap I have to put up with has always seemed worth it. If there comes a day when I can't say that, I'll know it's time to hang it up."

"Seems like a healthy outlook," I said.

"I try," he said, turning to me with a wry grin.

I heard Louis talking to his crew urgently like they were trying to negotiate something. Then he and Chris debated in French for a couple of minutes, pointing and gesturing at the sails. They seemed to come to a decision that satisfied Louis, who tipped his cap to me. "You are enjoying the boat?" he asked me.

"*Oui, vraiment*," I said, trying out a bit of the French I'd picked up. He smiled at me then nodded to Chris with a similar look to the one Marguerite had given him. I couldn't make myself believe that Chris hadn't been on this exact boat before, enjoying this exact vacation with someone else. Or many others.

"How many women have you brought out on this boat?"

He looked at me quizzically, as though unsure how our conversation had shifted to that. "I dunno. A couple. Why?"

"Just trying to get a sense of you. Your life."

His smile was more of a smirk. But it was still gorgeous. "And what have you gleaned so far—that my life consists of gazing at myself on the sides of buses and taking women out on sailboats?"

I couldn't tell whether he was amused or offended by the concept. I scooted back so I could look at him, putting a hand on his knee. "Chris. This week has been amazing. You're amazing. I'm just curious about what your life looks like outside of here. I only know you in vacation mode. Which is awesome, by the way. But what's it like the rest of the time?"

"Probably not that different from your life. If we're filming, I have call times, sometimes really early, and I work. The complicated action scenes take a lot of time, so it sometimes takes months to get everything filmed. And I'm still reading, thinking about what I want to do after that, sometimes preparing for the next thing if I'm not gonna get a break in between. Then when a film gets close to opening, there's the publicity tours and the premieres, so there's travel. Pretty much, I go where I'm told."

I nodded. "You forgot about the bus gazing."

He pinched my thigh right above my knee and I jumped. "Ouch." I swatted him.

"That didn't hurt."

"It might've hurt."

He shook his head. Then he kissed the spot where he'd pinched. Then he brushed his lips across mine and pulled me in. It wasn't until I felt his full soft lips claiming mine that a semi-absurd thought presented itself. After a moment, we drew back for air and the thought came tumbling out before I could stop it. "I'm a little worried kissing you is an addiction. I think I'm a junkie."

"I'm not sure I see the problem."

As if proving himself willing to feed my habit, Chris kissed me again.

WE'D SAILED SO FAR out into the Mediterranean blue that at one point I could barely see land. Chris brought our conversation back to my inquisition about his work life and turned the tables. "What is your life like when you're not seducing guys on vacation?" he asked.

We were sitting next to each other on a cushion at the back of the boat.

"Well, most of my life does consist of that, but in the off-season, when I head home, I'm a workaday stiff. I go to my office, put out press releases, or put out fires, depending on the day. Then I go home and hang out with friends or walk on the beach or stay in my apartment and watch art films or whatever's new on Netflix."

"Sounds like a pretty good life."

"Living the dream." I scooted back until I was lying on the bench with my head resting on his leg. He shifted as well so he could lean back against a pillow, and we floated like that for a while, feeling the waves under the boat.

"Do you love your job?" he asked.

"I'm good at my job."

"Not what I asked. I can see you're smart. I'm sure you're good at it. But do you love it?" he asked again. I didn't answer. I knew the answer but I didn't want to tell him after hearing how passionate he was about acting.

"I like it, and I like that I can do it well. But is it my life's passion to write press releases? I'd have to say no." I'd never admitted it out loud before. Maybe because no one had asked.

He was thoughtful a moment, nodding. There was no judgment in his expression. More like concern. "Do you have a life's passion?" he asked gently.

The problem was that I wasn't sure I did, and it had always bothered me. "I'm not sure." It was a sore spot and I blamed myself for not having figured out some essential career that I was dying to have. "I feel like a millennial cliché, like I'm casting about and trying to find myself. But I've tried a lot of things. I double majored in computer science and literature. I've worked in fashion, I've tried painting. They're all interesting and fine. It just may be that I just don't have one thing I like more than anything else."

"I don't believe that. You haven't found it yet."

"It may be that variety is my passion. I like lots of different things. I probably won't keep this job forever. Maybe I'll design wedding dresses. Maybe I'll go to veterinary school. I like that I have choices."

"I respect that. Choices are good." He picked up my hand and held it between his. I'd been staring at him as he spoke, mesmerized by his swoony eyes. Then his expression changed and he looked suddenly vulnerable when he spoke. "You still may find something you love more than anything else. And you'll know when you find it."

The way he said it, I wasn't sure if he was talking about my job anymore. I was kind of hoping he wasn't. "I think you're right. I'll know."

His eyes were stormy and focused on mine, maybe trying to read the same thing from my words. He looked at my mouth and reached for my chin, tilting it gently upward. His kiss was gentle at first, but it soon became heated and intense. It almost felt ravenous, as though a part of him needed to be fed, needed to be satisfied.

My hands twisted in his hair and I moved closer to him on the cushion, turning to face him more squarely. In seconds, he'd wrapped an arm around my back and pulled me harder against him, his mouth crushing mine, his tongue sweeping across mine. Consuming... Insatiable...

I heard his voice in a low growl against my lips. "Let's go downstairs."

"What's downstairs?" I asked, breathless, but curious whether he planned to have me in a tiny bathroom.

"Come," he said, not elaborating. He kept his arm wrapped

around me and pulled me up, his lips still on mine while he walked us down a set of stairs and into a full-sized bedroom below.

It was big enough to fit a queen-sized bed and a small sitting area. The quilt on the bed looked like it had just been fluffed. He walked me to the edge and lifted me to the center of the bed before he straddled my legs and sat up, assessing me. He looked like a puma deciding which part of his dinner he wanted first. I had no problem being his main course, but I still didn't know what had shifted to bring on his intensity.

"You make me crazy," he said, quietly. "I think I can control myself around you. I tell myself to let you relax enjoy the boat. Then I can't stay away from you."

I reached for his hand and pulled him toward me. He rested on his elbows, his eyes never leaving mine. "I am enjoying my day. Very much. And I don't want you to stay away."

He dipped his head down and slowly kissed up the column of my throat. When he got to my chin, his tongue traced a line along my jawbone. I just about lost my mind. "Oh my God, Chris. That sends me over the edge," I said, my voice shaky with lust.

He was hovering over me, his eyes roaming over my face, then downward, like he was trying to decide what part of me to devour. Abruptly we heard loud voices right outside the door, which we'd neglected to close. Chris froze for a moment, then rolled off the bed. "Hold that thought. Then I'm going to test the limits of every edge," he said.

He hopped over to the door and slammed it shut.

Then he made good on his word.

WHEN WE CAME BACK UPSTAIRS, Louis and the crew were

talking to each other at the stern of the boat. Suddenly the sails were starting to move and flap. Chris pointed up toward the mainsail. "We're getting ready to tack."

"What do I need to do?"

"You do nothing. You watch how beautifully this boat handles the wind."

One of the crew pulled on ropes, and the other helped him crank something on one side of the boat. The mainsail soon moved across the middle of the boat to the other side, where it refilled with wind, and suddenly, we were sailing in a different direction, parallel to the coastline.

"See?" Chris yelled something to Louis, who seemed to approve. "So that's called a tack. Turning into the wind. If we turn the other way with the wind pushing us more, it's called a jibe. Boat lingo is a whole other language, but you need to know it if you're captaining a boat, because everyone expects you to use the right terminology. You can't just say, 'Turn right.' It's all about where you are relative to the direction of the wind and relative to other boats."

"Interesting. Do you ever go out by yourself as the captain?"

"Sometimes, on a smaller boat. But it's work, and I wouldn't be able to sit here with you and drink champagne."

I nodded. The non-captain version of Chris was certainly nice. He refilled my glass from the bottle, which he'd stowed in an ice bucket built into the center of the table in front of us.

We spent a good part of the day heading toward Nice, where we dropped anchor a few hundred yards from shore and took a dinghy the rest of the way. From there, we walked into Old Nice, which was charming and packed with restaurants and centuries-old architecture. We had lunch at a small restaurant with an ocean view, sharing a plate of mussels and splitting an omelet and a pile of shoestring fries.

"This may be the best meal I've ever had," I said, knowing

that was only going to be true until the next exquisite dining experience I'd have in this country.

Chris regaled me with political trivia about the city, peppered with historical facts he couldn't have gotten without reading an obscure textbook. "The mayor here used to be a professional motorcycle rider. He raced in more than thirty world championship Grand Prix but never came in first. He got fourth a couple times. Evidently, politics offers better odds of winning."

"I doubt that."

"He's had a good run." Chris told me more about the mayor and some run-ins he'd had over a mosque that a businessman wanted to build. I was impressed by the depth of Chris's knowledge, which clearly had nothing to do with his day job.

The city beckoned to me with its Chagall Museum and Matisse Museum, and Chris did his best to indulge my enthusiasm for the large open market, where we bought fresh produce we could bring back to his house and a bag of apricots for Louis and the crew. Every so often, I'd catch someone looking at Chris, recognizing him and debating whether to ask him to pose for a selfie.

A couple of times, he was approached, and he graciously acquiesced, posing, smiling and thanking his fans in French or English, depending on what language they spoke. Nice in the summer had its share of American tourists, and some were delighted to have stumbled across an actor who was willing to pose in photos with them. I got a tiny glimpse of Chris Conley, celebrity, and I was impressed by how well he handled the attention.

"I don't think I have the disposition to be a public figure," I told him after the last gaggle of French teen girls had posed with him six different times before they were satisfied that their shot was Instagram-worthy. We'd plopped into chairs at a café and were having a glass of wine before meeting the boat.

"Oh, you'd be fine. You're good with people. It's just about being approachable."

"But I'd get annoyed if I was on vacation, trying to mind my own business, and I couldn't just walk down the street in peace."

"Is it annoying to you now, being with me?" he asked.

"Oh, not at all. I just feel a little bad for you. You can't even have a meaningless fling in peace. It seems like your life isn't totally your own."

"Like I said, you get used to it."

He took a long sip of his wine and didn't speak for a minute. Finally, he turned to me. "Is that how you see this—a meaningless fling?"

I hadn't expected that question, and I wasn't sure immediately how to answer. "Well, isn't it? We're both on vacation... and we're both going to opposite coasts and opposite lives afterward, so I just figured..."

"Meaningless fling ..."

"I... am I wrong?"

Again, he didn't answer. He had the same distant, slightly sad look on his face that I'd seen earlier. "I don't know... I just don't want to think of it like that. It sounds like something empty and frivolous, and I... like you more than that."

There was such vulnerability in his voice and his face. I hadn't even allowed for the possibility of my time with him feeling like more than a fun summer romance. The relationship could only end badly for me if I started to have feelings that could never be reciprocated in the real world.

I didn't want it to be a fling, but didn't it have to be one? Maybe that didn't need to be debated yet.

"I like you too. A lot. So let's call it something else," I said.

"I'm open to suggestions." He sipped his wine.

"Hot summer sex fest?" I suggested.

"Ah, that carries a lot more weight."

"So what do you want to call it?"

"I don't really want to put a name to it. I'm growing pretty attached to you. I like us together. And I don't want to cheapen a beautiful thing by calling it a fling," he said, and right then, I wanted him more than I had since I'd first felt his arm around my back on the bridge. And I felt something that alarmed me a little bit—the beginnings of falling for him. I sipped my wine and tried to push back that feeling because I knew it had no business intruding on our vacation.

"I'm good with a nameless lovely vacation," I said, careful not to let my alarming feelings show. "And one more thing... I have no idea what a *White Serpent* is." I figured I'd better just lay it all out on the table. If he decided that made me unworldly or uncultured, so be it.

Instead, he laughed quietly. "I kinda had a feeling. And I love that about you." There it was, that little word I'd been pushing out of my head.

Hearing Chris toss out the word *love*, even in that context, made my heart gleeful and sad at the same time.

AFTER LUNCH, we walked quietly for a while as I thought about what it would feel like to be recognized wherever I went, always on call to do a fan's bidding. Of course, I knew there were celebrities who were famously rude when fans approached for an autograph or a photo, and I actually understood their perspective. People didn't have a right to get in Chris's face and interrupt his vacation.

Or maybe he was right, and I was the one annoyed at having an intrusion into my fantasy vacation. I realized I'd need to adjust my expectations. This was his life, and if he was fine with it, I could go along for the ride.

We didn't have hours and hours to walk around because we still had to sail back before dark. I could have spent a week in Nice, but I knew I'd just have to visit the city my next time in France. I knew there would be a next time. I'd given Paris short shrift, and the people I'd been introduced to so far made me want to dig in deeper. I wanted to ride a bike through Provence and visit cheese caves in Normandy and taste wine in Bordeaux. It would take many visits to satisfy my craving for this country.

When the sailboat started heading back, with the sun following us on the right side of the boat, I felt more content than I had in years. I wanted nothing more than to be sitting next to Chris, under his arm, watching the glow of the setting sun on the water as we sailed back to Antibes. The wind began dying down by the end of our sail, so Louis eventually turned on the motor to get us the rest of the way into the harbor.

I'd heard stories about boat maintenance from friends who occasionally sailed, and they always detailed the work done right after the boat docked in the slip, washing down footprints, cleaning the seawater off the visible parts of the hull, covering all the wood, tying all the lines, and returning the boat to pristine condition before heading home. I knew without asking that Louis and his crew were paid to do that work and all we had to do was thank them and make our way back to Chris's house.

"I was a little worried all this produce was gonna go bad on the boat," I said, lifting the full bag from the farmer's market in Nice. "Should've figured there'd be a fridge on the boat."

"All your wants and needs… we try to accommodate," he said as we rode in the hired car back to his house.

I wondered why he didn't just use Uber, but I figured someone in the film empire that hired him had to be footing the bill. And what did it matter, anyway? "I had an ulterior motive, buying all this," I told him. "I'm cooking tonight."

"Not gonna fight you on that. And I'll even volunteer as your sous chef. What are we making?"

I looked into the bag of luscious produce, which I'd bought without a real plan for how I was going to use it. As much as I could eat a big salad any day of the week, I wasn't sure that would work for Chris, so I had to get more creative.

"I'm not sure yet... but I have a feeling your elves have already figured it out for me and stocked the kitchen with something I haven't thought of."

"They're good that way," he admitted.

I wasn't sure if he'd think it was strange to ask, but I'd been feeling awkward about this couple who lived on the property and always disappeared into the night when we were around. "Would it be weird to invite Clothilde and Henri to eat with us?"

"Well, they'll probably yank the knife right out of your hands and take over the kitchen if I invite them over... but if you don't mind being bulldozed by a pair of French grandparents, I'm game."

"Are you kidding? Bossy French grandparents with knives? That's all kinds of awesome."

But not as awesome as Chris.

CHAPTER TWENTY-FOUR

The Villa
Evening

CLOTHILDE AND HENRI were nothing like I expected. They really were like a pair of grandparents who looked out for each other and doted on Chris like he was one of their own. Apparently, they had three grown children and eight grandchildren living in various parts of southern France. But aside from appearances and grandparental demeanor, they were a couple of twenty-year-olds in spirit. Clothilde came over wearing a faded denim shirt over black yoga pants and immediately tied a long white apron over Henri's khaki pants and long-sleeved T-shirt so he could commandeer the kitchen. That left me to do minimal helping.

"He used to be a heart surgeon, then he retired so he could spend more time doing what he really loves," Clothilde told me in perfect English. Once again, I felt self-conscious of my own limited linguistic abilities. I vowed to myself to take a language class when I got home. I would need it because I planned to spend much more time traveling. "And this is it. He does all the landscaping, cooking, and odd jobs around the house."

Henri poured glasses for each of us from a bottle of Armagnac, then Clothilde retreated to the living room and began playing jazz piano. "She loves her piano," Henri said, looking at her with love and admiration.

"Is that her piano?"

"Yes. Chris was kind enough to let us move it here when we sold our bigger house."

"Kind enough? A piano and a pianist to go with it? I definitely got the good end of the deal," Chris said, and I agreed. Clothilde's playing was as good as anything I'd ever heard in a jazz club.

Henri completely took over the kitchen. Before I knew what had happened, he had chickens roasting in a white-wine-and-butter sauce, asparagus spears on the grill, and a pile of scalloped potatoes baking under a cheese sauce. He did, however, let me make a salad.

"I swear, I didn't say anything about you only knowing how to make a salad," Chris said when I smacked him with a dish towel. "I told him you were going to cook everything."

"I guess he has a sixth sense about these things," I said. Frankly, I was relieved. I knew my way around a kitchen, but the truth was, I didn't cook much for myself other than throwing vegetables over rice or chicken chili into a bread bowl. I often went out. Learning to cook multicourse meals had never held much appeal for me. Once in a while, I'd have a few friends over for dinner, and it would take me an entire day to coordinate the cooking and plating times to get a few courses on the table without burning anything. The best dish I'd ever made was cheese fondue, chicken paillard, and a beet-and-goat-cheese salad over a bed of arugula. I outsourced the desserts and drinks to my friends, and the whole thing had turned out moderately well.

My three-course-dinner party trick had only worked because I'd had time to look up recipes and shop. In Chris's house, I would have been left to scrounge through the well-appointed pantry and figure out what to do with the items on hand, like someone in an episode of *Chopped*. Standing in the kitchen of a gorgeous guy, I wished I had a few tricks up my sleeve to impress him. There was no arugula in sight, and I feared offending our French neighbors by turning some rare cheese into a pot of melting slop.

Henri didn't seem to care one way or the other. While Clothilde played, Chris hung out on the couch with his drink and read through a script. I knew he'd printed something out earlier in the day, but I hadn't realized he had work to do. It impressed me that he went so seamlessly between work and play, but I also found it a bit sad that he could never really unplug. He didn't seem bothered, so I didn't dwell on it. From where he sat, he had a good view of us in the kitchen, and every time I glanced his way, he was looking at me with a smile on his face.

"You know, he's smitten with you," Henri whispered to me as we were pulling the dishes out of the oven and looking for serving utensils. "I think you may feel the same way. It makes me happy—young love."

I didn't want to spoil his happy idea with the reality that it was more complicated than that. "He's a good guy," I said, looking over at Chris. I could fall for him. It would be so easy. We'd only had a vacation dream of a time together so far, the stuff of fantasy. I could let my mind wander to a place where my life consisted of coming home at the end of a workday to a sunset sail with Chris, a walk on a beach, and quaint dinner for two while staring at his lovely face. Instead, I reeled myself back in. I reminded myself of the philosophy I'd employed at the outset: Enjoy the vacation to the fullest, live the big moments, feel the breeze, but remember, it's just a vacation, and don't get too attached. I'd deal with heartbreak when I got home and was back at my desk with a pile of work to distract me.

Clothilde had left the piano and turned on an oldies playlist, which was now streaming through speakers that seemed to be in every room of the house. She knew the place better than Chris did, it seemed.

"*Bon appétit!*" Henri proclaimed, dinging a spoon against a copper pot and carrying the tureen with the chicken to the outdoor table, which Clothilde and Chris had set with the ceramic dishes from the kitchen and a mismatched set of utensils she'd bought at a flea market. I carried out my salad, which looked kind of lame next to the grilled asparagus and the delectable-looking potatoes, but the dressing I'd made with Dijon mustard and lemon juice gave it a nice flavor. Plus, the fresh vegetables tasted better than anything I'd ever bought in a grocery store.

"I don't think I've ever had a proper tomato before," I'd told Henri earlier.

"The market where you bought these was probably twenty kilometers from the farm where they were picked yesterday," he said.

Before anyone took a bite of food, wine was poured and toasts were made. "Salut," Henri said finally, and we dug into the piles of food. Henri's chicken fell off the bone and into the mouth-watering sauce. Everything else tasted fresh and divine, as if the menu had been planned for days, not on the fly after a long day on the water. We saved the salad for after dinner as a palate cleanser.

"You are in France," Clothilde said to me, as if I needed an explanation.

After that, Henri presented a cheese course he'd put together with some of the dozen cheeses in the refrigerator along with almonds and quince paste. I lost count after my third glass of wine, and although I felt tipsy, I never felt drunk. That had something to do with the smaller glasses, I remembered Guillaume saying. And maybe the lower alcohol content. I couldn't remember. All I could think about was how I was going to sleep really well later.

We cleared all the dishes, and Clothilde and Henri began dancing in the living room, having changed the music to swing. Chris and I moved over to one of the couches and watched them. "Aren't they cute?" Chris asked.

"Someday you'll be old and cute."

"Yeah. Someday."

"Right now, you're young and hot."

He looked at me, surprised. "How much wine did you have?"

"I think... a lot. And after being on the boat all day in the sun, I'm really sleepy." I folded myself into him, knowing that each time I felt him close to me, I was sinking in a little deeper, falling a little harder.

"Then you should sleep. I'm tired too and I can think of nothing better than falling asleep with my arms wrapped around you," he said, a sweet glint in his eye.

I started for the staircase. It was an impossible dream, imagining we could go on like this after our vacation ended, so I willed myself to stay in the present. We would never be Henri and Clothilde. I knew that. I just needed to take care of my tender little heart so I wasn't broken in half at the end of the week.

He said a quick goodnight to Henri and Clothilde who barely heard him because they were consumed with their dancing. Then he carried me the rest of the way upstairs.

CHAPTER TWENTY-FIVE

Antibes

Day After Glorious Day

BEAUTIFUL DAYS ROLLED into long warm nights until I lost track of the time. Saturday snuck up and, along with it, the night of the Cannes premiere. I couldn't stifle the nervousness I felt from the moment I'd woken up that morning, not knowing what to expect from the evening we had in front of us.

After our morning ritual of coffee, croissants, and peaches, a car picked us up to drive us to Marguerite's studio in Antibes's Old Town to pick up the dress. She was standing outside, waiting for us, drinking a tiny cup of coffee in the bright sun. Herding me impatiently into her studio, she insisted that Chris wait outside. Unfazed by her bossiness, he told her he'd take a walk around the block. I watched his back as he sauntered down the small cobbled street, running a hand through his still-wet hair. When I turned to follow Marguerite inside, I caught a knowing look on her face. Maybe she'd seen others fall for her "*cheri*," and maybe she anticipated the heartbreak I had ahead. She said nothing.

The dress hung on the curtain rod that separated the plain seamstress shop from Marguerite's magical art studio, a perfect cerulean blue that caught the light and shimmered like the sea. "Oh my God. Oh, it's really beautiful," I said, thinking it looked so good hanging there that it didn't even need to be worn.

"You must try it on. The final fitting I need to do on the body," she said as if talking about someone other than me, some body other than mine.

She handed me a strapless bra with an attached corset that sucked everything in. It fit, naturally. Given her years of experience, Marguerite knew my size without ever having asked me what it was. At first, I felt like an awkward teenager getting undressed in front of her. But she was so professional in her work that after a few minutes, I wasn't even me anymore but instead I'd been transformed into a dress model having a fitting for a fashion creation I couldn't have imagined wearing two weeks before.

Wearing black stiletto sandals with thin straps, also provided by Marguerite in the right size, I stood up on the box in the front room of the shop while she worked on the dress's floor-length hem, pinning it to the right height for the shoes. From where I stood, I could see Chris sitting outside a bench across the way from the shop. In his casual shorts, T-shirt, and sunglasses, he could have been photographed right there for a spread in an Abercrombie & Fitch catalogue.

Looking out at him made me less self-conscious about being fussed over by a woman who'd designed for Halston, so I allowed myself to stare, knowing he couldn't see me through the dark glass.

Marguerite went to the back for more pins and made a few tucks in the waistline, added an extra shred of fabric to the bust so I could breathe, then whisked the dress off me and went to the back with her needle and thread.

I stood in the corset and my underwear, still wearing the heels, looking at myself in the mirror and finding it mildly funny that I'd ended up in this shop in the South of France, wearing almost nothing. I badly wanted another cup of coffee from the machine on the back counter.

Strange where a person's mind goes.

"Marguerite, would it be okay if I made a cup of coffee?"

"*Bien sûr, cherie.* Please make a second one for me, *s'il te plaît.*" I obeyed, and no sooner had I set up our tiny cups on little saucers with the smallest spoons I'd ever seen than Marguerite was back with the dress. "I think it will be perfect now."

After she'd zipped me in, we admired the dress in the mirror. In the flowing blue strapless gown, I'd been transformed into someone who went to evening cocktail parties at high-end resorts and hung on the arm of a world-famous actor. Make no mistake, it was all that dress.

Chris came back, impeccable in his timing, almost like he knew how long it would take to turn me into his date to the Cannes premiere. The look on his face said he approved. "Marguerite, I didn't think it was possible to make her look any more spectacular than she already is, and somehow you managed."

She blushed then gave him a kiss on the cheek. "You are right about one thing. She is spectacular with or without the dress. But I'm glad you like the dress."

"I love it," he said, turning to me. "What do you think, Nik?"

"It's incredible. Marguerite, you are an artist."

She waved off my words and busied herself stirring sugar into her coffee. "I will need a few more minutes with the dress to make sure all the seams are tight. You two, go get some lunch, and when you come back, it'll be ready."

I had no way of knowing if she really needed to work on the

dress, but I could tell the compliments made her uncomfortable and she was eager to get rid of us. Chris and I left the shop and wandered through town, his fingers laced through mine, in no hurry to find a place to eat. It felt good to walk.

I was also aware of the nervous feeling I'd had in my gut since I'd woken up that morning, not really knowing what the red carpet of a premiere would be like but having a sense it would be like a prom on steroids. I needed to blow off steam somehow, just to keep my stomach from digesting itself. The last thing I needed was a three-course lunch weighing me down and straining the limits of that dress for hours to come.

By that point, Chris had gotten good at recognizing when I'd crawled too far into my head, plagued by some concern or other. He looked at me. "What's up?"

"I feel like I need to run around or something. I need to burn off my nerves. I don't wanna throw up on your tux."

He nodded. "Considerate of you. Okay, want to go down to the beach? Hit the gym at my house? What's good?"

"You have a gym at your house?" How had I not seen that yet?

He nodded. "Where d'you think I was going every morning before I showered?"

I hadn't even thought about it. I'd mostly been asleep, lulled into more dreams on the million-thread-count sheets. "Well, yeah. An hour on the treadmill oughta do it," I said as we started walking toward the waiting car.

Chris called Marguerite and told her his driver would be by later to pick up the dress. On the drive back, I bent toward the window like an animal eyeing its freedom. I couldn't recall the last time I'd gone this many days without some kind of workout. No wonder I was all wound up and restless.

We'd no sooner pulled onto the property than I was out of the car and running upstairs to dig through my clothes for a running bra and shorts. When I came back downstairs, hair in a ponytail, Chris was in the office, looking at something on his computer. He looked up when I asked him to point me in the direction of the gym then escorted me to a wing off the kitchen that had been equipped with a treadmill, rowing machine, elliptical, spin bike, multiple weight machines, and a rack of dumbbells. The guy didn't do anything halfway.

"This work for you?" he asked.

I nodded. Yes, I could definitely make something of this miniature version of a professional training facility by the sea. I looked straight out at the ocean as I revved up the treadmill, running faster than I would ordinarily because it had been a while since my feet had moved like this, and my adrenaline was sky-high. An hour was barely enough.

When I returned to the main part of the house, I saw a fruit platter and baguette sandwiches set out on the kitchen table, and I knew Henri or Clothilde was responsible. Chris sat at the table, finishing the remains of a sandwich and reading the paper. "Better?"

"Got all my stress out. For now. I think I'm good."

"Great. Make sure you eat," he said, getting up and kissing me on the cheek before heading upstairs. "Almost showtime. Gotta shower."

I grabbed a slice of melon and climbed the stairs slowly, my legs feeling the effects of my workout. I only had a half hour before a hairdresser and makeup artist were coming to the house. Chris had tried his best to cast a casual light on the fact that he had a crew of people responsible for making the two of us—mostly me—presentable for the paparazzi that would be out in full force later. I was secretly glad he'd hired a little help. I didn't know much about hair and makeup other than what I'd learned from a few video tutorials on accentuating my cheekbones.

I'd been sharing the master bedroom with Chris, but he'd insisted that the third-floor sunroom was mine to use anytime, "just so you have some space when you need it." So far, I hadn't wanted it, but it seemed like a good place to let the pros do their work. I wanted to surprise Chris once I was fully pulled together, hoping the effect would be impressive. I was normally lazy when it came to makeup so even I was curious what magic the makeup artist could work on me.

On the way to the upper set of stairs, as I was passing the door to the master bedroom, I heard the shower running. Then Chris's hand reached out and pulled me into the bedroom. He was wearing a towel around his waist. "Come with me, you sweet, sexy girl," he said, leading me into the bathroom.

The shower had filled the whole room with hot mist, and a therapeutic lavender-mint scent emanated from a fizzy salt ball in the corner of the stall. Chris helped me peel off my sweaty workout clothes, first lifting the shirt over my head, then the bra.

"I want you," he growled into my ear, tilting his head down and gently biting my shoulder, then running his tongue over the tender spot. "I want you slick and wet."

He gazed at my breasts and traced his finger over each one, circling the nipples but not touching them. My insides twisted with desire for his mouth on me. But he was teasing, making me wait and enjoying the lovely anguish he was causing me.

"Patience, lovely."

My head rolled back in agony because his hands were massaging but he was still neglecting the sensitive nipples which were swollen with want. I felt them harden and I almost reached for them myself. Then I felt his hot breath before he crushed his mouth to the center. Fire shot through my body and I leaned against the glass enclosure to steady myself.

When his eyes met mine, they were playful with an edge of roughness.

Two could play at that game. I lightly ran my fingers over his chest. Then I dragged my nails down his abs until I heard him suck in a breath. I stopped just shy of his triangle of hard muscle, working my hands back, lightly touching his skin but not dipping lower.

"Fair is fair," I said.

He raised an eyebrow. "You're in trouble."

He rolled my workout pants down my legs, but it was like trying to get me out of a wetsuit. "Hang on," I said, yanking them over my feet so I was free. "Okay, continue with your threats."

He smiled and looked me over from head to toe like he was trying to devise a seductive torture plan. But he was taking too long and that gave me other ideas.

I yanked off his towel and reached for his hard length, loving the feel of it in my hand. Rubbing slow circles around the head, I watched his face soften as he started to give in to me. Then he shook his head. "No."

Chris grabbed both my wrists and slowly walked me into the shower, where the jets doused us with water from multiple directions. His mouth crashed to mine and I freed my hands because I had to touch him. His chest, his arms, his back. I threaded my fingers through his wet hair as we kissed languidly under the streaming water like we had all the time in the world.

Then he started over again on my breasts, only this time, the hot water added friction. So did his tongue. "Oh God... you... amazing," I said, barely able to articulate words.

I slicked back his hair with my fingers and started to work my hands down his torso again, and again, he grabbed my wrists and held them over my head with one hand.

"Why can't I touch you?"

"Because you'll ruin me. I'm so fucking hot for you, I won't last."

He backed me up through the swirling steam to where there

was a bench—which every shower until the end of days needs to have—and he sat me down and eased my legs apart.

"Now you're gonna ruin me," I gasped, already halfway to orgasm under the heat of his touch. I couldn't get enough of him and he knew it.

"I intend to. Again and again," he said, taking a slow stroke down my center with his tongue. His very skillful tongue worked me from all angles and lightly sucked until I was moaning his name and likely promising him very expensive Christmas gifts. I wanted him totally. I needed him. The water coming from every direction added to the sensory overload.

But he wasn't done with his games. Just when he knew I was nearing the dizzying peak of orgasm, he'd move his mouth away and kiss me. It was painful because I always wanted to kiss him. But. Not. Now.

Not when I was that close. He smirked and went down on me again, this time circling and stroking with his tongue until my legs were shaking. "Please, Chris... please."

"I can't say no to you," he said. He slid a finger inside me at the same time his mouth was sucking and licking and possibly even biting. Until I was a writhing puddle of orgasm in his hands.

Oh... oh, wow..." That was the best I could do for words. I was actually slumped to the side, like he'd halfway killed me. Death by orgasm.

Then I felt his hand grab under me and lift me off the seat. He held me in his arms like I weighed all of ten pounds and swung around so he was sitting on the bench. I wrapped my legs around him as he lowered me down, filling me in the most beautiful way. We moved against each other slowly, perfectly. We kissed, our tongues circling in rhythm with our bodies.

It was different than it had been at the beginning of the week. Being together now felt like the sweet beginning of a real relationship. It wasn't just sex because it felt good. We were completely in sync with each other. We were connected. We were making love and didn't care if I'd be heartbroken later. All I cared about was the now.

~

I FELT a lot less nervous after the shower.

I left Chris to get himself ready and headed upstairs to work with my team of experts. It really took a team. Flora, a makeup artist from England, got to work on my skin, hydrating it with a steam machine and rubbing essential oils into my temples. Then George got to work taming my wet hair into dry loose waves that looked better than my best hair day at the beach. As he continued to fret and fuss over each wave, Flora swept layers of foundation, opaque powder, and contouring shadows over my face and added liner and rows of glued-on lashes that high-lighted my eyes and made them look enormous and pretty.

She packed lip gloss and foundation for touchups into a small clutch purse. Marguerite had dropped it off herself along with the dress, shoes, and a double-stranded diamond choker, whispering, "Don't worry, it's not real. But it will look *magnifique* with the dress." She wasn't wrong.

"Wow," Chris said as I descended the staircase, careful not to trip in my four-inch heels. "Just... wow."

"It's an amazing dress."

"It is an amazing dress, but it's just a dress. *You* are spectacu-lar," he said. Then he leaned in and whispered, "And I'm still picturing you in my shower."

His wolfish gaze made me blush. He stood there in a tux, his hair slicked back, looking gorgeous and hot and movie-star handsome. My nerves were doing a good job of pushing me to just shy of a heart attack.

Then I looked a moment longer at Chris, really looked. I reminded myself that he was the same normal guy I'd gotten to know over the past week, despite the premiere-ready exterior that made my heart race. Looking at him calmed me a little, maybe because of the placid depth of his eyes.

"Back atcha," I said.

As he grabbed my hand and walked me toward the door, I was awash in all the emotions I swore I'd protect myself from feeling. I'd have my work cut out for me when I got home and had to get over him. But there was nothing I could do about that now.

So tonight, I was all in.

CHAPTER TWENTY-SIX

ANOTHER TOWN CAR AND A RED CARPET IN CANNES

THE TOWN CAR that drove us from Antibes to Cannes was larger than the one that had been driving us around in town, but the same driver, Laur, commandeered it. We cruised along the twisting coastal road toward another city I'd only heard about but never considered visiting in a floor-length gown. The inside of this car had a stocked bar with cut-crystal glasses, decanters of various liqueurs, and a small fridge with chilled bottles of water and Perrier. We grabbed bottles of water and sank them into the cupholders carved out of dark wood on either side of our leather seats.

Chris was quieter than usual on the drive. I debated whether to try to make conversation with him or leave him alone. "So who does the studio invite to these premieres?"

"Press, French executives, agents..." he said.

We'd never had trouble finding things to talk about, but this felt painful. Eventually, I was reduced to talking about the weather, which seemed innocuous though a little sad. "Pretty day. I guess that's a redundant statement around here," I said, looking at him out of the corner of my eye. His mouth twitched, an acknowledgement instead of a smile. He said nothing. After another few minutes, I couldn't take it any longer. "You okay? I'm not used to the silent version of you."

That snapped him out of his reverie. "Yeah, I'm good. Sorry. Just stuff on my mind, I guess."

"I know you're in work mode," I said, trying to respect whatever his pre-premiere process was. "Don't apologize."

"Thanks."

I focused on the view, which never faltered. The water and sky met in a medium-blue haze out on a horizon I couldn't decipher in the afternoon light. I took a moment to let it sink in, grateful to be here. I couldn't have imagined any of this—the dress, the guy—when I'd decided to fly to France solo. The first week had been something out of a crazy dream, and I still needed to pinch myself to believe I was sitting next to Chris on the way to his premiere in the South of France.

We'd left the empty strand of beachfront behind and had entered an area of hotels with lines of matching umbrellas on the sand in front of each. One hotel had dark-blue umbrellas, the next had orange-and-white-striped ones in rows, separating sunbathers from one another. It was what I'd pictured when I imagined the beaches in the South of France, but Chris and I hadn't been to a beach like this. His cove was so private and perfect that we never considered going anywhere else.

Before long, we were pulling up to the Croisette in Cannes, where a wide red carpet was flanked with photographers with long lenses, and a set of bleachers allowed fans to crowd in and watch people exiting limousines and town cars like ours. My heart jumped into my throat even as I told myself that no one would be looking at me.

I felt nervous on behalf of Chris, seeing the gauntlet he'd

have to navigate. My respect for him grew as I registered the size of the crowd and began to hear the screams of excitement and shouts from photographers. His costar, Heidi Sanchez—an actress I'd read about furtively over the past few days while trying to make myself an expert in all things *White Serpent*—was already on the carpet, posing for the photographers, one hand on her hip and the other holding a beaded clutch. Her husband stood smiling as well, grasping her elbow, moving aside when certain of the paparazzi asked her to pose alone—a drill they seemed to know well. I got ready for our turn as Laur came around the car and opened the door on Chris's side.

He stepped out to a chorus of screams and people shouting his name. He smiled and put a hand up to wave then turned and extended his hand to me, helping me out of the car. I stood in blinding lights, trying to make sense of how to walk in a straight line.

I immediately felt overwhelmed and nauseated by the flashing bulbs, but I did my best to plaster on a smile that meant nothing and walk in my four-inch heels without face-planting. The least I could do for Chris was to make it past the carpet without incident.

He took my hand, and we started walking down the swath of red, stopping every couple of steps as another photographer called his name. He'd turn and pose for a specific camera, his hand never leaving mine, never relegating me to the side as his costar had with her date. He was gallant, and I was grateful.

"Just follow my lead, walk with me, and stay next to me," he leaned in and whispered. The smell of his cologne and the mint he'd swallowed a minute before we'd arrived brought me down to earth. He was movie-star Chris, but he was still the Chris I knew.

The carpet seemed to go on forever, populated with seemingly hundreds of entertainment reporters requesting a sound bite and a short interview in front of the cameras. They asked him questions about the movie.

"Will this be the final *White Serpent*?"

"How are you enjoying your new villa?"

"What projects are next for you?"

"Who are you with tonight?"

That stopped me in my tracks. I hadn't expected anyone to notice the noncelebrity next to Chris, but he took it in stride. "This is Nikki Woodford."

A few more flashbulbs went off as the paparazzi took in the sight of us together, hand in hand, but Chris was a pro at this. He answered the questions he wanted to but didn't linger for the ones he didn't. Before my brain could even process things enough to freak out, he'd whisked me down the remainder of the carpet, and we were in the theater.

The cool of the atrium hit me the moment we walked inside, but it was then that I finally exhaled. Much as I'd thought about it over the past few days, there'd been no way to prepare myself for the scene outside. Now that it was behind me, I instantly felt better. I'd gotten through the worst of it and come out unscathed. Maybe it wasn't even so bad.

Chris was staring at me like maybe I'd grown a second head. I swallowed and looked at him. "Yes?"

"You did great. Are you okay? Never want to be seen with me again?"

"I'm good. And excited to see your movie. Can we go in?"

We walked past a table with tubs of popcorn and drinks, and I grabbed both, but before we entered the theater, Chris's publicist pulled him aside and asked if he'd mind doing a couple of interviews with local media. "We can knock 'em out during the movie, and you can go right to the afterparty."

Chris looked at me, his eyes asking if it was okay. I wasn't about to be the one to get in the way. "Yes, go. You've seen it. I'm fine. I'll meet you after."

He kissed me on the cheek, and I headed into the theater. From behind me, I heard his publicist say, "She's hot. What's the story with her?" I didn't hear Chris's response.

WHAT COULD I say about the movie? Let's face it—I wasn't a superhero fan. It didn't matter, because what I got in that theater was a movie-screen-sized date with Chris. And the guy had talent. I could see that from the moment his face appeared, fraught with anger that he'd been betrayed.

Watching him work right in front of me was fascinating. I realized there weren't that many professions where a person was right there, laboring in front of an audience, baring something intimate in a big way. In the non-superhero mortal version of his character, he was unassuming and even a little nerdy. His acting chops impressed me, and I bought into his character's plight completely.

He lived two lives, and the trick was not letting them get in the way of each other, something the superhero version of his character made difficult. That side of him wanted to save the world more than he wanted to be a regular guy, so eventually, his regular self faded away, and he gave in to the larger calling.

Choosing that path made all the difference. The audience applauded when he put a knife through an old T-shirt that his alter ego used to wear. That part of him was gone forever. I hadn't seen the prior movies, but I could appreciate that this one, the fourth, represented his character's triumph over the forces of evil in the world. Like the rest of the theater, I cheered when he killed his nemesis after a brutal series of twists and turns that led to the final showdown.

It didn't matter that I'd never seen a *White Serpent* movie before. I barely noticed anything except Chris's performance in front of me and the several hundred other people with the same up-close view of him in the theater. It made me want him even more, seeing the power he commanded over his craft and the subtleties and human stakes he brought to his character.

Of course, he got the girl in the end. Heidi Sanchez didn't have anywhere near the talent Chris had, but it didn't matter. Her role was to be beautiful and hang off the side of a building in peril. When he rescued her, eyes flashing, the audience applauded again. I tried to fight a nagging feeling of insecurity.

He'd looked exactly the same way at me, and I'd believed he wasn't acting.

After the credits rolled, everyone streamed out of the theater, gabbing about the movie and looking for the signs that led to the afterparty. Chris was waiting in a corner off to the side, out of sight of people going the other way. I threw my arms around him. "You were incredible. I loved it."

"Really? Your first *White Serpent* film—did it measure up to the hype?"

"Are you going to give me shit about that forever?"

"I love that you only go to art-house movies. But yes, I will give you shit. So... you really liked it?"

"I really did. You've got some big talent. Everyone in the place was cheering for you. You must've heard the noise from out here."

He shrugged. "All I care about right now is what you think."

"I think you're brilliant," I said, realizing that in my giant heels, I didn't need to reach much to kiss him on the cheek. "And I think I just became your fangirl."

He seemed to like the sound of that. "Ready for a drink? Or six?"

"Yes, please."

He grabbed my hand and we left the theater, crossing the street to where a loud party was already in full swing.

CHAPTER TWENTY-SEVEN

THE AFTERPARTY WAS MORE like a crowded bar scene than anything else, with one difference—everyone in the place wanted to talk to Chris. He didn't need to work the room, because the room came to him. Mostly, we stayed by the bar, and he would introduce me when someone he knew came over.

"John, meet Nikki. Nikki, John's done all the post for the *White Serpent* franchise."

"Your work was great," I'd say as though I even knew what it meant to *do post.*

Chris would chat and smile, accepting every hug, handshake, and kind word with self-effacing appreciation. He knew how to make everyone in his orbit feel good to be near him and lucky to have a few minutes of undivided attention. I knew my job was to smile and nod and be equally gracious if someone included me in the conversation, which mostly consisted of them beaming at Chris and asking me, "Wasn't he great?"

If someone he didn't seem to know well came over to gush

about his performance, he mostly said his thanks, ever grateful for the compliments and adulation. He was friendly at all times, accessible to everyone, and patient even when having the same conversation for the fifteenth time.

On the whole, he'd leave details about me out of the conversation, just introducing me by name but never with an explanatory phrase—which was fine. What was he supposed to say? Nikki is "the goddess I've fallen for," "someone I've been spending time with," or "the woman I swept off her feet in Paris?"

Of course, this awkward moment was hardly the time to put words to what I might or might not mean to him. It wasn't like we were dating. When he'd get into a longer conversation about some abstract aspect of the film, I'd drift a few feet away and top off my drink.

The bartender was moving at lightning speed, efficiently taking orders and mixing drinks, spinning across from one side to the other, and never leaving anyone hanging for long. He reminded me a little bit of Johnny, ever the solicitous host, making sure everyone's glass stayed full. And thinking of Johnny, even with the charismatic film star standing just a few feet to my left, made me feel a little nostalgic.

Over the past month, I'd gained a little perspective on why Johnny and I never had a future. It wasn't his fault. He'd never pretended to be anything he wasn't, and he would probably go on to have a happy, albeit alcohol-soaked life because he never wanted more than a good time, living in the present.

He had a lightness I could never hope to harness. I was the one who took everything seriously, and to his credit, he'd never found fault with it. Watching the bartender spin around reminded me that there had been good parts to our year together. However, those didn't include being an unapologetic asshole and cheating.

"Mademoiselle?" he asked after I'd been watching him for a while.

I decided on another glass of champagne. The first had gone straight to my head, probably because I hadn't eaten since... I couldn't remember. Breakfast?

"*Merci*," I said when he handed me a refilled glass, generously poured. It went down easily, and I remembered that I hadn't really hydrated after my hour on the treadmill. In fact, I'd gone straight into a steam shower. No wonder I was thirsty. But instead of being smart and asking for water—*un carafe d'eau*, as Guillaume had instructed me to request—I finished the second glass of champagne and started on a third.

I wasn't sure when it happened, but at some point, I looked up and noticed that Chris was halfway across the room, holding court amid a group of admirers who were hanging on his every word. I looked around the room at the attractive crowd of actors, producers, and who knew who else, and it hit me hard.

I didn't belong in this room.

Chris had thought he wanted a date to take to his premiere, but now that he was busy being swept along in congratulations and expensive festivities, he just needed to be what he was: a celebrity. Maybe it was because the bartender reminded me of Johnny, but I was suddenly transported back to the high school reunion more than a month earlier, when I'd felt like a lame hanger-on while Johnny "had a lot of catching up to do."

This wasn't Chris's fault. I shouldn't have come. And with my head starting to throb thanks to the fourth glass of champagne I'd grabbed from a waitress, I desperately wanted to leave before Chris had a chance to realize what a big mistake he'd made inviting me here—before he saw me differently, like dead weight at a party where he'd rather be having fun than having to introduce me to everyone.

Or explain who I was. Or what we were. Because we were nothing.

Feeling drunker than I wanted to be, I pushed my way through the crowd and tapped Chris on the shoulder. He turned, and I could tell he didn't expect it to be me. He thought I'd be another admiring fan.

"I'm gonna go back. To the hotel," I said.

"What? Why? Are you... okay?"

I wasn't going to lie, so I said nothing. Because of the crowd of people already jockeying for his attention, he couldn't have a conversation with me or do much to try to stop me. He seemed to understand that.

So he nodded. And I left.

I DIDN'T EVEN KNOW which hotel we were staying in that night, but I knew Laur could get me there. Halfway down the now-empty carpet, I moved quickly in my stupid four-inch heels, which I'd been doing my best to ignore until that point. They were killing me, and I tried to run toward the row of town cars, not certain in my blurred state which one was ours. Fortunately, a woman in a floor-length cerulean blue dress is easy to spot.

Laur looked up from where he'd been reading a book and hurried over. "Mademoiselle, *ça va?*"

"*Ça va*, but I want to go to the hotel. Can you take me?"

He didn't ask questions or check with Chris. He just nodded, the kind of guy who was apparently familiar with the wayward desires of women at fancy parties where they didn't belong. It was a short drive to the Five Seas Hotel—two blocks, actually—but I'd never have made it in those shoes.

He made a quick phone call while he drove, saying something I didn't understand. When we arrived at the hotel, a bellman was waiting to open the car door and escort me straight to our penthouse suite, where our luggage had already been delivered and a plate of chocolates sat on a table. *Félicitations* was handwritten on the edge of the plate in chocolate scrawl. As soon as the bellman wished me a *"bonne soirée"* and closed the door, I picked up two of the chocolates and threw them at the door.

I looked at the time and calculated the hour in San Francisco, dialing Annie to FaceTime her before I'd done the math to be certain she'd be awake. It didn't matter. Whether it was day or night, we'd always been there for each other.

"Hey!" she answered in seconds. "How's the life of the rich and famous?" Whether it was the champagne or the sound of her voice, I couldn't have said, but the tears started rolling down my cheeks. "What's wrong?"

"I don't know." I really didn't. And I was too drunk and upset to sort through it all.

"Hang on, back up a second. Lemme look at that dress," she said. Priorities. I obliged, holding up the phone. "No, I want to see the whole thing."

"How can I do that? Okay, hang on," I said, the distraction drying my eyes out for a second. I went to the full-length mirror and showed her the head-to-toe version.

"That is ah-mazing!" she said. I told her where I'd just been, and I could hear my media-savvy friend typing on her computer. "Okay, wait... now I see it all."

"What?" I asked.

"On social. There are pics. Oh my God, you're such a gorgeous couple."

"Where are you looking?" I asked. It hadn't occurred to me that there would be pictures of Chris and me that my friend across the world—and apparently, lots of other people —could see.

"All over. Lots of great pics of you guys on the Croisette. Seriously, you make a great couple... though... ugh, have you seen this stuff? Is that why you're crying?"

"Seen what? What are you looking at?" I couldn't talk to her and look at social media on my phone at the same time, so I had no idea what she was seeing. But it didn't sound good.

"Oh, it's nothing. Probably why celebs say they never read the tabloids."

"Annie, what? What are people saying?"

"Just a lot of stupid crap about 'Chris Conley's latest flame' and 'Who's Nikki Woodford?' and 'Chris Conley's vacation romance' and some not-nice things about your hair."

"What's wrong with my hair?"

"Nothing. I think it looks great. People are saying it's messy."

"It's supposed to be beachy."

"Who cares what these trolls are saying? You were on the red carpet with Chris Conley. Was it fun?" she asked.

The tears started again. "No, it wasn't. I mean, for a minute, maybe it was, but... I'm not built for this."

"Oh, honey, I know. I love you, but this isn't you."

"It's not. But why is it not? What's wrong with me? Why can't I be spontaneous and easy-going?"

"What does that have to do with dating a celebrity? I just meant you don't like flashy designer clothes and shallow people."

"It's true, I don't. But I take everything too seriously. We're supposed to be having a fling. And I'm falling in love with him."

"Of course you are. Who wouldn't? He's super dreamy."

"Not helping," I said.

"Does he know? Have you told him?" she asked.

"Are you kidding? That's the last thing he wants to hear."

Annie sighed, one of her characteristic moves before she was about to bestow some philosophical advice. I readied myself for a proverb or some Shakespeare. What I got was actually pretty solid. "You should fight harder for what you want," Annie said.

My response was equally solid. "I'm not sure I know what I want, so how can I fight for it?"

"You do know. You always know exactly what you want and I admire that so much about you. You're just afraid to say it out loud, in case you don't get it."

And as much as I wanted to come back with a pithy retort, I knew she was right. I couldn't say it out loud because I was certain my feelings wouldn't be returned. The premiere party only reinforced that impression. "I can't tell him I'm falling for him. Especially after tonight."

"Maybe he feels the same way."

"No. I don't belong with someone like him. Tonight was stressful, and I couldn't have felt more like an outsider."

"Don't you think that's how Amal Clooney felt? She's a brilliant lawyer, and she got dragged to all kinds of dumb celebrity events."

"Kind of you to compare me to Amal Clooney."

"To me, you will always be Amal Clooney."

It made me cry. Again. My perfectly applied eyeliner began to drip down my cheek, tears heavy in my fake lashes. "I drank a lot of champagne, and I didn't eat," I admitted, a knot stuck in my throat.

"Rookie mistake. But you're out of your comfort zone. Cut yourself some slack."

"Why do you always take my side even when I'm wrong?"

She looked at me with sympathy from her apartment a billion miles away. "Because you've done it for me."

I had. I always would.

There was so much more I needed to unload. It had been a

mistake not to check in with her sooner. Maybe she could have talked me through things and helped me figure out what I was doing before my emotions ran roughshod over everything. Now there was no going back.

But just as I was starting to rewind and dump my emotional load on her, a keycard slid through the lock. Chris stood there in his tux, looking every bit as put together as I looked a mess. He also looked upset.

"I gotta call you back," I told Annie.

She didn't need to see Chris through her phone to know the reason. She nodded and mouthed, "Love you."

CHAPTER TWENTY-EIGHT

The Five Seas Hotel, Cannes
Late at Night, or at Least it Seemed Late

I KNEW HE WAS MAD. I knew I had to apologize. I'd probably ruined his night, as evidenced by the fact that he'd left his own party to see why his date had run off in a champagne-driven hissy fit. And at the same time, I didn't want to tell him I was sorry. I didn't know if I was. It was better not to talk at all.

I just wanted to leave. Maybe he would just let me go without us having to hash anything out.

I turned away from him and looked at the small Louis Vuitton overnight bag that contained the few things I'd tossed in for our "night away." I didn't own the bag, just like I didn't own the dress or the fake eyelashes. I could take my things out and shove them into a plastic laundry bag, leaving the luggage behind with Chris. No strings.

As I was considering this, he took a few steps closer to me. I went to the closet to look for a laundry bag, thinking about what to say and how to get out of there with the least number of words needed in explanation.

But he spoke first. "I'm so sorry."

It was so unexpected that I stopped what I was doing. In my drunken haze, I wasn't even sure I'd heard right. "What?" I turned to look at him.

"I'm sorry." He put up his hands like he was at a loss as to what else to say.

"Why are you sorry?"

He took another couple of timid steps closer, as if I might lash out at him. "For being an asshole date."

"You weren't an asshole."

"I left you alone where you knew no one, in a country where you don't speak the language, at a party where everyone is a shallow suck-up but only if you're famous. Sounds like an asshole to me. Isn't that why you left?"

I felt confused. No, none of those reasons were why I'd run out of there. My reasons had nothing to do with him, though it was kind of him to take responsibility. "I didn't want to stop you from having a good time."

He took that in. Then he nodded his head. "Well, you did."

I fought back the tears, which seemed to keep insisting their way past my lashes. I wasn't sure whether I could wipe them or if the whole eyelash would come off, so I let the tears roll down.

I hadn't cried at the end of a year-long relationship with Johnny, and there I was, practically sobbing over the end of a non-relationship I'd had for just over a week. The champagne wasn't helping.

"Sorry," I choked out, going back for the bag in the closet.

"I had a shitty time because these things are always a nightmare. But I had an exceptionally shitty time because you left." He came over to where I was and touched me on the arm, making me stop searching and turn around. "I wanted you there with me."

"Why?"

He looked confused. I took that moment to back away. Having him touch me wouldn't help me distance myself, and I needed to do that. He took his cue and retreated to the beige settee with the pink pashmina throw blanket. "Are you... have I been reading this wrong? Are you not having a good time... with me?"

He looked vulnerable, but I didn't let that stop me from saying what needed to be said. "Of course I am. But I don't belong here with you. That's what hit me tonight. You and I have been hiding out in your house and on the boat, and it's been great. Normal. Isn't that what you said? But tonight, I caught a glimpse of your real life, and it was clear I didn't fit into it."

"Because...?"

"Because all those cameras made my skin crawl, and I didn't want you to resent me—for lamely standing next to you, making you introduce me to people and explain who I am, your 'new flame' or your 'vacation romance' or whatever."

"I don't even know what that means." Of course he didn't. He made a point of staying off social media.

"I just think... maybe our vacation fling, or whatever you want to call it, has run its course. Maybe it's time you go back to your world and I go back to mine."

I felt mature laying it out like that. I'd taken the high road and given him an out, so he wouldn't have to feel bad about going back to his party. Laur would probably drive me back to the house, where I could pack my things.

But Chris gestured at me to sit next to him on the soft pashmina. My mind wandered for a second, wondering if people ever took those shawls home with them. "Remember how I said I don't live in some kind of world that's different from yours?"

I sat. And nodded.

"It's still true," he said.

"That was easy to believe when it was just the two of us on a beach, but come on. What I saw tonight—that couldn't be more different from my life. And I'm not judging at all. This is what you do, and you do it well. I just don't think I do it so well."

"Okay, I hear you." He looked like he understood because he slid a little farther away, which I needed just so I could straighten out my thoughts without feeling magnetically drawn to him. "But you have to realize this is all in your head. I never said a word about needing you to be anything other than yourself. Yes, my job involves a lot of bullshit celebrity stuff that I have to do—"

"And I get that." I knew I was interrupting, but I had to get everything out. "I see how fun it must be to be you, and I don't want to take anything away from that or make you enjoy it any less because I'm easily freaked out. It's okay for you to enjoy it without me."

"I don't want to. You fit into my world perfectly. But if you feel differently... at least own that."

"Own what? One minute you were next to me, and the next, you were across the room with a bunch of people who were laughing at every word you said."

"Yeah, and you were talking to the bartender. I tried to get your attention several times, but you didn't even notice me. You looked completely lost in the conversation."

Did I really talk to the bartender so intently that I didn't notice Chris? Just because he reminded me of Johnny?

Jesus.

"So I figured you were enjoying yourself, and I didn't want to pry you away. But I've got to tell you, it made me jealous as hell."

"I was... he seemed like he didn't fit in there either. I guess I felt comfortable with him."

He exhaled a long breath and shook his head. "Why didn't you just tell me how you were feeling? I had no idea. So I made small talk, like I always do at these things, and figured you'd come find me when you were ready. And then you bolted. So I came here to apologize because I knew something had upset you... but I kinda hoped I could read the tea leaves and figure out what it was because, frankly, I had no idea."

I couldn't believe I'd read the whole thing wrong. And despite me bailing on him in a huff of emotion, he'd been the one to apologize. If anyone was an asshole in this scenario, it was probably me.

"I'm sorry," I said, slumped and defeated. I suddenly felt very tired from the champagne. "I projected all my insecurities onto you." Tentatively, he put a hand on the pool of cerulean satin on my lap. He turned it upward as a suggestion, and I slowly put my hand in his. "I really am sorry. And I have a headache from crying. And from the champagne. I'm kind of a mess." I flopped backward to where the settee met the foot of the bed and lay my head on the cool duvet.

"For a mess, you're sure beautiful," he said, pushing himself up on to the bed so his head faced mine, leaning his chin on his palm. I couldn't help it—new tears rolled from my eyes. I vowed to never drink champagne again.

Chris went to the bathroom and came back with a plush white bathrobe. He unzipped the back of my dress and unfastened the painful stays on the corset so I could slip the robe on. He tied the sash then picked me up and deposited me higher on the bed so my head sank into the pillows. He lay down next to me and rubbed one of my feet where the straps had left a mark. It felt great. And I felt terrible.

"How can you continue to be so nice when I was such a jerk? And I made you leave your party early."

"Are you kidding? I was dying to get out of there. You gave

me the perfect out. I just wish you'd waited so I could've made my excuses and left with you."

I finally exhaled a day's worth of breath I'd been unknowingly holding in behind the corset. I didn't know what made me doubt that the guy I'd come to know over the past week was still that same guy at the movie premiere. I traced his cheek down to his jawline, marveling at the contour. "You know, Michelangelo's sculptures have nothing on you," I said, the anxiety I'd been fighting all day fading into calm. "I really should've eaten something today."

He shook his head at me. "Didn't I tell you? What did you do with all that food in the kitchen?"

"I left it there and went up to meet with my team of beauty handlers."

Chris rolled off the bed and grabbed a heavy leather-bound book from the desk in the other room of the suite. Then he dialed room service, speaking quickly in French, and asked them to bring up something I couldn't translate. He came back to where he'd been on the bed. We lay there for a while, looking at each other, not talking.

"We can go back to my house if you don't feel like staying here tonight," he said after a while.

"No, I'm okay here. Why?"

"I just thought if you'd rather hide out at the house, we could do that tonight. Laur would drive us back."

I rolled over to look at him. "Please. Don't feel like I'm such a shut-in that I can't be taken out in public. I just want to make sure you really want me there."

"What else do I have to do to make you believe it?"

I thought about it. "Nothing. You've done everything."

"That has been my goal since I met you."

"You've more than exceeded it. I'm done looking for problems where there aren't any," I said.

"Promise?"

"I promise." I really wanted to keep my word.

There was a knock at the door, which Chris answered. He tipped the room-service attendant. Instead of inviting him into the room to set up the table, Chris brought in a tray with covered dishes and silverware wrapped in heavy cotton napkins. The salt and pepper gleamed in tiny glass vials. I hoped it wouldn't be something too French, like escargots, which required special tongs and forks and a separate ritual for the sauce. But I vowed to eat whatever he'd chosen. I'd already done enough that night to act like a pain in the ass.

A half bottle of wine sat on the tray, but there was no way I'd drink any more. "For me," he said when he saw me eying it. "Believe it or not, you're not the only one who gets stressed out at these things." He uncorked the bottle and poured himself a glass.

"À santé," I said, holding up an imaginary glass.

Chris brought the tray over to the bed, so I didn't even have to get up. He spread out a picnic on top of the white duvet and unveiled the plates, on which sat two croque madame sandwiches—basically grilled ham and cheese with a poached egg on top—sliced in half, accompanied by fries. "I figured you might like some comfort food," he said.

He always anticipated exactly what I wanted. I felt my eyes starting to well up. He looked at me with sympathy even though he couldn't possibly understand what was going on with me. I didn't really understand it myself.

CHAPTER TWENTY-NINE

THE NEXT MORNING, I had a clearer idea of why I'd felt so emotional. We were long past the midpoint of our time together and had only a few days until I had to fly home. I couldn't believe the past week had flown by so quickly. The days that followed spun by in an equally rapid series of beach walks, time by the pool, trips into town, and sunset dinners.

Before I knew what had happened, only two days and two nights remained before my flight back to the real world. I didn't even want to think about my life back at home. The routine of going to work, going out with friends, and hanging out on my couch paled in comparison to what I'd seen the past couple weeks. Going home felt like moving backward instead of forward.

We spent the morning on the boat, just sailing south toward Saint-Tropez but not docking or dropping anchor. The point was to be on the boat in the sun, lounging side by side on matching yellow-and-white-striped towels in the front of the mainsail, feeling the salt air on our skin, and forgetting that the day after tomorrow would ever come.

I'd finally relented and tried on the expensive swimsuit with the cutouts and strings, and I had to admit, I felt glamorous wearing it.

Chris almost dropped his coffee when I came down the stairs in it, the caftan tied around my waist like a sarong. "Holy cow, I think my heart just stopped."

"Turns out maybe I am a caftan kind of girl."

I did my best to focus on the present because I didn't want to waste what little time we had worrying about how I'd feel when I got on the plane. No point in that. I rolled onto my side and looked at Chris lying on his back with a second towel rolled up under his head, his sunglasses reflecting the sails, his whole body evenly tanned. He looked content. He'd created a nice life for himself, which I now understood was a needed respite from the crush of publicity tours, twelve-hour, filming days, and paparazzi at every turn. I couldn't blame him one bit for living the way he did.

"I see you looking at me, but I'm too comfortable to move," he said. "Everything okay?"

"Everything is great. I was just thinking about how glad I am that I was clueless about buying fruit. Otherwise, I'd never have met you."

"I'm gonna let you in on a secret," he said, still not moving a muscle. I couldn't tell if his eyes were open behind his sunglasses. "I noticed you standing there at Monoprix, and I'd pretty much decided I was going to say something to you—I just didn't know what. Then you gave me the perfect opportunity. So thank you."

It made me happy, although I wondered why he hadn't he told me that before. I rolled closer to him and kissed him. I didn't feel like I could do more than that without thinking about how our time was running out. And I wanted to do whatever I could to avoid thinking.

I'd finally gotten more comfortable on the boat whenever it heeled, believing it would stay afloat with its giant hunk of metal underneath acting as a counterweight. Later that day, when the breeze kicked up, we sat on the low side, reclining, while Louis and the crew let the sails out and the boat zipped along under the warm sun.

Chris opened a bottle of Sancerre like we'd had the first night in Paris, and we sipped the cold wine and looked out over the hypnotic blue water. I couldn't imagine ever getting tired of the view or the feeling of the wind and sun on my face.

A couple of hours later, the boat pulled into the slip, and Louis and his crew went about their post-sailing ritual while Chris and I went back to the house to change for dinner. He'd suggested we pull out all the stops and eat at a Michelin-starred restaurant in Juan-les-Pins, not far from his house. How could I say no? Earlier in the week, Laur had driven me to a fancy shopping area, where I'd splurged on a summery yellow-patterned dress that was perfect for a nice night out.

Chris nodded appreciatively when I came down the stairs in it. "Bought a little something the other day. Like it?" I asked, twirling to show him the sash tie in the back.

He nodded. "The dress is great, but like I said before, I like the person in it."

I took in the full picture of him, tanned and gorgeous in his off-white linen pants and blue shirt. There was never a moment when he didn't look good. Yes, it was going to be hard to say goodbye. But first, dinner.

CHAPTER THIRTY

La Passagère, Antibes

THE RESTAURANT WAS on the terrace of a hotel, and our table overlooking the water's edge was set with a white tablecloth and small plates and place settings. A couple was posing for a picture by the rail, which was covered in creeping-ivy leaves and opened out to the same span of water where we'd sailed earlier.

We opted for a tasting menu and wine pairing, which meant we were served an uncountable number of plates with tiny exquisite arrangements of foods in swirls of sauce, sprinkled with herbs and accented with a grapefruit slice here, a cucumber swirl there. With each course, the waiter poured a different half glass of wine meant to bring out the flavor of the food. I ate slowly, wanting to taste every nuance of the oyster, the scallop, and the shaved watermelon radish.

"What do you think?" Chris asked after our second course had been served.

"Everything is delicious. Have you been here before?"

"Once. And before you get all crazy wondering which leggy blond starlet I was here with, I'm gonna tell you I was here with my mom."

"Thanks for supporting my paranoia, but I think I'm over it now."

"Good to hear." He lifted the second glass of wine, which had appeared next to his plate before he'd made a dent in the first. "I'm kinda thinking the wine pairing was a mistake. Neither one of us can keep up."

"Think it's too late to just go with wine by the glass?" I asked. He shook his head and called over our waiter, who was more than happy to make the adjustment.

Despite the never-ending parade of dishes, each described in detail by our waiter, I never felt too full, and the wine didn't overpower me. I was all too aware that the clock had begun ticking on my last hours in France—my last day on the boat, my last sunset. I had to stop torturing myself.

"This two weeks has been incredible. I really can't thank you enough for sharing it with me," I said.

"It's been my absolute pleasure," he said, looking at me the same way he had every day since we'd met.

"So... what's next for you? Is there, like, a worldwide tour to promote the movie?"

"Something like that." He looked uncomfortable, but I didn't care. It had been eating at me all day.

"Can you elaborate?" I asked, hoping there was a shred of a possibility this wouldn't have to end just because my vacation was over. Maybe he'd have to be in LA for a week. Maybe he'd want me to meet him...

He inhaled deeply. Then he exhaled and told me more than I wanted to know. "I have more interviews and more publicity in

Europe coming up. Then we have the US premiere and a bunch of press in New York, talk shows and stuff, but that will wrap up in a month or so. And... that script I read, the one my agent's been all over me to make a decision on... I decided to do it. We film on location in Ireland starting in September."

So I had my answer. There was no point in talking logistics —"Maybe you could fly to visit" or "If you'll be in LA some-time..." He was headed into back-to-back commitments. That was his job. And I had mine.

"Sounds like you'll be busy," I said.

"Always." His was a life of one.

Our dinner ended with not one, not two, but three desserts. First we were served a small bowl of sliced strawberries in a balsamic reduction. Then we had a sliver of lemon sorbet sealed under a crust of hard sugar. And not to be outshone by fruit, two chocolate mini tortes filled with a mocha ganache arrived on a bed of coffee beans. Looking out across the water, I could see Île Sainte-Marguerite and the coast where we'd been in Cannes the night before. It felt like a world away.

"Are you ever in New York? Or would you want to visit?" he asked.

My heart skipped a beat. Of course, I wanted to say yes. With every fiber of my being, I wanted to know I'd see him again, and I didn't want this to end. He reached out for my hand across the table. The sun was starting to set over the water in the distance. The clouds were perfectly placed to capture the yellow and pink glowing light in the sky.

"I think that might be too hard," I said.

"Yeah. I know you've got a job. I just figured you might have more vacation days."

"Sure, in a year. I pretty much used up everything to come on this trip." That wasn't what I was talking about when I'd said it would be too hard. I couldn't be the friend he caught up with on a visit once in a while. I'd never get over him that way.

"Right. I hear you."

"I wanna see you again... but..."

Maybe I didn't really have a good reason to turn him down. If we made plans for a visit sometime in the future, I'd have something to look forward to, and leaving might not seem so bad. Instead of goodbye, it would be "See you soon." That always felt better. Then we'd have a great weekend together in New York, and we'd have to say goodbye again. We'd end up right back where we were now, with him going off for six months to shoot a movie and me going back to my job. I'd feel like I was going in circles. I'd feel like there was no future, just a spread out series of *fun in the moment.* I'd already had that with Johnny. For once, I needed to feel like I was moving forward.

"I'm not sure it makes sense," I said finally. "I think I need closure."

He nodded as though in full agreement but his eyes burned with a pain I understood because I felt it too. He ran a hand through his hair, like he was trying to come up with another way this could go. I'd already thought through the possibilities—I'd been thinking for days. There were none.

"The way I feel about you... it's not some fling. But my life is... complicated," he said.

"Because of your job? Or because of some actual dark side you still haven't told me about?"

"They're kind of the same thing. I've been blessed in my career. I'm doing what I've dreamed about since I was eight, and I never take it for granted. If anything, I'm a slave to it because I'm afraid to lose it."

He'd said it earlier: "If you slow down, they forget." I remembered the words, but at the time, I hadn't realized they had him in a stranglehold. It didn't matter if the fear was real; it was real to him.

"I look at my parents, their marriage... they've been together for thirty-six years, and they'll be together forever," he said, looking away from me. I didn't say anything. I was glad he'd finally opened up a little bit, even if what he was saying didn't bode well for me. "I don't think I'll ever have that."

"Because you'll never feel that way about a person or because your work comes first?" I wasn't sure I wanted to know the answer, but I needed to hear it. He didn't speak for a couple of minutes. His gaze never left the water. He seemed to be working out what he wanted to say.

"I'm not sure," he said finally. "I always thought it was both. Acting takes everything from me emotionally. I'm sure it doesn't seem like that's required for some of the roles I take, but—"

"I'm not questioning. I never even tried out for the middle school play. I have no idea what it takes to do what you do."

He nodded but still didn't look at me. "So, the only way I know how to do it is... I give everything I have to the work. I have to invest in it fully if I want to do it right—I've always believed that. But in the last few days, I've been wondering if that's just something I told myself to let myself off the hook. So I didn't have to invest in people. Or relationships." He looked at me for a second, then his gaze went back to the ocean. "Life is pretty easy that way, actually. I'm always in control, and I never go out on a limb, because I'm not looking for anything. You've made me think differently about that for the first time."

My heart overflowed with love for him. I wanted him to say what it seemed like he was trying to articulate. I reached out gently, like I was trying not to scare a timid animal, and touched his cheek. When he turned to look at me, I could see the agony in his face. "You've made me think differently too," I said. But he didn't look relieved. It seemed to make things worse.

"But I'm not at a place where I can change what I'm doing. Too many people have a stake in the outcome. It's not just about me."

"Shouldn't it be? You're not a robot. You get a say. It's your life."

"Maybe someday. Just not today."

My heart sank. I'd learned my lesson from dating Johnny that it was better to let people be true to themselves than to try to change them. I had no interest in trying, only to end up exactly where I'd started.

But it made wonder if I'd ever find anything more permanent. Would there ever be a man in my life who could have fun in the moment *and* dig in for the rest of it?

"If you slow down, they forget," I repeated, remembering the words of his agent, which seemed to be a guiding principle. "Yeah, I understand."

Did I? Less than two months before, I'd upended everything, breaking up with Johnny and leaving to travel alone, not sure where that would lead. If I could do that, so could anyone. So could he. At the same time, I knew I'd only broken up with Johnny because I'd been pushed. I'd seen the truth for the better part of our year together, but the harsh words and the cheating gave me the excuse to act. I understood why Chris couldn't veer from his path. He wasn't ready. Maybe he'd never be ready.

By that point, I knew what I'd been feeling for him verged on love, if only because I'd been doing my level best to hold back the flood of feelings that would have pushed it over into forever love. I couldn't do that to myself. If I invested any more, I'd never get over him. If I'd just gotten a tiny inkling that he felt the same way, I might have considered seeing him again. But if he was feeling it, he kept those emotions hidden deep belowground. I decided I could do the same. I could stay even-keeled and be mature.

"Having a career like yours is a one-in-a-million lucky break. You have to go with it, even if it means making some sacrifices right now. You have a... larger calling," I said.

"You have no concept of how hard it's been," he said, bordering on angry. "Knowing everything I feel when I'm with you has a deadline. Knowing it has to end."

"But it has to," I said, though a shred of me hoped that somehow I was wrong. I could have folded and given in to what I was feeling, but by staying resolute, I was convincing myself as much as I was assuring him. "I don't see how it can't."

It was an opportunity for him to change his convictions, but how could I expect him to do that? "I know. It's just sad," he said.

It was more than sad because if I was honest, I doubted any guy I'd ever meet would measure up to Chris. How could he?

I'd have thought the rest of our evening would unfold beneath the dark weight of that conversation, but in fact, it was a relief to have finally brought everything into clear light. I didn't have to wonder anymore about what to say or when to broach the subject of what we could or would be to each other after these couple of weeks together. Now that I knew, I could relax and try to enjoy what was left of my South of France vacation. With our time together fleeting, I wanted to lose myself in these moments with Chris while I still had them.

We stayed at our table until the sun had long since set and the sky had gone from orange and pink to midnight blue. Then we walked on the beach, carrying our shoes and letting the gentle surf run over our feet. Chris rolled up his pants, but I could see water marks along the bottoms. He didn't seem to notice.

I didn't care if the hem of my dress got a little damp. I was focused on kissing him under the small crescent moon that shone brightly in the dark sky. There was a gentle tentativeness like what I'd felt on the bridge in Paris, edging deeper as we both responded without needing any more words. We'd said enough.

I wrapped my arms around his neck and felt one hand on the small of my back, the other running lightly through my hair. I have no idea how long we stood there, locked in that kiss. I didn't want to know.

CHAPTER THIRTY-ONE

ANTIBES

Later that Night

AS WE DROVE BACK, a thought struck me, and the more I thought about it, the more I knew it was the right thing to do. "I think I'd like to take the train back to Paris tomorrow morning." I told Chris. He looked surprised for a moment then nodded. "It's not that I wouldn't have an incredible time with you if I stayed one more day. It's just—"

"I get it. You haven't seen Paris." He nodded.

"And I think it would be good for me to take a day there and just... have some alone time before I go home."

"Right. Makes sense," he said, though his brow stayed furrowed, and it seemed like he didn't really understand why I'd made that decision.

"Of course, you know I'd love to be here one more day with you. It's not that," I said. "But it would just make it harder to leave."

"I know." He picked up my hand and held it the rest of the

way home, eyes focused out the window so I couldn't see his face. I didn't feel like he was punishing me, but he was shutting me out just the same.

It would have been easier if Chris had acted like an asshole after I left the premiere party. I'd have seen an ugly side of him that I could cling to, telling myself it was good riddance. But life's not like that and he was a better guy than that. It was on me to stick with my convictions, simply because they were my convictions. I didn't need to say something spiteful to Chris so he'd be angry and would say something to make me hate him. The truth was sad enough.

I'd reserved a tiny glimmer of hope for the possibility I was wrong about Chris and his commitment to his job and his life of one. Maybe he could surprise me and fight for me, for us. If he felt what I did, he'd want something more.

"I could go back to Paris with you. We'd have one more day," he offered. That was his attempt at more. One more day was all he could give.

While the idea of one more day lit up my heart again, the organ was starting to ache from the abuse—love him, ignore feelings, get over him, repeat.

I couldn't do it. "Look, we both knew this would end," I said. Then I took a stab at spite, trying to create some distance. "We barely know each other. It's an escape. It's not real."

He looked stunned at the harsh words but found his own. "It felt real to me. But if that's how you see it... Two weeks on vacation—"

"Is cute and romantic. It's vacation love, and then it ends." How could I expect him to fight for me when I wouldn't do the same. I wanted more, but I was afraid to ask for it.

He looked like he wanted to argue with me, but he didn't. His silence confirmed I was right.

That night, we both slept fitfully. Whenever I rolled over and realized I was awake again, I would look over, and Chris seemed to be half-asleep and moving around as well. We slept intertwined, then separately, then curled up together again. I wasn't used to being this disconnected from him, but it was one more sign we were finished.

CHAPTER THIRTY-TWO

A Town Car and a Train Back to Paris
Morning

CHRIS WAS quiet in the morning as I pulled my stuff together. Maybe it was significant that I hadn't unpacked my bags the whole time I'd been at his house. Maybe a part of me knew it was better if I kept one foot out the door for an easy getaway. Or maybe that one foot was what kept me from investing even more of my heart in a losing proposition. Either way, that made it easy to pack up and get ready to go.

I didn't have much of an appetite, even for the breakfast I'd loved so much every morning. I took a couple of sips of coffee, but even that was hard to choke down. Chris tucked a peach into my bag. "In case you get hungry on the trip."

"Thank you," I said, feeling awkward, suddenly, after having been so comfortable in his presence for two weeks. My heart was starting to take care of itself, sealing itself off from feeling more.

I insisted on taking the train. I also insisted that Chris stay at the house while Laur drove me to the station.

"You can take the jet. Please, let me do this for you," Chris said. It seemed like he was grasping at a way to make it easier for me and less painful for him.

"Really, I'm fine. The train will be nice. I'd like to go a little slower and see the countryside." I'd caught a glimpse of it from high in the sky on our flight, and I wanted to see it on the ground. Where I belonged.

"I just thought you'd want more time in Paris instead of six hours of travel."

"I know. I appreciate that. I'll still get some quality time there this afternoon. And I plan to visit Paris again," I said.

"Maybe we can meet again there someday," he said, though we both knew it was unlikely our schedules would match up. I nodded, not wanting to make things harder. Better to pretend our paths would cross. "Sure. Sounds good."

"So..." he said, reaching out to give me a hug.

I knew if I stayed a minute longer, I'd start to cry. Chris seemed to be swallowing back his own anguish. The sadness in his face was genuine. But then, I told myself protectively, he was an actor.

Chris made sure I was tucked comfortably into the town car. He leaned in through the window, touching my shoulder. I was hoping he wouldn't say something that would make our parting harder, but he seemed to know there was nothing else to say. He kissed me once more, but this time, there was kindness and closure instead of promise. I convinced myself I was okay with that as the car rolled down the cobbles of the driveway, leaving Chris behind.

I didn't turn around. There was no point. My only direction was forward.

I made sure I purchased the *supplément*, which allowed me to ride the TGV and get away from the South of France and my feelings for Chris as quickly as possible. I was hoping the adage "out of sight, out of mind" would prove true, but I quickly found that this dream, like all my others over the past couple of weeks, was based on wishes without substance. I spent most of the train ride rehashing the time I'd spent with Chris, reliving it in my mind like a movie I could rewind for the best parts.

Eventually, I settled in, mesmerized by the passing farms and fields and stands of trees and marveling at the lush countryside that looked so different from the arid mountains in California during summer.

CHAPTER THIRTY-THREE

I HAD no trouble navigating from the train station to the Hotel des Écoles, where I had booked my single room online during the train ride. Sylvie handed me my key, and I lugged my bags up the four flights of stairs and shoved them onto the bed, barely taking time to look in the mirror and wash my hands before heading out again. I only had the afternoon in Paris. I had to make it count.

I dropped my room key with Sylvie and raced out toward the Seine, desperate to gaze into its grey-green waters and let it direct me across the Île de la Cité, where Notre-Dame stood proudly, to the right bank. I wanted to stroll through the small streets of the Marais and find the Picasso Museum. I knew I couldn't spend long there, but an hour allowed me to gorge on early sculptures and paintings I'd never even seen in pictures and follow his progression through his blue period and portraits of his muse, the photographer Dora Maar.

I grabbed a falafel and savored the pita rolled with fried chickpea cakes and tomato-cucumber salad. I walked through the Place Vendôme, not stopping to walk into any of the art galleries that surrounded the square park in the middle, then passed the Centre Pompidou, with its spinning fountain and odd tubes marking the exterior of the modern museum, on my way to the Opéra Garnier. That was where my journey in Paris had begun two weeks earlier, when I'd felt so tired and daunted and confused, and I wanted to revisit the spot with fresh eyes.

I went straight to the café where I'd first met Guillaume. He was unloading a tray of drinks for a table of four when I sat at a table near the end of the row. I watched him bend down to hand *l'addition* to a customer and turn to collect a few coins in tips from a now-vacant table. He deposited the coins into a pouch around his waist before checking the row of tables for new arrivals. Then he spotted me and came right over.

"Do you remember me?" I asked, momentarily afraid he wouldn't.

"Ah, Nikki, *oui! Bien sûr*, I remember you." He kissed me on both cheeks. "You've been outside in the sun, I see." He looked me over. "You look great, *ma cherie*. Tanned, relaxed. You look happy. And sad. Sad to be leaving Paris, I imagine. That's normal."

I felt a lump form in my throat. He'd think it was strange if I burst into tears, even if he chalked it up to me being sad about leaving Paris. I wanted to tell him about Chris, but the café was bustling, and I could tell I was already keeping him from his job. "Do you have any time later? It's my last night here. Maybe we could meet for a drink."

"*Oui*. Yes, I am free. Maybe Jean-Yves will join us?"

"Oh, please. I'd love to meet him."

We agreed to meet at La Palette, where we'd had chilled red wine on my first night. I loved the idea of my time in France coming full circle. I stayed for a quick cup of coffee, this time with milk, and looked over a map on my phone, trying to plot where I'd go next. I didn't want to rush through the sights. I knew I'd have to come back. I chose a couple more places I wanted to visit and decided I would linger as long as I wanted at each one.

First, I walked through the Tuileries Garden next to the Louvre. The flowers lining the squares of green lawns were immaculately manicured in pinks, purples, and whites, some allowed to grow taller, others close to the ground to provide a dense, lush garden that repeated around each area of grass. Kids were sailing boats in the fountains there, too, as they'd done in the fountains of the Luxembourg Gardens. Similar green chairs reclined all around the fountains, and almost none sat vacant. But I found one.

It felt great to stop moving and soak in the warmth of the cloudless day amid Parisians who understood the importance of spending time outside when the weather was nice. It struck me that living in Los Angeles made most of us take the nice weather for granted. In France, where the fields were green because it rained throughout the year and got cold in the winter and early spring months, a sunny day was not to be squandered. I wanted to return home with a little more of this perspective. I vowed to take time each day with a real coffee in a real cup, rather than a to-go cup in my car on the way to somewhere else.

I'd come to appreciate the ritual of sitting with other people and having conversations. I'd need to find ways to get out of the house more and be social. And I wanted to learn a language or two so the next time I traveled, I wouldn't feel so inept for only being able to speak English. In a short trip, I felt like I'd covered a lot of ground mentally.

A couple lay on the grass together, a woman about my age resting her head on the stomach of a man. She had her knees bent and was reading a book while he lay there with his sunglasses on, possibly asleep. It could have been me with Chris. It could have been so many other people.

I felt at peace, believing it would be me again someday. I had to trust that I'd find the right guy eventually. Maybe not in a bar, maybe not in Paris, but somewhere.

After a while, I felt ready to walk some more, so I followed the gardens to where they ended at the Place de la Concorde, admiring the symmetry of the giant traffic circle around the gold-tipped obelisk that had originally stood at the entrance to the Luxor Temple in Egypt and was given to France in exchange for a mechanical clock that apparently never worked.

I positioned myself in a central spot, where I could see the obelisk straight in line with the Arc de Triomphe at the end of the Champs Élysées. I admired the symmetry of the straight line that extended from the Louvre to these monuments, ending at the arch in La Défense at a point I could barely see.

The city had been planned with such thoughtfulness. Granted, much of it had been for the benefit of monarchs and the Catholic Church, but the footprint left behind was awe-inspiring.

I didn't want to leave Paris without seeing more of the Eiffel Tower. Walking along the right bank, I had a perfect view of the tower as I drew closer to it. I didn't think I needed to climb it or stand beneath it. I just needed to get near enough to feel it looming large. It took walking past several more bridges before I was close enough to appreciate its size and impressive ironwork. When I'd gotten as far as the Pont de l'Alma, I changed my mind —I wanted to go all the way to the base of the tower.

Just a short walk across the bridge took me to the park at the base of the tower, which was crowded with people standing in lines to go up to the second-floor restaurant or to take the elevator to the top. Bike tours were gathering and setting off to see the city, and tourists were posing for selfies with the tower in the background. I wasn't above joining them, and I found a couple of Americans who didn't mind snapping a picture of me so I'd have the memory of this day.

I stood for a while and marveled at the engineering feat of the giant structure, which soared upward at an angle that made it impossible to see the top from where I stood. It was hard not to think about the view from the terrace of Chris's rented apartment and the days that seemed to spring from the magic of the sparkling tower.

I pushed those thoughts aside, making a new association with the Eiffel Tower that was only mine.

Somehow, the hours had flown by, and I realized that if I didn't move fast, I'd miss meeting Guillaume and Jean-Yves at La Palette. Reluctantly, I turned and walked through the Champ de Mars. As I crossed the park, I turned around every so often to catch a new view of the Eiffel Tower as it receded into the distance. The shortest route to the restaurant took me past La Fontaine de Mars. Passing that familiar spot was almost like intentional torture. I had to peer in at the restaurant where Chris and I had shared a bottle of the delicious red wine he'd ordered.

The table where we'd sat was occupied by a cute couple about my age—a dark-haired guy in sunglasses and a blond woman wearing a sunhat. He was drinking red wine. She had a beer. I wondered where the rest of their evening would lead and whether they were on a first date. Maybe they'd been together for years. Or maybe they were just friends meeting after work. Another couple, another day, another set of lives unfolding.

I walked faster toward my destination.

The Louvre beckoned from across the river, tempting me with more incredible art that I'd never see anywhere else in a traveling exhibition. If I wanted to see the Venus de Milo, I had to do it here. But in the time I had left, a visit to the Louvre was impossible. It would take something like a hundred days to see every piece of art in the museum, and that was assuming I looked at each one for only thirty seconds. Even if I didn't intend to see everything, the overwhelming amount of art I would want to see put the Louvre into the column with other sights I'd have to save for next time.

Montmartre was also too far off my walking path, so I put a pin in that entire neighborhood as well. It would all be there for me later.

CHAPTER THIRTY-FOUR

La Palette

GUILLAUME AND JEAN-YVES had already gotten a table when I arrived. Guillaume made introductions like he and I had been friends for years. We kissed on both cheeks, and I no longer felt like an American poseur for doing it.

I looked around and noticed that people filled almost every table. "This place is popular."

"Always busy," said Guillaume. "Now, tell me about your vacation. I'm dying to know where you went."

"We are always looking for a way to live vicariously," said Jean-Yves, his English perfect and barely accented. I unfolded my entire saga, from the first meeting in Monoprix to our date that night to the whirlwind trip on the jet that followed. Jean-Yves was agog.

"I know your Chris Conley. He's a huge film star, even here. *Très beau.*"

"He tries to make me jealous," Guillaume said. "But I admit I share his view this time. Chris Conley is…"

"Magnifique," Jean-Yves finished. They hung on every detail of our time together and wanted a play-by-play of the film premiere night. I gave them the high points and explained how it had all ended in our emotional goodbye the day before. I kind of expected us to move on to other topics once I was done, but they both looked at me in confusion.

"*Je ne comprends pas*," Jean-Yves said to Guillaume.

"We're confused. Why are you walking away from this man? It sounds like you love him."

"I... I don't know what I feel. I just need to get some distance from it all, let my life get back to normal. I have a full day of work on Monday."

"That doesn't answer my question," Guillaume said.

I explained some more about our different lives in different cities. Slowly, Guillaume started nodding, accepting reality as I eventually had. Jean-Yves needed more convincing. "It's just different here. Work is important, but so is living. That's why we have government-mandated vacation of three weeks a year. There's an understanding that work can never be everything to a person. And if it is, maybe it shouldn't be."

He was right, and if I'd learned anything during my time in France, it was to have a little bit of perspective and slow down. But that didn't change anything about the reasons why Chris and I were an impossibility.

"Jean-Yves is a romantic," Guillaume explained.

"So am I. But some romances don't work out," I admitted.

"Sometimes life gets in the way, I know," said Jean-Yves. "It's just too bad."

I didn't really want to talk anymore about Chris, and they seemed to sense the need for a second round of drinks and a new conversation. Guillaume started prattling on about his boss at the café while Jean-Yves signaled for our waiter.

"He bought the café a year ago, but he doesn't seem like he wants to run a business," Guillaume said.

"I keep telling him, your issue is not with the owner. I'm not sure Guillaume wants to work there anymore, no matter who owns the place," Jean-Yves said.

Guillaume sighed. They'd had this discussion before, clearly, and were airing it in front of me, maybe presuming my objectivity could help tilt the balance.

"Is there something else you'd rather do?" I asked.

"I think I'd like to give voice lessons. Maybe teach *au lycée*, the littlest kids."

"Is that an option?" I asked.

Jean-Yves sighed, bracing himself for a conversation that apparently annoyed him.

"It is... it's just—"

"It's a big change," Jean-Yves said. "I think he's not ready."

"Maybe not," Guillaume said.

"When you're ready, you'll know," I said. I believed that was true of everything. It was why I hadn't ventured abroad before this trip. I hadn't been ready. Now I wanted so much more.

Our next round of drinks arrived, and we sipped them and chatted about talking about a model train collection Jean-Yves had started as a kid. "You should see how many he has now," Guillaume said. "Our apartment has one wall with eleven shelves, each of them containing trains all the way across."

"I am a collector. There will always be another wall I can fill," Jean-Yves said.

"He's like me, only my love is books," Guillaume said. "The shelves that don't have trains are filled with my old books. You should come back with us, and we can both regale you with the stories behind our collectibles."

"Oh, yes. Do come. We can have dinner together before you leave Paris."

The idea of a cozy dinner at the home of these two Frenchmen on my last night sounded lovely. I thanked them heartily but declined. I still hadn't gotten up the nerve to dine alone, and that night would be my last chance to do it. I needed to climb that mountain before I left Paris.

So we talked for another hour, the sky turning from pink to pale blue. We walked down by the Seine before Guillaume and Jean-Yves left me to make their way home. The night had gotten darker and brighter as the lights on all the bridges and buildings came on at *l'heure bleue*. The Eiffel Tower began its hourly light show.

"Dammit," my heart seemed to say. "Is everything until the end of time going to remind you of Chris? I can't take it." I put a hand on my chest, as though in sympathy. We would get through this, my heart and me.

I walked into a small bistro with no more than twelve tables. At this hour, only half of them were filled. "*Une personne*," I told the maitre d', who didn't bat an eye at the request for a table for one. He led me to a two-top by the window and handed me a menu.

At first, the seat across from me seemed obviously empty, like it stood waiting for the person who would fill it. Eventually, though, a waiter came over and asked what I'd like, and he didn't ask if I was waiting for someone else. He didn't feel sorry for me for being alone. I didn't feel sorry for myself. I felt liberated.

I'd overheard a woman at the table next to mine order her coffee, and I imitated the words I heard her say, only I substituted an item from the menu for the coffee.

"*Je prends du soupe a l'oignon.*" I could tell from the waiter's expression that I hadn't gotten it completely right, but he understood what I wanted. I also ordered a small steak and fries. Why not? It was my last night here, and I didn't feel like I had to eat and run. I'd have two full courses with a glass of wine and maybe even dessert. I felt fine sitting there by myself. I liked my own company.

The soup was a little salty, and the cheese was a little gummy on the floating piece of bread, but the steak was delicious. And I could have eaten a barrel of those fries, which were thinly sliced, just crispy enough, and salted to perfection. By the time I'd finished, a couple of tables had emptied and a few more had filled. There was no rule on how late the dinner hour had to be, especially in summer when the sun set late and the air stayed warm.

It turned out dessert was a no-go. I'd done my damage on the steak and fries. "*L'addition*," I told the waiter, who responded, "*Oui*, mademoiselle." I hadn't had anything qualifying as a conversation with him, but my small effort at using a bit of French had succeeded. He didn't need to help me along in English.

I didn't feel like I'd summited a mountain, exactly, but I was on the path leading upward. There was no reason to go back.

CHAPTER THIRTY-FIVE

A Bridge Over the Seine

I HAD ONLY one more item on my list for the day, one thing I couldn't miss before turning in for the night—the light show at one in the morning. I walked back toward the Seine and positioned myself on a bridge, prepared to stand there as long as it took to reach the early-morning hour when the Eiffel Tower lights would dance a final time before turning off for the night.

I still had a half hour to wait, which was fine.

Leaning over the ledge, I looked down at the water, where the Bateaux Mouches still plied the narrow river and tour guides pointed out the sights over loudspeakers. In the distance, I could see the bridge where I'd stood that first night with Chris. At least, I thought I knew which bridge it was. Like all the memories from the prior couple of weeks, that one was starting to fade, out of necessity. I would never forget him, but I'd have to put this whole chapter of my life in the past, where I could look back on it and smile.

A few couples had joined me on the bridge, all anticipating

the light show that would start at any minute. Of course, they would kiss and wrap up in each other's arms. That was what I'd do if I were them. Public displays of affection no longer seemed strange.

I looked down at the dark swirling waters below, thinking about how many people before me had stood on this bridge, making decisions about their lives, and how they'd live them better now that Paris had gotten under their skin. I heard a collective "Aaahhh" and looked up to see the sparkling lights of the tower. They kept dancing and flashing for what seemed like an extra-long finale, allowing me to wring the last drop from my time in France.

As the bulbs flashed, I felt almost like they were reassuring me that they'd be there every night even when I was home in LA, so I'd be able to picture them sparkling and beckoning me back. I couldn't look away until the lights went out.

As I walked back to the Hotel des Écoles, my heart felt full. The trip hadn't been anything like what I'd imagined when I'd bought the tickets for Johnny and me a few months earlier. The time away had confirmed for me that I was absolutely done with him. It also confirmed that I didn't need the happy ending of a new romance to make myself whole. I felt self-sufficient and independent, something I couldn't get by clinging to the wrong relationship. I knew that when I got home, after a few weeks—or months—of patching the hole in my aching heart, I'd be okay.

It was Saturday night, I realized as I passed several packed outdoor bars on the Rue de Buci. No one seemed in a hurry to call it a night, so I decided I had one more round in me as well. I didn't think anything about sitting at a table by myself, and I only looked around at the other tables in the interest of people watching, not to check whether anyone else sat alone. It didn't matter, and I didn't feel alone.

I ordered a final glass of white wine, not caring if I only slept a few hours that night. I'd have plenty of time on the plane, and maybe I'd become an airplane sleeper after all. I no longer felt like I had to define myself in the ways I had before.

While I watched the dozens of people enjoying the warm night, a trio of musicians moved into the middle of the street with an amplifier and began to play. A woman who looked a bit younger than me set up a microphone and sang some Ella Fitzgerald jazz classics while her bandmates played a violin and a horn. Silverware clinked against plates, and voices in multiple languages accompanied the music, and I couldn't have felt more at home. It never occurred to me to look around to see if Johnny or Chris or some other guy was coming my way to save me from being alone. I didn't need saving.

CHAPTER THIRTY-SIX

A PLANE, ECONOMY CLASS – CHARLES DE GAULLE AIRPORT

UNLIKE MY FIRST night at the hotel, I slept like a rock until my alarm woke me in the morning. Sylvie wasn't at the front desk, but it was almost easier to say my last goodbyes to a stranger. I turned in my key with the long attached piece of wood.

This time, I took a taxi to the airport, and the march through the security checkpoints was uneventful. I bought a jar of Dijon mustard at the duty-free shop and a box of butter cookies for the plane. Everything went smoothly. I'd even downloaded my boarding pass onto my phone. Soon, it was time to board. With my luggage stowed under the plane and a paperless boarding pass, I felt like I'd mastered international travel.

I found my seat toward the back of the plane. The experience was a far cry from flying on the private jet, but it was best to stop making comparisons, I decided. That had been a once-in-a-lifetime thing. Starting at that moment, it was back to the real world for me. I was better for having made the trip, with a new thirst for travel and adventure and the memory of a whirlwind romance. I would do it all again if I got the chance. My time with Chris had become part of the magic of France for me, and the memory of it would lure me back. *Je ne regrette rien*—no regrets —I reminded myself. I wondered if that French saying originated from people leaving love behind after visiting France.

The seat next to me was empty, as was the one by the window. *I could get very lucky,* I thought. Maybe no one would sit in either seat, and I could spread out across the whole row. Or even if just the middle seat ended up free… I began to dream about the nap I could take on the ride home, because despite the decent sleep the previous night, I was still emotionally drained and exhausted.

"*Excusez-moi,*" said a female voice in the aisle next to me.

I looked up at an older woman, who prattled on in French and gazed down at me with consternation. I shook my head, not able to answer her questions. She then held out her boarding pass for me to see, and it became clear why she was standing there—I was in her seat. I got up and showed her the boarding pass on my phone as proof that I was in the right place, but she shook her head, unconvinced.

Eventually, a flight attendant came over to mediate. She looked at the set of three boarding passes the woman produced for all the seats in my row, and I began to sense that I was on the losing end of the battle. I showed the flight attendant my electronic boarding pass, which I'd felt so worldly for having procured, but it did nothing to convince her I was in the right.

"*Non,* mademoiselle," she said, looking at the three tickets proffered by the family members who were waiting to take the row of three seats. "There was a mix-up. These seats are taken. We will have to see if there is another seat for you."

Confused and defeated, I relinquished the seat I'd thought was mine. Couldn't I just get out of the country without a final snafu that proved I didn't really have what it took to be an international traveler? I couldn't imagine what had gone wrong. I went over the details in my mind. I hadn't confused my travel times or dates, and the airline had let me past the gate.

Now I'd have to go back to the desk and figure it out. Maybe there was a bug in the electronic system, or maybe it was because I was so late checking in...

The flight attendant waited while I grabbed my carry-on from the overhead bin then led me up the aisle as other passengers looked on at my walk of shame. She stopped me in the galley area of the plane, where another flight attendant was readying the drinks cart and stowing it away, locked behind a metal bar.

The two of them conferred, pointing at me and discussing my predicament. One of them picked up a phone and asked a question then explained to the other what was going on. Neither of them bothered to let me in on the conversation. The few words of French I'd managed to pick up weren't part of their conversation, so I stood and waited, watching as a few more passengers shuffled past me and found their coach seats.

I tried to cheer myself with the possibility of spending one more night in Paris. I could see another museum and eat some more cheese. But the idea failed to lift my spirits.

When I looked back at the cabin, I saw that all the seats were occupied. The chances of going home on this flight were dwindling as the two flight attendants chatted in incomprehensible French and I stood there like a moron.

"I think I'll get off and ask at the desk. Maybe I can get on a different flight..." I said, trying to move things along. Hunching in the galley in limbo wasn't doing me any good.

"Ah, mademoiselle, non. We have found the problem." This came from the second flight attendant, who'd been handling the drinks. Maybe she had seniority.

"Okay, great. Is there a seat somewhere I can just hop into?" I asked. I'd have been happy to sit with the luggage under the plane. I just wanted to go home.

"Yes, follow me. We have a seat for you here."

She led me in the other direction from where I'd come, passing through a second section of economy seats, which looked equally occupied. I was scanning ahead to see where the empty seat was and assuming I'd get stuck in the middle of a row. I didn't care.

Then she passed through a curtain and into a cabin where the seats were suddenly a little bigger. My seating blunder had somehow gotten me an upgrade to the only available seat, which seemed to be in business class. "Voilà. You may seat here."

She pointed to an empty pair of seats. Well, one of them was empty. On the other sat a painting, presumably belonging to my seatmate. I settled into the aisle seat and glanced over at the colorful watercolor to my right, curious but not wanting to be nosy. I assumed its owner would be back at any second.

That was when I really noticed the subject of the painting—a woman in a cerulean blue dress, looking out a window, an expression of pure adoration on her face for whatever she beheld. And I knew exactly what—or who—that was. I just had no recollection of when Marguerite had taken the photo from which she'd painted this gorgeous watercolor.

"I asked her to paint you when we first went to her studio," said a voice behind me. Chris. He was standing in the row of seats across the aisle.

I couldn't imagine what had brought him there. My brain was having trouble computing the discordant elements in front of me—the business-class seat, the painting, the guy. He was supposed to be at his house in Antibes, not here. "What's going on?" I managed to extract from the jumble of thoughts, feeling an unexpected wave of light-headedness wash over me.

"Marguerite delivered this to me last night. She just finished it. It's beautiful, don't you think?"

"She's... really talented," I said, having a hard time looking at myself in the painting as I remembered that day. "You came to bring me a painting?"

"I came because... when I saw this... I looked at the expression on your face, and I thought you looked more beautiful than at any time I'd seen you."

His words melted me. But I couldn't go back to three days earlier. He couldn't ask me to do that. All the things we'd talked about were still true. I was on the plane, pushing myself forward to get over him. He was making it nearly impossible, but I had to maintain my resolve for my own heart's sake.

"The look on your face... I couldn't stop staring at it. Then Marguerite told me you were looking out the window at me."

I felt a little embarrassed, wishing she hadn't told him that. But I remembered so well how I'd felt that day, looking at him. It all came flooding back, and the feelings crushed me.

"Yeah. I was."

He closed his eyes like he was relieved to find it was true. Then he looked at me. "Seeing this, I thought... for the first time, I thought maybe... you might actually feel about me the way I've been feeling about you pretty much since the moment we met." His eyes never left mine. "So I'm here because I had to find out."

It was everything I'd wanted to hear. But it didn't change things from how we'd left them. Even if I spent a few more days with him, eventually we'd have to go back to our separate lives. I didn't see the point of making it harder. "Of course that's how I feel. But—"

He grabbed my hand and put a finger over my lips. Just the feeling of his touch made my skin tingle like it was skimmed by a hummingbird's wings, but I had to set him straight.

"It's still impossible. Chris, I just—"

"No." He moved closer and held up a hand, stopping me from objecting.

I shook my head at him. It didn't make sense. Nothing had changed. Despite this grand gesture, nothing was any different...

"You're different from anyone I've ever met. And you're normal in the way I wish my life could be. I want to be with you. I want... you."

It was sweet gut it was also crazy town. "Chris... dating me isn't enough to make your life normal. Your life isn't normal."

"It could be."

"Then you wouldn't be you. You're a superhero."

"I know you don't see me that way. And that's why I like you. It's why I'm goddamn falling in love with you."

It was torture. I wanted to reciprocate everything he was saying but I couldn't. I had to protect my heart. I couldn't get by on a visit to New York here and there and the occasional night out at a premiere. "Chris, I can't be all those things you need. I get intimidated by paparazzi and fancy dresses and iced tea spoons. I'm not a superhero."

"You are to me." His eyes sought mine and I had to look away.

I shook my head. He was caught up in the moment, and it *was* a beautiful moment. But I had to make him see reality for what it was. If nothing else, I was good at being rational. I started to formulate my argument, gathering all the evidence of what I knew to be true—that we were lucky we'd had two weeks, that we had to be realistic, that I wanted more. That was the crux of it. I wanted more and there was no way for him to give me that.

Except that he was talking again before I had a chance to say any of my rational words.

"I'm not done with you. And... maybe I'll never be done," he said. He cupped his hand around my cheek and made sure I was looking at him. "So it occurred to me that it would be easier for me to see you as much as humanly possible if I sold my place in New York and relocated to LA."

"I... wait, what?" I couldn't have heard him right. What I'd thought I heard sounded insane. My heart started racing as the blood flooded my brain. "That's crazy. Why would you do that? You love New York." Then I stopped looking for excuses. "You... would do that?"

He cupped a hand around my cheek. "I think I'd love to do that."

I found myself at a loss for words. If I had allowed myself to dream up the exact thing I wanted Chris to say, this would be it, and I couldn't even respond. I looked around self-consciously, wondering if we were making a scene, but no one was paying attention to us.

Chris pulled me closer. "Are you okay with that? It would mean this isn't just a two-week fling, or whatever you called it."

I started to laugh. "I think I called it vacation love."

"I think you did. Well, you got the love part right." Then he kissed me, and this time, I didn't think about holding something back in order to make it easier to get over him.

Chris leaned toward the window seat, where the painting sat, and moved it. "Hope you don't mind. That's my seat."

"Wait, you're really doing this? Flying to LA with me? What about your next movie and prep or whatever you said you had to do?"

He put his hands up, as carefree as a person whose life was carefully orchestrated could possibly be. "I'm trying to push it back to November. I don't know what this all looks like exactly. I still have all those commitments. It might take some logistics to get our schedules in sync. But I'm willing to try if you are." He settled into the seat and extended his hand to me.

I hadn't let myself consider the possibility of anything

beyond our two-week vacation, but now that it was staring me in the face, I couldn't imagine doing anything else. I had a feeling his assistant was going to have a busy day.

I plunked into the seat next to him. It wasn't lost on me how much bigger and nicer it was than the coach seat I'd just left.

"So is that a yes?" He turned to face me and picked up my hand. He brought to his lips, then held it against his cheek. A thousand watts of light emanated from his eyes, along with the extra special sorcery that had me nodding like a zombie.

"Oh my God, absolutely. Yes, please."

The flight attendant closed the curtain, shutting off the people with regular coach seats and preventing them from getting a look at what they were missing in business class. She started making preparations for departure in the small kitchen behind us, pouring champagne into real glasses and carrying them on a tray through our section. Another flight attendant came by with soft blankets and pillows.

But I barely noticed any of that, because when Chris leaned in to kiss me, the rest of the world faded into the background. Everything that wasn't the two of us—our lips, his hands, my skin—disappeared from view.

At least, I wanted it to disappear.

Unfortunately, there's no such thing as being off the grid in Chris's world. Our kiss was lovely, passionate, sweet. Then it was cut short by the incessant pulsing of his cellphone.

He groaned and reluctantly pulled away from me and fished it out of his pocket. When he looked at the screen, he scowled, showing me what he saw: six missed calls from a blocked number.

"That's my assistant," he said. I didn't ask how he knew the blocked call was from her. He just knew. From the expression on his face, he didn't seem to think she'd called six times to ask him what color file folders she should buy.

"Give me a sec," he said, standing up. Before he moved away, he bent down once more and completely covered my mouth with his, giving me the kind of kiss that made me drop a few IQ points and sigh his name. While I sat with a dumb grin on my face, marveling at what had just happened, he called his assistant back from a more private area in the front of the cabin.

He wasn't gone long, but from the look on his face, that wasn't a sign of success. He didn't settle back into the seat next to me. He didn't look like the carefree Chris I'd been falling for over the past two weeks. He looked stressed. All he said was, "We have a problem."

THE END

FOREVER WITH HIM, Part Two in the Summer Heat Duet, will be released in August 2020.
PREORDER on Amazon.

READ ON FOR A SNEAK PEEK...

ABOUT THE AUTHOR

Stacy Travis is an author of contemporary romance novels and romantic suspense fiction.

Stacy lives in Los Angeles with her husband, two sons and a poorly-trained rescue dog who hoards socks.

She loves to hear from readers so please connect with her on social media.

Don't miss a Travis thing: join Stacy's Social Club for all the newsletter goodies, including exclusive bonus content, swag giveaways, info about upcoming books, and excuses to drink margaritas.

SIGN UP at https://bit.ly/3cUT55Bnewsletter!

And join my facebook reader group at https://bit.ly/2B1psS4

www.stacytravis.com

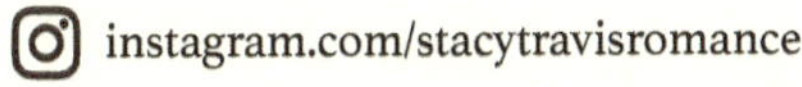

COMING IN AUGUST, 2020

FOREVER WITH HIM - BOOK TWO IN THE SUMMER HEAT SERIES

SNEAK PEEK

FOREVER WITH HIM

Chris didn't have much time to think about missing New York before New York was beckoning with an urgent plea. He'd gotten a call an hour after I'd shown him the entirety of my one-bedroom condo—the walk-in closet, the tiny bonus room I used as a home office, the kitchen—and learned that production on a film that was supposed to start in November was starting ahead of schedule. His agent wanted to know if he was available.

"Are you available?" I asked, wryly, expecting him to say no. He'd already spent part of the plane ride communicating with his manager to finesse the start dates of another project and committed to a second project because it would be shooting on location in LA. He still needed to do publicity for his latest White Serpent movie, but some of that would take place in LA, where he'd also do some talk shows.

He didn't answer right away and I could suddenly tell that everything had shifted. Gone were the sweet whispers of an hour before when Chris was telling me wanted to stay inside me forever. Reality had quashed any plans except those relating to his job. I felt a pit settle into my stomach. Here it goes, I thought.

"Yes. I mean, no. I can always say no." He smiled, like he could treat his career with the cavalier tone he was using, but we both knew the truth.

"You don't have to say no. If it's something you want to do, you should do it." I felt strongly about that. I'd never want him to turn down something he wanted to do, especially out of consideration for me.

He looked torn. "I kind of want to do it." I nodded. It would be fine, I told myself. "But if you tell me not to do it, I won't."

"Oh no, that's not how this is going to work. If we have a chance at all of being together, you need to work and be happy. I have a job. It's not like I'll be sitting here all day, waiting for you in an apron. I've got a career to manage too." I tried to sound like a badass, but I wasn't sure I was pulling it off.

I didn't like the way he was looking at me, like he felt guilty.

"Please. Let's get this right at the outset," I told him. "Go to work. Be your best self. And when you're not at work, come be with me."

Chris sat on my blue denim couch and put his head in his hands. "Ugh, I hate this. You know I want to be here, right?"

"Yes. Chris, I know."

"I could say I'm not available until the November date. They work around my schedule."

"If they could do that, wouldn't they have kept the original date?" I still didn't know enough about how the movie business worked to understand why they moved things around but I knew that did it for a reason."

"Right. It's a co-star issue. She can't do November and if we don't shoot now, we wait a year."

"Sounds like you have your answer if you want to do this movie."

"But all the things I said... I still mean them. I really do want to be here. With you."

"I appreciate that. But we have to start things off right or we're doomed. Let's make it simple. You were planning on taking this role when it was shooting in November. And you don't have anything—other than me—to keep you from doing it now."

"What if I'd rather hang here with you?" I went over and sat down next to him. He really seemed distraught over his choices. "Chris, that's a lovely thing to say. And I know you mean it. But I'm not gonna let you start turning down jobs for me."

"So I should go to New York."

"You should."

"Will you come out?"

"I mean... How? I have to work."

"Even for weekends. I can get you on whatever flights you need, so you can time it with your hours at work." Of course I would try to make that happen. I wanted to be with him. It was worth some redeye flights and a little schedule juggling.

"Of course. Sure I'll come out," I said, having no idea how I was going to do it. I knew I'd be returning to a full in-box and a lot of small fires no one had put out in my absence. The last thing I could do was take more time off. But I had to give Chris the affirmation he wanted. He seemed unable to move forward without it. "I just need to look at my calendar when I get back to work."

Chris looked elated. Finally the sad, guilty look was swept from, his face. All I had to do was convince him his life didn't have to change in order to be with me.

The reality was that his life hadn't changed. After one night back in LA, during which we'd fallen asleep on the couch despite trying to enjoy our last few hours together, he'd flown to back to New York on a private jet.

He'd unpacked his suitcase in his own apartment and made plans to meet the director the next day over lunch. He'd gotten coffee from a place on Thompson Street where he usually went and talked to the baristas there because he was that guy, always friendly, even though he was famous. A few people pretended to take selfies but were actually snapping pictures of him from a distance. Those pictures would end up on their Instagram feeds and soon he'd have tabloid photographers trailing behind him after getting tipped off about where he'd be.

It was almost as if he'd never left. Almost like we'd never met.

PREORDER Forever with Him